YACHT
OF THE DAMNED!

"You're not the Coast Guard!" Captain Valaczek said in a hard voice as the intruders took position on deck. "What the hell is this!"

"Drop your weapons! Now!" Cuesta, the leader, repeated loudly.

But Valaczek could never give over the *Maria Isabel* without a fight. Knowing he was outgunned, he raised the shotgun.

Jake Parrish, who along with McGill knew these men, thought of the PPL in his back pocket and realized he would never be able to bring it into play. "Don't!" he shouted at the captain.

But it was too late. Valaczek squeezed down on the trigger of the big gun just as Cuesta dropped into a crouch and fired his M-16. The shotgun went wide as Cuesta's gun exploded. Valaczek was blown off his feet to the deck.

Parrish knew the gig was up now. The rebels had the yacht—and they had its precious cargo.

DEEP RUN

Ralph Hayes

TOWER BOOKS NEW YORK CITY

A TOWER BOOK

Published by

Tower Publications, Inc.
Two Park Avenue
New York, N.Y. 10016

Copyright © 1981 by Tower Publications, Inc.

One

Good morning, loyal citizens of Ecuador. This is
Iberama International reporting to you directly from
your Ministry of Public Information in downtown
Guayaquil. According to last-minute communiqués,
there has been heavy fighting through the night between
our brave government forces and Reform Council
guerrillas at Quito, Riobamba, and Montecristi. In
Quito, where undisciplined opposition hooligans are
massing in large numbers, eyewitness accounts disclosed
wanton and senseless killing in the streets by guerrillas,
with many innocent civilians being shot, knifed, and run
down by commandeered vehicles. Fires rage centrally,
with foreign businesses a favorite target of violence.

At least two regular army units are reported to have
traitorously joined the guerrillas in Quito and also in
Loja in the south, under the infamously dissident
generals Perez and Linares, lending moral as well as
tactical support to the criminal Alvaristas. At Quito,
Latacunga and Loja, guerrillas and dissidents are now
reportedly in control of airports and government
facilities, but in Riobamba and Montecristi regular
army forces have stymied the aggressive thrust of the
guerrillas, killing many and forcing the surrender of
entire units.

There are late reports of incursions into the area of
the capital from the south, but these are unconfirmed

5

rumors at this time. Residents of outlying villages, however, are urged to stay off the streets until further notice. A curfew will be in effect in all districts between Loja and Guayaquil this evening, from eight p.m. to six a.m., and will continue indefinitely. Further reports will be coming to you throughout the day.

Luther McGill snapped the radio button off with an abrupt twist of his wrist, and then sat glumly staring across the blossom-grown patio to a stucco wall where morning sunlight irradiated the red bougainvillea. On the breakfast table, covered with white linen, papaya, mango and pineapple lay untouched in their silver serving dishes. McGill's Ecuadorian wife, Ana, and their daughter, Nita, both watched McGill's face closely, as if it had been he who had delivered the news account rather than the anonymous voice on the portable radio.

"Did you call Tony out here?" McGill broke the silence abruptly, speaking to his wife.

"He'll be right out, Luther," Ana told him. Not much over forty, Ana looked younger, with dark thick hair and a chiseled Spanish face that made men look twice at her when she entered a room. She had been considered one of the most desirable debutantes, and there had been much local resentment among Guayaquil bachelors against this presumptuous American-in-exile who had *stolen* the finest fruit of Ecuadorian womanhood from their midst.

"It all seems so silly and pointless," Nita said, a silver fork poised over uneaten papaya. "If Alvarez manages to oust Biaza, it will all be the same in the long run. Nothing ever changes here, really." She glanced at her mother. "Well, does it?" She looked very much like her mother had at the age of nineteen, except that Nita's hair was not as dark, and she had McGill's blue eyes and strong chin. A beautiful girl, she had already done some modeling in New York and Mexico City. She was as

6

popular with the local young men as her mother had been, but none of them interested Nita. She and her twenty-two year old brother, Tony, had both been born in the States during a temporary return there by McGill under company orders—Ana had longed for Ecuador during those years—so both of them were American citizens. The whole family was bilingual but spoke English amongst themselves.

"You've always sided with your father in his criticism of Ecuador," Ana said quietly. "Your brother likes it here, why don't you?"

Juanita Maria Elena McGill made a face, looking even prettier. "I like it here, Mother. This is my home." McGill glanced quickly at her, studying her sculptured features as seriously as she had regarded his moments before. "But you must admit that despite all these political upheavals, nothing ever changes, except the faces of the people in Guayaquil."

Before Ana could reply, Tony McGill came out onto the patio; McGill's and Nita's eyes went quickly to him. Like his sister, he was dressed casually, wearing a T-shirt and shorts. He was tanned and taller than McGill, with sandy hair and brown eyes, an athletic healthy-looking young man. He joined them at the table. Antonio Roberto had gone off to college in Chicago for two years, but was finishing his degree at the university in Guayaquil. Unlike Nita who planned to live in the States as soon as McGill gave his permission, Tony wanted to make his future in Ecuador. He had close ties with the sons of the rich and powerful in Guayaquil, and he liked being a member of the elite.

"Well. . .a family gathering," Tony smiled, a bit sleepily. He leaned over and kissed his mother on her cheek, then looked around at the unconsumed food. "My God, did everybody wait for me?"

Nita made a sound in her throat. "Nobody is hungry," she said.

7

Tony cast a sober look toward McGill, and McGill reached and touched his son's hand reassuringly. "I hope we didn't hurry you, Tony. I wanted to have us all together this morning."

McGill rose from his chair and walked over to the blossom-studded garden wall. He stood ramrod-erect and gave more the appearance of a military man than a rubber company executive. His dress was casual at the moment—bright sport shirt over slacks, and sandals on his feet. His slicked-back brown hair had traces of gray in the sideburns and temples, and there were new lines in his face.

When McGill first came to Ecuador as a young man, he had been very independent and idealistic. He had seen the inequities around him—beggars in the public markets and homeless children in the streets, while the elite few purred behind estate walls. But then, as he himself grew more comfortable and secure, socializing with those in power, McGill had begun looking the other way. The status quo seemed impermeable to change; so he relaxed, accepting invitations to embassy functions and official banquets, joining powerful business associations, and regularly visiting the States to retain his citizenship. Now, as a vice-president of the Ecuadorian-American rubber company known as Ameco, and manager of its Guayaquil area plants, McGill was not just allied with the local establishment—he was an integral part of it.

McGill turned from the wall. "The garden has been so beautiful this year." He looked down, and Ana's brow furrowed. "We're going to have to leave," he added, almost as if it were an afterthought.

Ana made a little gasp in her throat, a sound like someone strangling her. "Oh, God," she murmured.

"Leave?" Tony said incredulously. "Leave Guayaquil?"

"Leave Ecuador," McGill said heavily. "Return to

the States."

Nita raised her dark eyebrows. Every expression she made, every look that came on her lovely face, was photogenic. "Good. Most of my friends are in New York and Mexico."

Tony rose slowly from his chair. "Why? Because of a few harebrained rebels?"

McGill cast a level look at his son. "In the first place, they're not harebrained. Alvarez has three generals on his side now. Maybe you haven't heard. . .his troops now hold half the towns in this country, and they're threatening the capital. I spoke to Enrico Fuentes last week. He confided to me that President Biaza himself is making plans to leave. So are a number of other high-ranking officials. Apparently they have more respect for Alvarez than you. Those at the top are saying that the government could fall, one way or another, within sixty days."

"Hell, what if it does?" Tony argued. "What difference would it make to us?"

"There, you see?" Nita said triumphantly. "Tony agrees with me. A change of government would make no difference at all. Things would go on just the same."

McGill cast a sober look at her. "Except for one thing. Biaza and all pro-Biaza people will go. The Reform Council has already announced that they will try all Biaza supporters as criminals and traitors, and that the death penalty would be appropriate in most cases. Whether you know it or not, Nita, we're considered Biaza people by Alvarez and his rebels. He has specifically mentioned foreign businesses as criminal sponsors of the Biaza government, and Ameco is possibly the largest foreign interest in Ecuador."

Tony slumped back onto the chair. "Oh, hell."

"If Alvarez should topple the Biaza government in the next few weeks, we would all be in the gravest danger. Perhaps the best thing that might happen to us

9

is that we would be arrested by guerrilla forces and held on trial for treason. The worst is that a band of hot-headed, gun-happy guerrillas might storm into this house one bright day and kill everybody they find here because we're considered dirty capitalist financiers of tyranny.''

A heavy silence fell over the patio, like a night fog off the Guayas River. Ana's eyes were suddenly moist. "Are you sure, Luther? Are you quite certain we must pull up roots and leave our home?"

"You've scared her, Papa," Nita told McGill. She always called him Papa, in the Spanish way, and Tony called him Dad. "Why are you trying to scare her?"

McGill moved over to his wife and put a hand on her shoulder. She was wearing an expensive, wispy dress that made her seem very fragile. "I don't want to scare any of you," McGill said, "but I want you to know how it is. The company wrote to me a month ago, asking me to come back to New York before the situation worsened. I delayed, thinking things might get better. Instead, they've gotten worse. I wrestled with it all through the night, and I see no alternative. I already have our air tickets to Miami. We'll be debriefed by Wade Sumner at our Miami plant before going on to New York.''

"When will we leave?" Nita asked him.

"Early next week, probably Tuesday, if flights are on schedule. We could be in Miami Tuesday night.''

Tony turned away angrily. "Well, the rest of you can run if you want to," he said bitterly, "but I'm not going. This is my home. My future is here. There's nothing for me in New York.''

McGill came around the table to Tony, and caught his eye with a steady gaze. "You're going, Tony. We're all going. I wouldn't consider leaving you here.''

Young Tony glared at his father. "I don't like running. Do you think Jake Parrish would run? Is he

10

running?'' Tony referred to an old friend of the family and ex-employee of Ameco who had been McGill's top assistant for a while in Guayaquil.

Nita laughed softly. She had always had a crush on Jake Parrish, as a younger teenager. ''Jake has probably joined the rebels!''

''Oh, Nita! Don't say things like that!'' Ana said in agitation.

''Jake Parrish doesn't have a family to consider,'' McGill told his son. His tone told them the discussion was finished. ''I don't want any more argument, Tony. You'll help us pack this weekend, and you'll be there at the airport with us when we leave.''

Tony's heavy sigh revealed his acquiescence to McGill's wishes. ''Oh, hell,'' he said.

''We won't be taking anything but clothing and a few personal effects,'' McGill went on, turning away from the table and staring pensively across the sunny patio. ''I'll arrange to have the furniture sent later, if it's possible. The house will be closed up, and I'll try to get Pablo to watch it. I'll decide later whether it will have to be sold, if Alvarez leaves us that choice.''

''If we sell the house,'' Ana said quietly, ''or if they take it from us, we'll never come back. Will we?''

McGill did not want to lie to her. ''It would be unlikely,'' he said almost inaudibly.

''So we're just going to give the guerrillas our home and land and everything you've worked for here,'' Tony said glumly.

''We'll hope to salvage something from it,'' McGill said, ''but that's all incidental, Tony.''

''Incidental?'' Tony said with a hard look.

''Yes,'' McGill said with certainty. ''There's something else that is primary at this moment. Our lives.''

Neither Tony nor the two women responded; McGill had convinced them. A chapter of their lives was finished, and it was time to acknowledge that fact. For

11

McGill, it was a time for going home.

That weekend was a busy one for the McGills. Ana supervised the packing and closing up of the house, while McGill wound up things at the company plant for the duration of the emergency. Everything seemed to be going smoothly, although there were further reports of guerrillas in and around the area of the capital. Most of the Americans had left Ecuador, and some government officials had packed up and gone. On Monday morning, after a hectic weekend, McGill stopped at the Customs and Immigration offices on Malecon Simon Bolivar to pick up Ana's visa. He was ushered into the office of a small, dumpy man with slick, greasy hair and a thin mustache. His name was Zamora.

"Of course, you will not be able to use the visa at this time," he told McGill from across a littered desk.

"What in the world do you mean?" McGill exclaimed. "We expect to leave here tomorrow on Aeroperu flight 451. It's all arranged."

Zamora shook his head. "Apparently you have not heard the news this morning, Mr. McGill. Simon Bolivar Airport is under attack by guerrillas. Government troops have blocked off all access to it. Commercial flights are still arriving, but none are leaving at this time."

McGill felt a weight grab at him from inside. This was a complete shock to him; he had had no idea that such a thing would have been possible in so short a time.

"But surely some flights will be leaving Guayaquil," he said a little hostilely. "Especially with evacuations of government personnel. I happen to be a personal friend of Minister of Finance Enrico Fuentes who has assured me that there will be flights available for evacuation."

Zamora smiled an ugly smile, his face oily with a light perspiration. A ceiling fan moved slowly above them, but the room remained oppressively hot and still. "Mr.

McGill, I do not make the rules. The government has cancelled all flights from the air terminal here. Soon, I suspect, all incoming flights will be diverted. What you must understand, Mr. McGill, is that the airport is under siege. Bullets are flying there. In a matter of hours the guerrillas may hold it. Then they will decide whether air traffic moves or does not move."

McGill's cheeks flushed hot. He was not a coward, but neither was he a hero, especially with a family to protect. He swallowed hard, and the room seemed to close in on him.

"Listen," he said. "What about other airports nearby? Maybe we could hire a small plane to Riobamba or Montecristi. Government troops are still holding those areas, aren't they?"

"Yes, they are. But I know of no area airports that would be safe for you to travel to. I'm afraid you are stuck here, Mr. McGill, until this fighting is finished one way or another. I suggest you relax and hope for the best. Maybe our loyal government troops may yet prevail, yes?"

The conversation was suddenly like some awful nightmare. The company had told him to get out, and he had delayed; that delay had put his family in grave danger. McGill rose numbly, staring past Zamora toward a shuttered window where light forced its way past louvers in hard bars of brilliance. He squinted as if searching for his future in the harsh sunlight.

He stuck the visa into his pocket and stared at Zamora. *I'm afraid you are stuck here, Mr. McGill.* Sweat dotted his upper lip.

"Thanks for processing the document," he said in a voice he did not recognize. "I may be in further touch with you, Mr. Zamora."

Zamora grinned again. "If you get no answer here, you'll know we've had to close down." A small man in a small position, he was enjoying this American V.I.P.'s

13

discomfiture. "Please be careful on the streets, Mr. McGill."

McGill sat in his car for almost an hour after leaving Zamora's office, trying to get his new situation settled in his head. His first impulse was to go get Ana and Nita and Tony and start driving toward Riobamba, just to get away from the capital, but such a trip would be dangerous. Also, getting to Riobamba or Montecristi was not getting out of Ecuador. Since Guayaquil was a port, he thought of possibly leaving by sea. But there were no passenger ships in port at this time, and it was rumored that Alvarez spies were all over the waterfront.

Finally, McGill knew what he had to do. He had done some favors for a number of his big-wig friends in government, including his closest one, Enrico Fuentes. Now maybe it was time to ask for a return on his investment.

The Ministry of Finance was not far, just a block off the waterfront. McGill drove there quickly, seeing everything differently now. The Indians, sitting on the sidewalks in the shade of the government buildings selling their country wares, did not seem colorful to McGill that morning. They symbolized the primitive aspect of Ecuador. You could not count on security, stability. You paid for favors in hard cash under the counter, and, after twenty years, you still could not drink the water. You were and always would be a foreigner. He saw harried-looking officials going and coming, soldiers with automatic weapons slung onto their backs, and an armored car at the edge of the lot where McGill parked his car. There was no shooting yet in the capital, but there was an air of tension that was almost palpable.

Inside the building with its high ceilings and tapestries, there were more soldiers. Fuentes' suite of offices on an upper floor was relatively quiet. A guard admitted McGill. He identified himself to a secretary in the reception office, a male one who did not know him

14

by sight. Then McGill was being received loudly and warmly by Enrico Fuentes, and ushered into Fuentes' inner office. "What a pleasure, Luther! I've been thinking about you a lot in the past week. How is Ana? Your beautiful family?"

Fuentes occupied a large plush office with thick draperies at sunlit windows, potted palms, and oil paintings of ancient Ecuador on the walls. In a glass case on an end wall were displayed Inca artifacts—pottery and a couple of gold figures. The two men exchanged pleasantries, and then Fuentes mentioned the advance of guerrilla units to the outskirts of the capital.

"It's a disgrace, Luther!" McGill was now seated beside Fuentes' long, heavy-looking desk with its marble ashtrays, silver letter opener and gold-encased photos. "Biaza should have taken action much sooner than he did. Now it looks bad, old friend. Perez and Linares are a couple of our best generals, and now they fight with Alvarez. That gives the whole movement a different feeling. Peasants are rushing to support the opposition forces in some sectors. What must the world think of us? It's a national disgrace!"

"It's all come as quite a shock to your American friends here," McGill admitted to him. "I knew there was unrest, but I never dreamed anything like this could happen in the foreseeable future."

Fuentes frowned slightly. He was a thick-set, swarthy fellow with balding hair and heavy bags under his eyes from regular drinking and rich living. He was dressed in a dark business suit, with a diamond stick-pin affixed to a narrow dark tie. He looked like a minister of finance, and that had helped keep him in office through the vicissitudes of Biaza's iron-fisted regime.

"Why are you still in Guayaquil, Luther?" he asked McGill now. "I heard that you and your family had already left for the States. I'm frankly surprised to see you still here."

15

McGill sighed wearily. "I should have left a couple of weeks ago, Enrico, but there were so many things to do. I had to make sure the company would survive an economic crisis. If Ameco has trouble, all of its Ecuadorian stockholders have trouble, and some of them are my friends."

Fuentes clucked his tongue, nodding. "You have always been so responsible, Luther."

"I've been irresponsible toward my family, I'm afraid," McGill said quietly. "The airport is under attack, Enrico. The most expedient way to leave the country is gone. I have my flight tickets, but I can't even get to the airport. And if I got there, they won't let the planes leave."

Fuentes leaned back in his leather chair and rubbed his chin. "Yes, I see what you mean. A number of our own officials were counting on the airport, too. It's surprising how bold these rebels have become. There's panic in the capital today, Luther. Many government offices have already closed down. Others have only clerks left in them. The machinery of the country is running down. As for those fleeing, not all will find safety beyond the city, I'm afraid. Some roads are open in two directions, but the situation changes every moment. Biaza is gone, incidentally."

McGill was surprised. "The president has fled?"

"That is not the way he characterized it," Fuentes smiled nicely. "But, yes, he has fled. He is in Iquitos, Peru. He is in constant touch with his generals here, and attempts to direct both their activities and ours from there. It is, of course, impossible."

"When will you leave?" McGill asked.

Fuentes shrugged thick shoulders. "For those of us in power, it is in our best interests to fight until the very last moment, is it not? Our generals have not given up. If we lose, we lose everything our lives have stood for. We lose our entire futures, if not our lives. So, despite

16

Biaza, we stay on and show our loyal generals that they have someone behind them. It could make a difference.''

"You don't sound very optimistic,'' McGill said.

"The consensus of opinion in high circles is that the Alvaristas will be swarming these buildings within two weeks, possibly less. If that happens, I hope to make my departure from Guayaquil in time. My wife is already in Iquitos. When the time comes, I've made private arrangements to fly out on a small plane at an airstrip hopefully unknown to the Alvaristas. I could take possibly one of you with me, Luther, but no more. Anyway, you should not delay your leaving. You have no reason to.''

"Do you have any suggestions, Enrico?'' McGill said, leaning forward on his chair now. "I understand ships are still coming and going here. Could I get aboard any of them?''

Fuentes pursed his lips. "No passenger ships are coming here, and the freighter traffic is light, mostly local stuff. Also, Alvarista spies, it is rumored, are watching the port, in case one of us big fish tries to leave that way.'' He grinned slowly.

"Then is there no way out for us?'' McGill asked with dismay.

Fuentes stared at McGill for a long moment, then his eyes narrowed. "Maybe there is, Luther. I just recalled, there is an old friend of mine in port at this very moment, the captain of a small freighter called the *Maria Isabel*. His name is Valaczek, a gentleman of the sea with an American passport and, I understand, questionable parentage. He has no facilities for passengers, and no license to carry them. But he is operating at the moment with a skeleton crew of just a few men, and could find the space for you, I'm sure.''

Hope flooded into McGill's chest. "My God, Enrico, that would be great!''

"I spoke with Valaczek just a couple of days ago. He is having a minor repair made and expects to leave Guayaquil in four more days. He will sail to Panama, pass through the canal, and make a stop or two in the Caribbean. Then he will head for Miami."

McGill could not believe it. "Miami! Why, that's perfect! I could have my friend Wade Sumner meet me there, just as I had planned!"

Fuentes grinned easily. "It is a rather good idea, isn't it?" he said. "Your family should be in no real danger in the next four days."

The bright look now flickered in McGill's face, though. "But will Valaczek take us? You said he had no license."

Fuentes took a thin cigar from a box and offered McGill one, but McGill declined. Fuentes lighted the cigar, and puffed on it for a brief moment, sending balls of white smoke aloft between them. "I think I'll be able to persuade the good captain. He owes me a very old debt, you see. Now he will have the opportunity to repay that debt by doing us both a favor."

McGill squinted down. "Both of us? I don't follow you, Enrico."

Fuentes sucked on the cigar, then rolled it between his finger and thumb as he blew a perfect smoke ring upward. "There are certain. . .documents here at the ministry, Luther, that must not fall into the hands of these guerrillas and traitors, should they take the capital. Documents that must not be destroyed, but saved. They would help us fight back even after a defeat, from exile. Do you understand?"

McGill nodded slowly. "I think so, Enrico."

"Well," Fuentes went on. "If I can get you aboard the *Maria Isabel,* it occurred to me that you might do me the favor of taking these documents and papers with you when you go, Luther. I have a cousin in Miami to whom you would deliver the papers when you arrive there. He used to be a commissioner of police here and would be the proper recipient and guardian of such important material. His name is Victorio Salazar.''

"I'd be happy and proud to deliver a few papers to your cousin in Miami, in return for this grand gesture toward my family,'' McGill told him. "But wouldn't you prefer to take the documents with you when you leave for Peru?''

"Yes, I would. But if I were to fall into the hands of Alvaristas, the documents would, also. If I handle your boarding of the *Maria Isabel* correctly, the things I give you will go aboard inconspicuously as a part of your luggage.''

McGill frowned. "Surely there will be little time between my departure, if Valaczek agrees to take us, and yours. Maybe as little as a week. I suggest that you ought to leave with us, Enrico, on the freighter. When you get to Miami, you can fly to Peru later to join your compatriots there, or they can fly north.''

Fuentes smiled. "A tempting notion, Luther. But even if I wanted to give up on our defense of Guayaquil, I have my orders from Biaza. If I should leave, and then our troops should hold and turn this fighting around, I would be subject to the severest criticism and discipline, if you follow my meaning.''

"Even if you were trying to save the documents?'' McGill wondered.

"Even with that excuse, I'm afraid. No, I think I must keep to my original plan for evacuation, Luther. But, if I can get you out of here in the next few days, perhaps I can also save things of importance to an exiled government that Biaza has not already taken with him.''

"It would be my pleasure, believe me, Enrico,'' McGill said. "When will I know about our passage?''

"I will get in touch with Valaczek today,'' Fuentes told him. "I think there will be no problem.''

"My God, that's just wonderful,'' McGill said. "Ana

will be so relieved. She must know by now that the airport has been cut off. I'll go right home and tell her.''

"Of course, this will be a very hush-hush operation, Luther. You must travel incognito, or Alvarez' spies may try to stop you. I'll have false papers made up. Maybe you'll be a Caribbean importer who brought his family on a buying trip to South America. Valaczek will know your I.D. is false, and he will know about the documents. His crew will know nothing.''

McGill sat there, nodding, all of it sounding bizarre to him, as if it were happening to someone else.

"You'll need protection, too," Fuentes added, puffing the cigar.

"Protection?" McGill frowned.

"A couple of men who know how to use guns. I can furnish them. They will go all the way to Miami with you, and then fly to Peru from there.''

"But I thought that when we got away from here—"

"Believe me, Luther. It doesn't hurt to have protection.''

McGill sat there thinking. Remembering Jake Parrish, and how Parrish had handled himself so well in an incident involving hill bandits in the back country a few years ago. Parrish had probably saved McGill's life. And then McGill had had to let him down, later, when Parrish got into trouble with the company.

"Tell you what, Enrico. Give me just one bodyguard of the two, and allow me to supply the other man. I have in mind a friend of the family, if I can find him, and if he's interested. Ana and Nita would feel more comfortable with at least one of the two a familiar face.''

Fuentes rolled the cigar in his hand. "Guns and men who carry them do tend to make women jumpy. Very well, Luther. If you think this friend of yours is a man you can trust with your lives. I prefer you take two men I know to be qualified, but I will leave this to your discretion.''

"Thanks, Enrico,'' McGill said.

"I will give you a man named Rueda, an experienced policeman and bodyguard. He knows several Alvarista agents by sight and should be able to smell trouble well in advance.''

"It sounds as if we'll be well taken care of,'' McGill said, grinning again.

Fuentes rose, and McGill did, too. "I truly hope you will, Luther. I'll be calling you later today, perhaps this evening. There will be a fee for Valaczek, of course, but I'll make sure he keeps it reasonable. The thing you must impress on your wife, and your son and daughter, is that this must be discussed with absolutely no one outside your family, except for this man you intend to hire. One slip to the wrong person, and you may not leave Guayaquil at all.''

"You can rest assured that we'll all exercise the utmost caution, Enrico.''

Two

Only a couple of hours' drive from Guayaquil, the oil camp, Punto Segundo, was a festering sore on the bank of a muddy tributary of the Guayas River. Corrugated iron shacks and flaking stucco buildings dotted that jungle clearing steaming in the sun. Beyond the buildings were a dozen oil wells with black-steel, tyrannosaurus-type derricks, some working and some not. There was a sizeable dock at the river's edge, and a dirt road, paralleling the river, that led to the nearest town, a few kilometers down-river. In the camp itself were two company office buildings, an annex, storage facilities, barracks for the workers, a tiny store, and a bar.

The store was a dark little hovel where a black Ecuadorian displayed gray mysterious objects of toiletry on dark shelves, unlabeled cans of fruit, and dusty packages of razor blades. In the bar, a greasy company bartender swatted flies without enthusiasm and watered the few bottles of Guayaquil liquor available to camp men. The streets of the camp were always litter-clogged and dust-blown, and a stench of urine and feces came from the direction of the barracks buildings. Black, scrawny buzzards sat on rooftops like misshapen shooting gallery pigeons, their claws scratching on the corrugated metal as they waited and watched for something to scavenge. Some of the buildings had been boarded up and, like the derricks, were no longer in use.

The two barracks buildings that housed men were dilapidated structures with torn screens and paint-spray graffiti decorating their exteriors. Inside, there were a few old cots, each draped in a mosquito netting, a toilet that did not work, a couple of wash bowls. There was the incessant humming of insects in and around these places, and a scattering of company workers sprawled under netting canopies—dirty, unkempt, blank-looking, sweating away their lives.

Jake Parrish was one of those blank-faced men. Outside the temperature was almost a hundred, and it was not much cooler where Parrish lay. His netting was coiled above him in a ball, and a couple of mosquitoes and flies had found him, but he did not notice. In his right hand he held a bottle of the watered liquor from the bar, and he had consumed almost half of it. At Punto Segundo it was necessary to immerse oneself in alcohol in order to make one's surroundings more bearable.

Parrish rarely drank hard liquor when he had worked for Ameco, under Luther McGill. Those were the days when he had control—of his life, his future. He had been a junior officer under McGill and a rising star, just a few years ago. During a visit by McGill and two other company executives to a Montecristi rubber camp, there had been a scrape with local bandits, and Parrish had led the counter-assault to drive the hill thieves off; McGill had been very impressed. Parrish had been rather surprised himself at his own audacity. He had been treated like some kind of hero by McGill's family then, especially by growing-up Tony and Nita. Life had been good.

But there had been a cresting of Parrish's life at that point, it seemed now, looking back on it. He had blundered into an affair with the young wife of an elderly Guayaquil politico, and had thought he was in love. When the affair was uncovered and the politician vented his outrage, the young wife dropped Parrish like a hot Ecuadorian platano, and the politician demanded Parrish's hide. The company requested McGill to fire him, and McGill, too concerned with his own future with the company, made no defense for Parrish, one of the best young men the company had working for it in Ecuador.

Parrish had been caught off-guard by McGill's lack of loyalty. He had depended on it, and was mildly shocked when McGill let him go. McGill assured him that it was only business and that he wanted to stay on friendly terms with Parrish, but Parrish cut himself off from McGill completely. He did not return to the States, but moved to Loja where he invested all of his money in a failing banana plantation, and lost it.

Those two setbacks, so close to one another, did something to Jake Parrish. He lost his self-image. He began drinking more regularly. He took a job with a competing rubber company, a small one owned by Ecuadorians, got into a raging argument with a superior over procedures and heatedly quit. The next job was with a poorly run rubber and oil company, and it marked the third trauma for him in a brief period, perhaps the worst one. Working as a field foreman, Parrish had been on duty one hot afternoon when a fire broke out in a rubber warehouse, trapping a half-dozen men inside. Three of them got out, but three remained behind the wall of flame, with nobody knowing how to save them—except Parrish who was responsible for them. He knew that if he risked his own life to break down a rear door, he could probably get to them. He hesitated too long, and a roof collapsed; none of the three survived.

Before the Ameco firing, Parrish knew that he would not have hesitated. Now he had become a coward as well as a failure, and, without knowing it, he had come to dislike himself.

24

He had resigned after the fire. Nobody at the camp had accused him of cowardice, but there were those who had seen his missed opportunity, and he could not look into their eyes.

Drinking even more heavily then, Parrish finally landed this job at this oil camp. As a foreman of a small crew, he delegated the repair of rusting-out pumps.

Parrish lay there sweating on the lumpy cot, staring at the crude-beam ceiling, wishing he had saved enough money to buy a ticket back home. He was tired of Ecuador, tired of speaking Spanish. Lying there in soiled shirt and pants, a stubble of beard on his square chin, he thought Ecuador might be his tomb. Nobody bothered about visas in the back country. He would rot away here, and one day the vultures would come down off the rooftops and finish him off.

"Hey, Parrish!"

The voice came to him from the ceiling, the walls, from under the cot. He squinted his dark eyes and grunted, propping himself up on his elbows. "Huh? Who is it?"

A form against the front screen was silhouetted by a bright, flat-iron sun. "The boss he wants to talk with you." In Parrish's native language, to show off his English. Then, in quick Spanish: *"Venga conmigo en seguida, por favor."*

Parrish swung his legs off the cot and rubbed a hand across his chin, looking at the watch on his sweaty wrist. "Hell, okay. I'll be right there."

The straw-hatted figure turned and disappeared into the hard sun.

Parrish set the bottle down beside the cot and rose to his feet. He did not feel drunk. That was the trouble nowadays, he could not seem to throw enough of it down him to make any difference. Of course, when they doctored it, you never knew how much you were getting for your money.

He walked to one of the wash bowls and poured some brownish water into it from a pitcher, and splashed some onto his face. He was a tall athletically-built fellow in his early thirties, with dark brown hair and eyes, and a handsome, angular, masculine face. A light scar crossed his chin on a diagonal, and the chin was slightly cleft. He had played football at Kansas State a thousand years ago, and then had fought a war for his country, a war in which he learned more about killing than he ever wanted to know.

Parrish toweled off and focused on himself in a cracked wall mirror. He made a face at the bearded, pouchy fellow who stared back at him. "Jesus!" he muttered.

Picking up a battered straw hat from a rickety table, he went to a side door, kicked it open, and stepped out into the flat, hard sun. It knifed his eyes. He grunted and walked toward a nearby stucco building where the field office was located. A skinny yellow dog cowered out of his way, and a fly buzzed about his head. Down at the muddy river bank, a couple of women—wives of company workers—were jabbering in some Indian dialect. And always, the eternal thumping of the oil pumps.

He stepped into the building, his eyes adjusting to the dimmer light again. Parrish's boss was slouched behind a desk-table, one booted foot up on its edge. The table was littered with crinkled papers, some of which had oil-stain fingerprints on their surfaces. The sizeable room had white-washed walls and an overhead fan that moved too slowly to be of much use.

"Ah. Parrish," Gonzalez said. He was a square-shouldered man with heavy, thick features. He wore a black mustache, and the lobe of his left ear was gone, cut off in some long-ago brawl. He was bare-headed at the moment, showing thick black hair, and his khaki shirt was unbuttoned down the front. He placed the remainder of a greasy sandwich on the table, wiping his hands on his shirt.

"You wanted to see me?" Parrish said, sitting down on a straight chair near the desk without being asked.

"It is five-forty, Parrish," Gonzalez told him in a backwoods Spanish. "Your siesta was over at five."

"Oh, Christ, Gonzalez," Parrish said. "It's still a hundred degrees out there. The crew will raise hell if I roust them in this. Give us a break, for God's sake." His voice was tougher than he meant it to be.

Gonzalez wiped a sleeve across his mouth. "You're drinking too damned much, Parrish. You don't get to work when you're supposed to, and you don't pay attention to what you're doing when you're out there on the derricks. You're costing me and the company money."

"Oh, shit," Parrish muttered.

'I've had to send a report in about you," Gonzalez told him. "I hired you because these men have respect for a white gringo like you, and they will work hard under such a foreman. But they are losing that respect, Parrish, because of the drinking."

"To hell with respect," Parrish grumbled. "What good is it, anyway? What did it ever buy for anybody?"

"It got you your job here," Gonzalez told him. "And the loss of it can take that same job away from you."

"Are you threatening to fire me, Gonzalez?" Parrish said harshly, his face flushing under the beard stubble.

Gonzalez took his foot off the table and leaned forward on his chair. "You're the best foreman I've ever had here. You know how to keep our machines going. But I'm not getting enough out of you, Parrish. Stop the heavy drinking, or I'll have to let you go. I mean it."

Parrish rose off the chair. "No backwoods Indian tells me how much I can drink, goddamn it! I'm getting your goddamn pumps repaired! What more do you

27

want, for Christ's sake?''

"I want you at top production capacity," Gonzalez said evenly, ignoring the insult to him. "And I want you to be an example to the other men. At this moment, you are neither of these things."

"If it gets to where you don't think I'm earning my wages," Parrish growled, "just let me know, and I'll haul ass. But don't interfere in my personal life, god-damn it!" Without waiting for a reply from Gonzalez, he turned and left. Gonzalez stared moodily after him.

That evening after his post-siesta work was done, he dismissed his three-man crew of local Indians, borrowed a rusty old vehicle and drove to the village, just to get away from Punto Segundo for a few hours. The village was called Santa Rosa de Santiago. It had a population of about a thousand, but it was a real island of civil-ization in comparison with Punto Segundo. There were two cantinas, three stores, an Indian market, and a central plaza, just above the river. Under the shade trees boys sat on benches drinking soda and listening to the radio music from the cantinas. There were also several whores in Santa Rosa, but Parrish had not patronized them. He came to Santa Rosa to buy good booze, get a good meal and maybe a bath at one of the cantinas—to dissipate the feeling that he had isolated himself in the ugliest hellhole in the world.

Parrish went directly to the largest of the cantinas, bought himself a bottle of real Gordon's Gin, and sat by himself in a dark corner sipping the gin from a short water glass the proprietor had furnished him. If he lost the job at Punto Segundo, he had no idea where he would go to get another. He remembered Ameco in Guayaquil, when the world belonged to him. One mis-take and everything went bad from that moment on. If he had not allowed himself to get involved with the petite, good-looking wife of the deputy minister of foreign affairs, he might be a high-ranking officer of

28

Ameco now. He supposed that Luther McGill was long gone, sipping his liqueurs in New York and reading about the civil strife here in the *Times*.

"Ah, Mister Parrish. What a pleasure it gives me to find you here, sir."

Parrish glanced up. He was a boy still in his teens, dressed in white cotton and holding a straw hat in his hand. He looked like a banana farmer, but he was the local pimp for at least three of the village whores. He had approached Parrish before, on many occasions, but Parrish had always turned a deaf ear to his offers.

"Oh, Christ," Parrish groaned. "You again, Lazaro? I told you before, your women don't appeal to me. Take them in a truck up to Punto Segundo, maybe you'll make out there. Or feed them to the fish in the river, for all I care."

"Ah, sir, I fully understand how you feel about the ordinary whore this miserable place has to offer such a man of the world. I would not have come to you with the offer of such a woman, sir. I have something completely different for you. Special, sir, and new."

Parrish met his gaze blankly. In the cantina across the plaza, a radio blasted out a rich flamenco music. "Special?" Parrish said sourly. "New?"

"Exquisitely special, and absolutely new," Lazaro said, grinning broadly. "Actually, a second cousin to myself, sir, just recruited into the profession. You would be the first—well, almost the first—man to have her."

Parrish narrowed his dark eyes slightly. "How old is this cousin?"

"Oh, she is of age, Mr. Parrish. Absolutely. It is the law. She is a woman, you will see. She is both innocent and willing, a fine combination, I think you'll agree. When I mentioned you to her, before coming over here, she was very excited about the prospect of serving you."

Parrish rubbed at his stubbled chin. The boy, Lazaro,

was getting to him with his descriptions of the young whore.

"This one you must see, sir," Lazaro insisted. "Her name is Linda, a real clean girl. Would you like to see her now?"

"Oh, hell," Parrish grunted, swigging a half-glass of the gin.

"I won't bother you anymore, if you will just see this one," Lazaro insisted. "As a small favor for old times, yes?"

There had been no "old times" from the business standpoint, though. The old times had consisted of Lazaro's having an occasional drink at Parrish's expense, while pleading with him to spend an hour with one of Lazaro's women, and with Parrish always declining.

Parrish met the young man's gaze with a tired one. "All right, Lazaro. I'm bored tonight, anyway. I'll take one quick look at this girl, if you'll quit bothering me with all this every time you see me. Agreed?"

"Yes, agreed, Mr. Parrish," Lazaro said quickly.

Parrish rose with his bottle and left the place in Lazaro's company. Outside on the square, there was just a slight breeze coming from the direction of the river, and there were knots of young men gathered under the plane trees, talking and laughing quietly. The Latin music from the other cantina was louder out there and sounded more tinny. Parrish followed Lazaro down a dark side street to a two-story dwelling with cracking stucco on its exterior. There was the odor of the barnyard on the first floor. They went up a narrow broken stairway to an upper corridor, and passed a couple of doorways, closed. Finally Lazaro knocked on a third door, and waited. When it opened, a young girl stood there.

Lazaro had been right about her. She was pretty and innocent-looking. She looked past Lazaro to Parrish.

30

Lazaro turned to Parrish. "Please." He gestured for Parrish to enter the girl's room.

The room was small and dimly lighted by two kerosene lamps. Most houses in Santa Rosa had no electricity. There were two chairs, a sizeable bed, and a washbowl in a corner. Over the bed hung a faded lithograph of ex-president Ibarra. Parrish liked that; it was a political statement, and in Ecuador one did not make political statements.

"I'm pleased to meet you, Mr. Parrish," the girl was saying to him.

Parrish turned to her. She was petite, dark-skinned, doe-eyed. Almost pure Indian, he figured, but pretty. She spoke Spanish well, with no hint of tribal accent. When you got down to the Amazon basin, Parrish knew, there were Indians who had never heard Spanish spoken.

"Same here, little flower," Parrish said, affecting the Spanish manner. He reached out and touched her brown cheek, and sighed. She might be sixteen, but might not. In this part of the world, though, a man's values changed. She was truly a woman, in every sense. It was only because of Lazaro's care that she had gotten this far without being used up. That was the way it was in the back country.

"You like her, yes?" Lazaro grinned, showing a gold tooth at the corner of his mouth.

"You're very pretty, Linda," Parrish said.

"You see? I told you, Mr. Parrish," Lazaro reminded him.

Parrish turned to him, took some sucre bills from his pocket, and counted off several and handed them to Lazaro. "This is as good a place to drink for a while as the cantina."

"You will not regret it, sir," Lazaro said happily.

Linda had averted her dark eyes at the exchange of money. Now she gave Parrish a lovely smile.

31

"Call me Jake. We're business associates now, you can both please call me Jake."

Lazaro, still grinning, tipped his straw hat and went to the open door. He paused for a moment. "Ah, I almost forgot. . .Jake. There was a man asking about you. At the plaza tonight. I hadn't seen you then."

Parrish furrowed his dark brow. "What man? Somebody from Punto Segundo?"

"I don't think so. I can inquire, if you'd like."

Parrish stood there thinking for a moment. "No. To hell with it. See you later, Lazaro."

"As you wish. . .Jake."

A moment later Parrish was alone in the room with the girl. He sat down heavily on the edge of her bed and swigged the gin from the bottle. She sat down beside him. She was wearing a cotton blouse and skirt, nothing on her legs or feet. Her long black hair was down on her shoulders, and she smelled like crude back-country soap. "You want to take your clothes off?" she suggested.

Parrish glanced at her. She had big dark eyes and a very sensual mouth. She began unbuttoning her blouse. In a moment it came off, revealing her perky breasts to Parrish. She avoided his eyes, stood up, removing her skirt and cotton underclothing.

"Is it all right? Do I please you?"

She was beautiful to look at, and Parrish was reminded how easily beauty comes to youth, and how flagrantly youth displays it. Her skin was perfect, her muscle tone delectable. The dark nipples awaited his touch, the warm dark place between her thighs was ready to enjoy his caresses. Young flesh was so easily aroused, too. There was always a readiness for orgasm, a hot hopefulness just under the surface.

"Yes, honey. You please me." She was just about the age of Nita McGill a few years ago when she had had a crush on Parrish, and Parrish had had to keep her at arm's length. It had taken an iron will some days to ward off a bikini-clad bundle of sex like Nita. But Parrish had had an outlet for his physical urges at that time, anyway, in the deputy minister's young wife.

Linda was unbuttoning Parrish's shirt, and he did not try to stop her. But he drank as she worked, and he was getting quite a bit of gin inside him, now. That was what he wanted, to get enough inside him to forget what he had become, to forget Punto Segundo and the dirt and the heat.

In a short while, Parrish was on his back on the bed, his trousers still on, the bottle on a night stand. Linda was propped beside him, and her warm flesh was in his hands, her hungry mouth on his. She kissed him passionately, her supple curves on him, moving and moving, and for a moment Parrish thought he was in bed with the Guayaquil girl. There was some fumbling with his trousers then, and a hot handling, and then her hot mouth on him. But quite abruptly, in the middle of all of that, the liquor hit him hard, and he suddenly withdrew from her, rolling onto his side.

"Hey. Jake," she said quietly into his ear, touching it with her tongue.

But now he was breathing deeply, and was lost to her.

She sat up on the bed beside him, frustrated. "Damn," she said to herself in the darkness of the room. She sat there for a long while, hearing his deep breathing. Then she lay back down, apart from him, on her back, and let her right hand fall naturally to the still-hot place between her bronze thighs. In just a moment, the hand was caressing the place, inflaming it, and just minutes later the bed shook with her climax, her throaty cries rising above Parrish's soft snoring beside her.

When Parrish woke, an hour later, the girl was sound asleep. He got up without waking her, found the gin, and swigged some of it down. He had no idea whether they had had sex or not. Sex and women were not important to him nowadays. Almost nothing seemed important, except for the booze.

Parrish got dressed awkwardly, and the girl rolled over once but never woke. He left her an extra sucre bill on the night stand and departed quietly, with his bottle.

When he got out on the street the moon was up, and it was later than he figured. He had to get back to Punto Segundo. He stumbled against a building wall, and got his balance there for a moment. As he hung there on the wall, he saw the dark figure come up to him, out of the shadows.

"Jake Parrish."

Parrish squinted into the darkness. "Who is it?"

"I've been looking for you, Jake Parrish."

Parrish saw another dark figure come up from behind him, and then another materialized. They were *mestizos*, wearing the narrow-brimmed straw hats of the area, and they looked like oil or rubber camp men.

"What the hell's going on?" Parrish said in a slurred voice. He raised his hand to wipe the sweat on his chin, and the bottle slid from his grasp, shattering on a flat rock at his feet. "Christ!" he muttered.

The first dark figure came closer, and now Parrish saw that he held a wooden club in his hand. "I am Salgado," he said. "The nephew of a man by the same name who lost his life in the fire at the San Luis rubber camp."

Parrish sobered up. He looked at the *mestizo* and remembered that there had, indeed, been a Salgado killed in the fire at San Luis.

"I remember," he said thickly.

"You let my uncle die," Salgado said.

Parrish glanced toward the other men and saw that each of them held a short club of some kind. They had moved within a few yards of him.

The liquor in Parrish made him belligerent. "So?"

"So now you must pay for that crime," Salgado told him. "An eye for an eye, Parrish. Debts do not go unpaid in these parts."

"Christ, go home and sleep it off," he said querulously. He started past the fellow called Salgado.

In that next moment, one of the men moved in and slammed a club against Parrish's neck and shoulder.

Parrish grunted under the unexpected impact, and hit the building wall again. In his head flashed a jungle scene from the war, and he was in hand-to-hand combat with a Cong. He hit out blindly with the heel of his hand, missing his assailant, and another club descended on him, from Salgado this time. It struck him across the side of the head, splitting his scalp over his ear, and then he was on his back on the dirt, almost unconscious. Now came kicks in his side and back, and the clubs came down again and again. He realized that they intended to beat him to death, but he could not defend himself.

"Hey! You men! What are you doing there!"

Parrish vaguely heard a voice, and feet running. One last crack across his head and neck, then nothing but pain. Two pairs of boots came up and stood beside his head.

"Ah. The gringo."

"Look at the blood."

"I think his name is Parrish. He drove a car here this evening."

"I know him. He's always drunk. He's one of those Punto Segundo gringos that they hire there. No good."

Parrish opened his eyes, and saw the gunbelts of the local police. "It was Cong," he said thickly. "They had AK-47's. They're down in the rice paddy now."

"He can't drive the car back," the first voice came.

"There is a Punto Segundo truck here this evening. A few Indians on it. He can ride back with them."

"We ought to leave him right here. What good is he

to anyone, I ask you?"

"I'll get the truck," the other one said.

"It all happened so fast," Parrish was saying thickly, on the ground. "There was all that flame. And then the roof just came in. It just came in on them, for Christ's sake."

The remaining policeman was paying no attention to him, though.

Whatever the drunken gringo had to say could be of little importance.

They had had quite enough of him at Santa Rosa.

Three

In the blossom-scented coolness of evening, they all gathered in McGill's study for a second family conference. Not wanting to alarm Ana, McGill had not turned on the radio all day, but he knew that the airport was now in control of the Alvaristas. He had gotten a call from Fuentes early that morning, and the Valaczek passage was confirmed. Valaczek would be leaving in two days as planned, and Fuentes was busy working on papers for McGill and his family.

"We're going to have to quit meeting like this," Tony said laconically, sprawled across a leather armchair. He had found a ripe slice of papaya in the refrigerator and was eating it with a silver fork.

"Oh, Tony!" Nita said impatiently. "This is important, for God's sake! Can't you fill your stomach later?"

Ana sat on the very edge of a Queen Anne chair, her hair pulled severely back away from her face, her dark brown eyes lined with fatigue. "All right, you two. Let your father speak."

McGill sat on the arm of the sofa, at the opposite end from his daughter. Behind him were rows of bookshelves, a desk, and another easy chair. At the French windows, the heavy drapery was pulled aside to allow as much air from the garden as possible. Dusk had just fallen, and the temperature had already dropped.

"I'm sure you all know," McGill began, "that the airport is controlled by the guerrillas."

A heavy silence fell over the room. They could hear the clock ticking on McGill's desk and the slight rustling of the draperies as a breeze came in from the garden.

"Luckily, though, I've made arrangements for our departure," McGill added. Ana knew about the freighter, but McGill had given her no details yet.

"How?" Nita wondered.

"By freighter," McGill said.

"Oh, God!" Nita said, making a sour face. Her dark hair was standing out at the sides of her head in pigtails, and she looked about fifteen, except for her woman's body.

Tony narrowed his eyes. "What kind of freighter?"

"I don't honestly know," McGill said. "Except that its registry is Chilean, and its captain is an American. It's called the *Maria Isabel.*" He sat there, pausing. "Enrico Fuentes is setting the whole thing up for us. We're damned lucky he offered his help. We'll be taking some things for him, too."

"Does this freighter go to Miami?" Nita asked.

McGill nodded. "By way of Panama and Haiti. It probably won't be first class accommodations, but it will get us out of here."

"Hell, it sounds terrible," Tony groaned, setting the remainder of the papaya on the floor beside the chair. "Let's wait for something better."

McGill turned to his son angrily. "We will go now, damn it! There isn't anything better! This is our safety we're talking about here, Tony, can't you understand that? These Alvaristas mean business, and they hate our guts! Do you want to end up in prison?"

"Or standing up before a firing squad?" Nita suggested.

"Please, Nita!" Ana said heavily.

McGill turned to Ana, watching her lovely face

38

closely as he spoke. "She's right. Or they might not be so formal. Near Quito, a French businessman and his family were locked up in their house and it was set afire."

Tony grunted. "I don't believe all those stories."

"Well, believe them or not," McGill said harshly to him, "the guerrillas have declared foreign investors as their enemy. They may treat that enemy well, and they may not. Hopefully, we won't be around to find out. We leave on the *Maria Isabel* in two days' time."

Ana sighed audibly. "These things you are taking for Enrico. What are they, Luther?"

McGill shrugged. "He says they are papers, documents. There will be a piece of luggage which we will treat as ours, and we must speak of it to no one."

"Oh, Christ!" Tony muttered. "Fuentes always was a little bit melodramatic!"

McGill regarded Tony soberly. "There are Álvarista agents everywhere, Tony. If they found out we're leaving on the *Maria Isabel*, they'd try to stop us. Even without knowledge of the Fuentes papers. We must be very secretive about this. We'll travel under false papers and assumed names until we get to Miami."

"You're kidding?" Nita exclaimed.

"No, I'm not. Also, we'll have bodyguard protection." Ana looked quickly toward McGill.

"*Body*guards!" Tony said, his jaw dropped slightly open. "You mean. . .with guns?"

"Fuentes thinks there should be at least two. He's supplying a man from the police, and he's letting me pick another. I'm going to try to hire Jake Parrish, if I can find him."

"Jake?" Nita said, sitting up on the sofa. "Jake will be going along?"

"If I can get him," McGill said.

"Well, at least Jake would make the trip tolerable," Tony said. "I could get him into some chess games. We used to play some great games of chess."

"Jake Parrish," Nita said quietly. All the other three turned to look at her, and the anxious look on Ana's face melted slightly.

"You all know what I think of Jake, despite what happened with the company," McGill told them. "It would be nice to have an old friend along who has our best interests at heart. Jake was always good with guns, and you all know what he did at Montecristi."

"He saved your skin, is what he did," Tony offered. "And then you fired him."

"A man can't just take another man's wife, for God's sake, Tony. Not even in South America." Nita stared past him then, with a small wry smile. When she had heard of the Parrish scandal, she had envied the deputy minister's wife. When Nita was sixteen, she could not imagine going to bed with a man more desirable than Jake Parrish.

"I can't believe he'd go, after what the company did to him," Tony said. "I wouldn't."

"Luther," Ana said. "Do you think guns are necessary? I mean, once we leave Guayaquil, we will surely be safe."

"Fuentes isn't so sure," McGill said. "Alvarista reputedly has people training in Panama, for instance. And we know nothing of Captain Valaczek's crew. I can assure you that we'll have a pleasant, uneventful trip, Ana, but precautions are nevertheless wise."

"Fuentes was always this way, Mother," Tony said. "He's probably more interested in his papers than in our safety, anyway."

McGill scowled at him, but ignored the remark. "Tomorrow you will accelerate your packing. If things go well, we'll be leaving the following evening at about midnight. In the meantime, I must call Wade Sumner in Miami and tell him about our change of plans. I've worked out a kind of code with him, so the local oper-

40

ator won't know what we're talking about."

Tony shook his head. "I don't believe all this."

McGill continued to ignore him. "I'll also have to find Jake Parrish. The last I heard, he was working for a competing rubber company. I'll hope he's located where I can still get to him."

"Can I go with you?" Tony asked, "when you go talk with Jake?"

"No," McGill said firmly. "I want you here with the women. I don't want them left alone until the moment we leave."

"Oh, hell," Tony grumbled.

"A week from now we'll all be safe in Miami, and the worst of this will be behind us," McGill said.

"I pray to the Holy Mother for it to be so," Ana added quietly.

That same evening, in a military headquarters set up temporarily in a village south of Guayaquil, Idilio Alvarez held a brief conference with two advisors from his Reform Council and General Perez, a defected army general who had long been opposed to Biaza and his government.

They sat around a kitchen table in a confiscated villa. Alvarez, like the others, wore a green fatigue uniform and gunbelt. He was a bearded, masculine-looking man in his forties, taller than average, slim but muscular. His official title was Chairman of the Council, but he rarely used titles. An intelligent, uneducated man, he saw himself as a champion of the working class and peasants in Ecuador, and an independent revolutionary. But he had already accepted help from the Communist parties of Cuba and Panama, and was heavily in their debt. Alvarez wanted a better world in Ecuador, but he was not sophisticated enough to know how to go about achieving it. He saw all foreign investors as imperialists, exploiters, and pillars of President Biaza's reactionary

41

government, a government indifferent to necessary social reform.

A man who consciously modeled himself after Castro, Alvarez possessed the righteous piety of the reformer and the unshakable conviction that the heel of oppression must be removed. He no longer attempted to argue or to persuade; the enemy had to be destroyed.

On Alvarez' right was a shorter, darker-skinned man —General Perez. Perez had a fat cigar stuck in his mouth. He wore gold rings on his fingers. His sole motivation for joining Alvarez was the acquisition of personal power. Alvarez knew this, but needed Perez' troops. When the Biaza government fell, there would be time to deal with men like Perez. Perez sat there puffing on the cigar, his small eyes watching the other faces intently.

On Alvarez' left sat Torres, a man who had been with Alvarez from the beginning. He was stocky, with gray in his dark hair, and he wore a short beard. The fourth man, across the table from Alvarez, was a tough aide and council member named Jesus Cuesta, a kind of bodyguard to Alvarez. He was athletic-looking and wiry, with dark diamond-hard eyes and a thick black mustache. Cuesta was a killer, and a rabid slogan jawing rebel. Like Perez, he was a necessary evil to Alvarez, a man who could be dangerous after the shooting stopped.

"The villages to the east of the airport are now controlled," Alvarez was saying to the others. "Our guerrillas have secured all facilities in that area. And General Linares is progressing steadily from the north, along the coast. Regular army units are surrendering to him en masse, rather than fire on his troops."

"It's just a matter of time now," Perez said, puffing on the cigar. A tic at the corner of his mouth unexpectedly jerked his face into a lopsided grin. "My troops have completely routed the Biaza units at the airport and have control of the tower. We'll take Guayaquil within a week."

"It's too damned bad that Biaza got out," Torres offered. "He must stand trial for his crimes."

"I'd like to shoot the sonofabitch myself," Cuesta said. "Give me the word, Idilio, and I'll take a few men to Iquitos and do a job on him."

But Alvarez shook his head. "No, we don't need trouble with Peru. We'll let Biaza stew in exile. But let's try to keep the rest of the fish in our net. In the next week there will be an exodus from the capital, along the roads and from the port. I want to keep this to a minimum. We want some fish to fry in our reform court. All found guilty of treason against the people will be executed, including foreigners."

"Our troops are not taking many foreigners alive," Cuesta said with a crooked smile. "Somehow they don't seem to last through the arrest."

Alvarez eyed Cuesta sidewise. "There is no victory in mass slaughter," he said seriously.

"There is satisfaction," Cuesta said.

"There must be a properly established tribunal," Alvarez insisted. "The evidence of criminality must be brought forth for the world to see. Punishment through legal means will serve as the basis for a new social order."

"When you catch a snake, you kill him," Cuesta growled.

Perez grinned and puffed at the cigar. "Jesus has a point, Idilio," he said easily.

"I agree," Alvarez said. "But our mission in Ecuador is not just to kill snakes. We must vindicate our reform government, and establish the new order as a legitimate nation."

Torres turned to Alvarez. "My informants tell me that a few ships are still coming into port at Guayaquil, and then being allowed to leave. I think we should put

43

agents all along the waterfront. If a big fish tried to leave by sea, we'd have our catch."

Alvarez stroked his beard and nodded. "All right." He turned to Cuesta. "Jesus, would you like to take on that responsibility?"

Cuesta's hard eyes smiled. "It would be my pleasure," he said. "I'll put some men on it this very evening."

Torres grunted. "You're always so damned efficient in these matters, Jesus."

In Miami, it was almost midnight. Wade Sumner had received the call from the fellow named Salazar in mid-evening, and Salazar had insisted on a meeting at Sumner's place that night. Now, at 11:45, the front doorbell rang, and Sumner knew it must be Salazar.

Sumner's wife, Bette, was still up, and she started for the door, but Sumner asked her to let him answer it. "Who would it be, Wade?" she wondered. She knew about the McGills' coming, but Sumner had not told her about Salazar.

"It's a fellow to talk about Luther," Sumner told her without further explanation. Then he was opening the door and staring at the rather swarthy, heavy-set man standing there.

"You're Salazar?" Sumner said.

"Yes, that's right, Mr. Sumner." Just behind him stood a second man, a young fellow who also looked Latin, twenty years the junior of Salazar, and had the look of a highly paid pimp. Sumner noted a slight bulge under the young man's tropical suit jacket, and knew exactly what it was.

"Who is it?" Bette Sumner asked quizzically. She was wearing a robe and slippers, and had already put up her ash blond hair. A tired-looking woman in her late forties, she had lost all signs of youth in her face. When her children had grown up and moved out, life had

44

wound down for Bette. Her looks had gone, and her interests had waned, and her husband had begun seeing other women. Now, just recently, he had found one who just might ruin what was left of their marriage.

"This is Mr. Salazar," Sumner told her. "Please come in, Mr. Salazar. And Mr.—"

"Smith," the young man said, with no trace of an accent.

Sumner looked him up and down. "All right, come in, Mr. Smith."

They came in and the young man leaned against the closed door, without attempting to join the small group. Bette regarded Salazar and his young companion and turned to Sumner. "They're here about Luther McGill?"

"That's right, Bette. It's just a matter of arranging to meet Luther and his family down at the docks. Why don't you go on to bed?"

Bette gave Sumner a look. "All right, Wade. Glad to have met you, Mr. Salazar. . .Mr. Smith."

"The same to you, Mrs. Sumner," Salazar said in an oily, accented voice.

The young man with the bulge in his jacket nodded casually, and then Bette left for another part of the house. "Why don't you step in here, gentlemen?" Sumner invited them, gesturing toward the living room.

The men moved into the big room, with its Moorish archways, plush overstuffed furniture and potted plants. Sumner seated them on a velvet sofa, and he drew up a wing chair to face them. The fellow who called himself Smith never took his eyes off Sumner, and hardly spoke at all.

Sumner leaned forward on the chair. He was in his early fifties, fit and handsome, with some silver in his wavy hair. He had come up in the company with McGill, and, for a while, they had been assigned to the same office of the parent company to Ameco. He and

McGill were now both on the vice-presidential level, but Ameco itself was no longer a going proposition. Consequently, neither McGill nor Sumner were highly valued by the parent corporation in New York. Sumner had already been advised to offer McGill, on his return, with a lesser position with Ameco in Miami, or early retirement, and since McGill was not yet fifty, that was not much of an option. Sumner dreaded the idea of being the one to break the news to McGill. It had been Sumner who had had to fly to Guayaquil a few years ago and fire McGill's top assistant, Jake Parrish, and that had been unpleasant enough.

"So, Mr. Salazar. You came to talk about Luther McGill?"

Salazar nodded. He had slicked-back hair and pock marks on his lower face, giving the appearance of a drug boss or wealthy bookie. He was related to Enrico Fuentes by blood, and he had been a former strong-arm for a government previous to that of Biaza.

"You have been advised by Mr. McGill that he will be in the custody of certain documents and other items on his trip from Guayaquil to Miami? Things given to him by Enrico Fuentes, and belonging to the Ecuadorian government?"

Sumner nodded. "Yes, Luther mentioned that."

"You must understand," Salazar told him, "that Mr. McGill's escape from Ecuador has been procured by Mr. Fuentes at great risk to himself, and that Mr. McGill promised safe delivery of these documents to me here in Miami as an absolute condition of our assistance to the McGills."

Sumner frowned and pursed thin lips. "I see."

"And since it is important to your company, and to you personally that the McGills arrive here safely, Mr. Sumner, we're going to ask you to not only receive the McGills upon the arrival of the *Maria Isabel,* but also to receive the trunk of Enrico Fuentes that Mr. McGill will

46

have with him."

"I don't think I understand," Sumner said. "It will be with his luggage, won't it?"

"Aboard the freighter, yes. But when the *Maria Isabel* anchors out in the bay here, Mr. Sumner, in preparation to docking, the Fuentes trunk will be separated from the McGills' luggage, under Captain Valaczek's direction, and be transferred to a small craft in the middle of the night, so that it may come ashore without inspection. You own a pleasure boat, don't you, Mr. Sumner?"

"Why, yes. A converted Coast Guard cutter. I've owned it for several years now."

"The *Sea Witch*, I believe you call it?"

Sumner narrowed his handsome eyes on Salazar. "That's right."

Salazar sat forward. "On the night that the *Maria Isabel* anchors offshore, we will expect you to meet the freighter, Mr. Sumner, on your *Sea Witch,* take the Fuentes cargo aboard your boat, and transport it to a point up the coast a few miles that I will designate to you at the last moment, just before you are to leave."

Sumner was frowning again. "Is this illegal?"

Salazar shrugged. "It is done all the time by private parties, for one reason or another, Mr. Sumner. We cannot run the risk of having these documents impounded by some over-zealous customs official. You must understand our position. Without safe delivery to me here, Mr. McGill's agreement to bring the Fuentes trunk here means nothing to us."

Sumner nodded slowly. "All right. I see your point. But I'll have to clear this with the company."

Salazar shook his head sidewise. "I'm sorry, Mr. Sumner. Nobody else may be brought into this. If you contact one other person, the deal will be off, and your action will be regarded as very unfriendly by me and by Mr. Fuentes. Do you fully understand?"

47

Sumner glanced toward the silent young man. "I think so," he said quietly.

Salazar grinned broadly. "Then you will cooperate?"

Sumner hesitated just a moment. "What the hell. Okay," he said soberly. He owed McGill some favors. Maybe his involvement in their safe return to the States would soften the news Sumner had to unload onto McGill.

"Very good," Salazar said, rising. "I'm certain Mr. McGill's family will appreciate your assistance in this."

Sumner nodded. "Where can I get in touch with you, Mr. Salazar? Between now and the arrival of the *Maria Isabel?*"

"You can't, Mr. Sumner," he said impassively. "I'll get in touch with you."

Sumner glanced at the jacket-bulging young man who had an unnerving grin on his face.

"Well," he said uncertainly.

Salazar came up very close to Sumner. "It would be best not to mention this even to your wife."

Before Sumner could reply, Salazar and the young man strode quickly from the room.

A moment later, Sumner heard the front door close behind them.

Four

Captain Valaczek sat big and tough-looking in his blue
sea uniform, an old pipe stuck between his teeth, his
graying hair wild and uncombed. His lined eyes watched
carefully as Fuentes counted off a pile of American
dollars—Valaczek's payment for taking the McGills to
Miami.

"There, that's all of it," Fuentes told him in English.
"You can't complain about payment, Captain. You're
receiving top dollar."

Valaczek grunted, picked up the stack of money and
pocketed it. "I still don't like it, Enrico. I have no
facilities for passengers. They're going to get in the way.
They'll be asking for deck chairs, for Christ's sake."

"So, you will suffer some small inconvenience for a
few days," Fuentes said, shrugging. His heavy face
looked more lined than it had only a few days earlier,
and the pouches under his eyes were more pronounced.

"I've scheduled the ship to leave port at midnight,"
Valaczek said. "There should be no trouble at that
hour. The McGills should board at the last moment.
You mentioned there will be two men with them?"

"I'm sending a man with them for protection,"
Fuentes said. "And McGill is bringing a second man, I
believe."

"Aren't you being overly cautious?" Valaczek said.

"I'm sending some things along with the McGills,"

49

Fuentes said, "in a separate piece of their luggage. Papers important to the government."

"Ah," Valaczek said. "Now it comes clear."

"This trunk must not be taken off your ship at Miami with the other belongings of McGill," Fuentes said to him. "We are arranging to have it taken off while you anchor offshore, by a friend of McGill named Sumner. I'll give you more details later, before you leave."

"Hey, I didn't get paid for smuggling any trunk in at Miami," Valaczek protested.

Fuentes smiled and reached into a desk drawer and pulled out another pile of American money bound with a rubber band. Fuentes dropped it onto the edge of the desk near Valaczek. "I thought that would occur to you. I think you'll find this adequate for an additional favor."

Valaczek picked up the money and flipped the corners of the bills. His thick eyebrows raised slightly. "Hmmph. Those papers must be pretty important to you."

"They are," Fuentes said. "When Sumner appears, you will facilitate the trunk's removal from the ship. That is the extent of your involvement."

"You're not expecting any. . .trouble on this, are you?" Valaczek wondered.

"There shouldn't be any. We'll know who's going aboard, and you know your crew. You're only making a couple of stops on the way. It should be a very ordinary run for you."

Valaczek nodded doubtfully. "I don't know if you're aware of it, but there are a lot of characters hanging around the waterfront nowadays, watching the ships closely. I presume some of them are not government people."

"Alvarez has spies all through the city," Fuentes admitted. "We arrest them when we can."

"It wouldn't hurt if these guards, and possibly even

McGill's son, came aboard dressed as crewmen,'' Valaczek suggested.

Fuentes nodded. "A good idea. I'll mention it to Luther."

"How long will you be able to keep the port open?" Valaczek asked.

Fuentes shook his head. "I don't know. I am hoping indefinitely."

Valaczek rose. "I want to wish the best to you, Enrico."

Fuentes smiled weakly. "I'll take care of myself, don't worry. You just get my trunk to Miami. And, of course, the McGills."

"Of course. We wouldn't want to forget the McGills now, would we?"

That same morning, Tony McGill came rushing into the house breathless. Not finding anyone in the front of the house, he hurried to the kitchen, where Ana and Nita were preparing a light lunch for the family. All servants had been dismissed, cloths had been draped over most of the furniture, and windows had already been boarded up. Upstairs in the bedrooms, two trunks and some luggage had been packed for their leaving. The house had the feeling of hushed expectancy, as if something was about to happen there that was best not talked about.

"Where's Dad?" Tony demanded when he stormed into the kitchen. "Have you had the radio on?"

The women turned to him quizzically, wearing aprons and looking very domestic at a work counter, making sandwiches. "What's the matter?" Nita said.

"Isn't Dad at home?" Tony asked irritably.

"No, he'll be back shortly," Ana told him. "He's in town tracking down a lead on Jake Parrish. What is it, Tony?"

"I just heard it on the car radio," Tony told them.

51

"Guerrillas are moving into this area. We can't stay here until tomorrow night. It isn't safe for us here anymore."

Ana and Nita exchanged quick glances.

"Reports say the main road between here and town is already cut off. General Perez' troops are everywhere. They're looting, killing, raping. . ."

The women looked scared, suddenly.

"I didn't mean to tell you that," he said.

"Oh, God," Ana said.

"You know how these things are exaggerated by the press," Tony added.

"Where can we go?" Nita wondered.

"I don't know, maybe a downtown hotel," Tony guessed. "Or maybe Enrico Fuentes could put us up until tomorrow night."

"No, we couldn't go to him," Ana said. "That would be too dangerous for us. Your father made that very clear."

"If Jake were here, he'd know what to do," Tony said.

Ana gave him a look. "Your father will know what to do, also, Tony. Let's just try to stay relaxed until he gets here. He said he would be here for lunch. He will know all about. . ."

There was the sound of a car on the drive outside the house. "That's probably him," Tony said, running to the front of the house.

"I know, it's getting worse all the time," McGill said, as they grouped in the foyer. "I've already called the Humboldt and reserved two rooms for the night. Get the rest of your packing done this afternoon; we'll move downtown in early evening. I ought to be back here about six or seven."

"Where are you going?" Ana asked quickly.

"I've found Jake Parrish. He's working at an oil camp south of here, about an hour's drive, near Santa

52

Rosa de Santiago. I gather he's repairing oil derricks there, and. . ."

The telephone rang. McGill walked quickly into the living room and grabbed the receiver.

"Yes, McGill here. Oh, Enrico."

The voice on the other end was sober. *"Luther, it's all set for tomorrow night. But the situation in your area is changing rapidly. Our troops are not holding down that way. You're going to have to bring your family into town, and the sooner the better."*

"I've already phoned the Humboldt," McGill told him. "We're driving in later." He cupped his hand over the phone. "Enrico wants us in town."

"You'd better come immediately," Fuentes said. *"I want to tell you about the trunk I'm sending with you, and have you meet Pedro Rueda."*

"I'm driving to Santa Rosa this afternoon," McGill said, "to see Jake Parrish. Should I send the family on in?"

Fuentes sounded impatient. *"You should come with them! Forget this Parrish fellow, Luther. Didn't he get you into trouble once, anyway, with a local official? Believe me, you don't need him. Rueda is perfectly competent to protect you and your family. If you want me to find a second man, I can do so this afternoon. But don't go on a wild goose chase to Santa Rosa at the last moment. You owe it to your family to come on into town with them, now."*

McGill hesitated a moment. "No, Enrico. I'll send the family on to the Humboldt. But I've got to connect with Parrish this afternoon."

Fuentes' voice went hard. *"All right, Luther, it's your neck. Call me as soon as you get back to town."*

"I will, Enrico, I promise."

McGill stood by the phone for a long moment after he had hung it up. Then he turned to his family. "All right, let's start filling the Ford with our stuff. You're all

53

leaving for town now. I'll meet you at the Humboldt later."

"I want to go with you to see Jake," Tony said.

"No," McGill told him. "I wouldn't send your mother and sister into town alone. They need a man with them, Tony."

"I'll take care of mother," Nita said boldly.

Tony looked at her, and then at McGill. "Oh, hell. Okay, I'll drive them."

"Who needs you?" Nita said.

"You'll have no trouble if you keep to the east of the big boulevard," McGill told Tony. "I just came that way. Come on, let's get the car loaded."

"Hey, there are sandwiches in the kitchen," Nita objected.

"Wrap them and bring them," McGill told her. "Time is important."

Less than an hour later, they locked up their house and left it, with hardly a look back. There was no time for sentiment or fear. Tony drove away first in the Ford station wagon, and McGill followed them for a couple of miles in a small blue Toyota sedan, the car that Tony and Nita usually drove. McGill turned off to the east, honking his temporary farewell, and then headed south toward the river country.

McGill was stopped just once on the road, and that was by government troops. When he showed his I.D. and mentioned Enrico Fuentes' name, he was passed through the roadblock. He had no further contact with military forces the rest of the drive. He reached Santa Rosa mid-afternoon and was at Punto Segundo twenty minutes later.

McGill had seen some rubber and oil camps in his day, but he was surprised by Punto Segundo, surprised that Jake Parrish would be working there. It was siesta at camp, and nobody was out in the heat of the day. McGill inquired about Parrish at the small office, and a worker pointed out Parrish's barracks building to McGill.

"He just finished his shift. He should be over there resting, mister. What did you say your name is?"

McGill ignored the question and walked to the barracks building. Opening a busted screen door, he entered the place, pulling his tie down at the collar, sweating through his shirt. His nose wrinkled at the stink. He saw a crumpled form on a cot and went over to it, squinting down in the soft light. The figure wore a wrinkled pair of trousers, was unshaven, and looked filthy.

"Jake?" McGill said incredulously. "Jake Parrish?"

Parrish opened his eyes and squinted upward at McGill. He had run out of money until payday, so was sober at the moment. On his left cheek was a purple bruise from the beating at Santa Rosa, and he had a rib taped up. He looked as bad as he had ever looked, and felt as bad as he had ever felt.

"Hunh? Who is it?"

McGill glanced around the room. There were two other men off in a corner, asleep on their cots. McGill felt a trickle of sweat run down the side of his face.

"It's me, Jake. Luther McGill."

Parrish stared up at McGill for a moment. Then he sat up and swung his legs to the floor. "Luther? Jesus Christ. I thought I was dreaming."

McGill sat down on the end of the cot and looked Parrish over. He would not have recognized him if he had passed him on the streets of Guayaquil.

"What the hell happened, Jake?" McGill said quietly. "What brought you to this hellhole? Are you hurt?"

McGill looked about the same to Parrish. Like a colonel out of uniform. Neat, businesslike, in control. "I got into a brawl in Santa Rosa," he said. "It's nothing."

"And you're. . .working here?"

Parrish nodded. "I'm repairing some derricks. The pay's lousy, but look at the swell accommodations."

"I thought you had a good job with the Padron company," McGill said. "We all thought you were doing well."

Parrish gave McGill a look. "I am doing well. Can't you see?"

"God. I feel just awful about this, Jake."

Parrish grunted. He knew that McGill probably knew nothing about the rubber camp fire, but he felt that McGill could read it in his face, as if the history of the past three years were printed upon it. "Forget it. A man is responsible for his own life, isn't he? I had my chances after Ameco, Luther. I just blew them." But deep inside him, he could not forgive McGill for letting Wade Sumner come down from Miami and fire him. The punishment had not fitted the crime, and McGill had known that, if Sumner did not.

McGill looked at the foot of the cot and saw two empty liquor bottles. "Jesus, Jake."

Parrish turned to him. "What brings you out here, Luther? I thought you'd have taken the family and left the country by now. Things are getting rough around the capital, aren't they?"

McGill nodded. "We're about to leave, Jake. Tomorrow night, with a little luck. Enrico Fuentes has arranged for us to board a freighter heading for Miami. All hush-hush because of the Alvaristas. I'm taking some papers of Fuentes along, too. Fuentes thinks we ought to have a couple of guns with us, and I agree. He's supplying a policeman, and I told him I wanted you along, if you'd go."

Parrish regarded McGill studiedly. "You want me? As a bodyguard?"

McGill nodded. Despite Parrish's present condition, he would feel better with Parrish along on the trip. He trusted Parrish as he had trusted few men in his life. "That's right. You're good with a gun, you've proved that. I don't know which end to fire. The women would feel more comfortable with you aboard when we leave, Jake. So would I.''

Parrish was dumbfounded. He could not believe that Luther McGill could come to him to ask a favor, after what McGill had done to him, at Ameco. "I. . .don't know, Luther,'' he said.

"You'd be paid well,'' McGill said. He mentioned a figure, and Parrish regarded him in mild surprise. It was a lot more than he would have expected. "You sure wouldn't be giving up much here. And maybe it's time for you to get out, too. Maybe we've all overstayed our time here.''

Parrish rose and ran a hand across his stubble of beard. "How is Ana?'' he asked, not looking at McGill. "Tony and Nita?''

"They're all fine, Jake,'' McGill said, hoping they had had no trouble getting into town. "But scared.''

"I'll bet Tony's filled out. Did they manage to teach him anything at college?''

McGill grinned. "You know Tony. He was never much for book learning.''

"Nita must be a real heart-breaker now. She was a good-looking kid, Luther.''

"She's done some modeling,'' McGill said. "She talks about you a lot, Jake. You were always special to her.''

Parrish, self-conscious now about his appearance, pulled up his trousers and straightened his posture some. Suddenly, he wanted to get out of Ecuador and never set eyes on it again. He walked over to a nearby window where a big fly buzzed loudly.

"I don't even have a gun any longer, Luther. I'm not the man you knew back in Guayaquil. You've come to hire a different Jake Parrish. Can't you look at me and see?''

McGill rose and walked over to Parrish. "There are a lot of reasons for leaving Ecuador now, Jake. And we want you along. I know Ana and Nita will feel much more at ease if you're with us.''

Parrish turned to him. "If Fuentes is supplying you a man, I don't see why you would need me.''

"Rueda is Fuentes' man," McGill said deliberately. "You would be mine. I don't have to tell you the difference.''

Parrish stood there, peering through the busted window screen. It would be absurd to trust him with anybody's life after what had happened at the rubber camp. It would be a blatant fraud. It was all different with him now. He had lost confidence in his ability to act under pressure, and succeed.

A flash of memory skittered across his mind—a petite girl in bed with him, the feel of her warm flesh against his, and the scent of her in his nostrils. She had pledged her love to him, had said that her husband meant nothing to her, that Parrish was the only important thing in her life. Then when they were discovered, she had backed off completely, suggesting to her husband and others that she had been seduced unwillingly by this gringo, and that she was sorry she had ever given herself to him.

"I was railroaded, Luther," he said almost inaudibly. "The girl lied about how it was. I was in love with her.''

"I know, Jake.''

"Sumner wouldn't listen. He didn't come to listen.''

"He had his orders," McGill said weakly. "From New York.''

But you could have made a difference, damn you! You could have saved my job by standing up to them, Parrish thought grimly. "It doesn't matter," he finally said.

"It's Sumner who'll be meeting us at Miami," McGill

58

said apologetically.

Parrish turned back to him, shook his head and laughed. "God," he said.

"He's not really a bad sort, Jake," McGill said. "I can get you a gun, that's no problem," McGill went on. "Maybe I have no right, but I'm asking you for old time's sake. Come back to Guayaquil with me this afternoon, Jake, and board that freighter with us tomorrow night. I'm not just asking for me, Jake, but for Ana and Nita and Tony."

Parrish met McGill's gaze, and in that instant, with McGill's unabashed plea ringing in his ears, Parrish felt a strong, overpowering resentment toward McGill that was more pronounced than anything he had felt before. "All right, Luther. I'll accompany you to Miami."

McGill's face broke into a broad grin. "That's just great, Jake. I mean it."

"I want you to know, though," Parrish said, not returning the smile, "it's not for old times. It's for the money. And to get the hell out of this stinking place."

"All right, Jake."

"It's purely business, Luther," Parrish added.

McGill nodded. "I understand."

Twenty minutes later they were on their way to Guayaquil.

Five

The dining room at the Humboldt had few guests that evening. Tourists had stopped coming to Ecuador, and businessmen were no longer entertaining clients. Most of the white-jacketed waiters just stood about looking decorative, like the potted palms. Only three tables were occupied; at one large table sat the McGill family. They had been served a before-dinner wine, but were waiting to order until Parrish arrived. "Don't expect him to look the same. He's been through some rough times," McGill said.

"I don't understand," Nita said. Her dark hair was down long, her eyes were made up, and she was wearing a low-cut dress that showed a remarkable cleavage. The waiters kept staring at her from the four corners of the room. "You told us that Jake was doing well."

"I can't imagine Jake working for Padron," Tony put in. He wore a sport jacket over an open-collar shirt, and looked very All-American. Ana had her hair up and looked quite lovely in a blue gown.

"Well, just don't act differently toward him," McGill said. "This will all be a little uncomfortable for him. Let's just make him feel like one of us."

"Hell, he is," Tony said brusquely. "Why should we feel otherwise?"

"When you called Enrico," Ana said to McGill, "did you tell him the trunk had arrived here?"

McGill nodded. "Yes. He was glad it got here safely. He thinks it's important it goes aboard tomorrow night with our luggage."

"Did you mention the size of it?" Nita wondered. The trunk now sat in the middle of the room McGill and Ana occupied. It was the largest piece of luggage they would take aboard, and it looked more like a safe than a trunk. It was made of thick metal and had special locks built into it that looked impossible to open.

"I asked him about that," McGill said. "He said that he decided to send a lot more papers and files than originally intended. It should be no difficulty for us. We won't have to handle the trunk personally, and Rueda will be in charge of its security. Tomorrow morning I'm to take Jake to Fuentes' office and meet with Rueda. I'll get our papers and instructions for boarding. Valaczek is fixing accommodations for us, and everything is going as planned. If there are no changes in Valaczek's schedule. . ."

The others had stopped listening to McGill, and were staring past him. McGill turned, and his jaw fell open.

Parrish did not look like the same man McGill had wrested from that oil camp earlier in the day. He was clean shaven and bathed, his dark hair combed neatly back. He was wearing an off-white tropical worsted suit, with a dark tie, and a dark handkerchief in the jacket pocket. Except for the small bruise on his cheek and a few extra lines around his eyes, he looked like the Jake Parrish they had all know three years previously.

Nita's eyes widened slightly. "God!" she murmured to herself. Parrish was even more handsome than she had remembered him. He had a more worldly look now, and possibly a more masculine look. A small thrill worked through her as he came up to the table, and she was suddenly breathless.

"Jake!" McGill said, rising. "God, what a difference a shave will make!"

Parrish grinned wryly, as Tony also rose. "I'll be damned," Tony said. "You look great, Jake."

Parrish came around and took Tony's hand, and looked him over. "By Jesus. You're a man now. How's the chess game, buddy?"

Tony returned Parrish's grin. "It's fallen off, since we stopped playing."

Parrish turned to Ana. "Ana, you look younger than the last time I saw you. Luther must be treating you well."

"It's a pleasure seeing you again, Jake," Ana told him, "and thanks for the compliment. Luther isn't a bad husband when he finds the time."

Parrish turned at last to Nita, and his face changed slightly. "My God," he said softly. "Look at what's happened to you."

Nita blushed slightly under his open stare. "Hi, Jake. I've really been looking forward to seeing you again. I mean, we all have."

Parrish reached down and touched her cheek with his lips, and Nita swallowed hard. "I've missed you all a lot," he said.

"Nita has to fight the young men off," McGill said, grinning. "But she doesn't get serious about any of them, do you, baby?"

"Oh, Papa!" Nita said, turning her lovely face aside.

McGill offered Parrish a seat between him and Ana, and Parrish sat down. There was some small talk about the old days, and a waiter came and took their orders. Parrish found Nita staring at him when he looked toward her once, and he gave her a wink and a smile. But it was already bothering him inside, to be presenting himself to them as the man they had known three years ago. Maybe McGill deserved his cynical acceptance of their money and their trust, but they did not.

"We'll take a drive over to Fuentes' office at about ten," McGill was telling Parrish, "and get things finalized there."

"We'll all be traveling under aliases?" Parrish asked.

"Fuentes says you and Rueda may use your own names," McGill replied. "Frankly, I don't think it's necessary for us to go under assumed identities. But Fuentes wants it this way."

"It all seems so melodramatic," Tony offered. "What do you think, Jake?"

Parrish met Tony's gaze. "Well, I know that Alvarez would look unkindly upon your leaving, if he knew. He considers Ameco a cancer feeding on Ecuadorian society. He'll want to make an example of men like your father. Try him in a people's court, maybe. I guess precautions can't hurt."

Tony was slightly disappointed in the answer.

"Our consul pulled out yesterday," Nita said to Parrish. "There are almost no Americans left here."

Parrish caught her eye, and she held his look for a long moment, boldly meeting it, letting her reaction to him show itself.

"I don't see how the capital can hold out another week," Parrish said, finally looking from her to McGill. "I'm glad you've found a way to get out before it's too late. And I'll do everything I can to facilitate the move." His voice had gone somber and quiet. He studied his place setting for a moment, then looked back up at McGill. "This Rueda that will accompany us, is his first name Pedro, by any chance?"

McGill furrowed his brow. "Why, I believe it is."

"That's the name you mentioned to me, Luther," Ana told him.

Parrish nodded. "He's a policeman, all right. He's one of an elite guard that used to watch Biaza. His outfit had a bad reputation for a while, as you know, Luther. They mistreated some political prisoners badly."

A silence fell over the table.

63

"I didn't know the name," McGill admitted.

"That secret police guard," Tony said curiously. "Aren't they the ones who executed a dozen Alvaristas without a trial about a year ago, by publicly beheading them at Loja?"

All eyes turned on him, and a deeper silence hung over them.

"For God's sake, Tony," Nita finally managed.

"What?" Tony said defensively.

Suddenly McGill craned his neck and looked past them, putting on a falsely bright countenance. "Ah, here comes our dinner! The cream of the Humboldt's kitchen!"

The subject was quickly changed then, and Rueda was not mentioned again that evening.

It was all getting too close, now.

It was almost beyond discussion.

It was a muggy, overcast day the following morning when McGill and Parrish arrived at Fuentes' office in the big building on Malecon Simon Bolivar. The Guayas River was muddy-looking, and the trees looked gray in La Rotonda, and on Avenida Cinco de Octubre. Many office buildings were almost deserted, including the British Honorary Consul and the American Consulate.

Parrish had never seen so many troops in the capital. They marched along Diez de Agosto, clustered on street corners, and stood in formidable platoons before the government buildings, automatic weapons slung across their backs. Armored cars were parked at main intersections, with helmeted crews manning them, and at the Palacio Municipal soldiers were stacking sand bags along the perimeter of the grounds.

Inside the Ministry of Finance, clerks were hurrying through high-ceillinged corridors with piles of papers and files, worried looks on their faces. Parrish and McGill went directly to Fuentes' office, and were admitted by a military guard.

Fuentes was already in conference with Pedro Rueda and an aide named Esquinaldo when a secretary ushered Parrish and McGill into his office.

"Ah, Luther! I'm so glad you could get over here this morning. And this is Mr. Parrish, I presume?"

Parrish was introduced to the three of them, hands were shaken, and Parrish's and Rueda's eyes locked for a long moment. Then they were all seating themselves around Fuentes' desk.

"Well, we got together at last," Fuentes said. "I wanted Valaczek here, but he had business with the port authorities this morning." For the first time in McGill's memory, Fuentes was in his shirtsleeves, looking harried and tired. Even his balding hair was slightly mussed as if he had not slept all night.

"What time will we be boarding the *Maria Isabel,* Enrico?" McGill asked him.

"Esquinaldo here has just gotten it all arranged," Fuentes said, gesturing toward his small thin aide, a fellow in his forties with rimless spectacles on his nose and the manner of an accountant.

Esquinaldo nodded. "Valaczek is sailing at one-thirty, and he thinks you should arrive at the last moment. At one, he suggests." He reached for a parcel on the desk, wrapped with brown paper, and handed it to McGill. "There are two gray work uniforms of Valaczek's crewmen in here, for Mr. Parrish and also your son. Mr. Rueda will be similarly attired. One of you might carry a duffel for added authenticity."

"All right," McGill said, looking at Parrish.

Parrish cast a glance at Rueda who sat there silent. Rueda was a wiry-looking fellow just under forty, broad in the shoulders but with a slim build, and an inch or two shorter than Parrish. His complexion was light, lighter than Fuentes', and his features were aquiline. His eyes were intelligent and hard, his expression stony.

65

He had rather long, thin brown hair, and there was a hole in his left earlobe where it had been pierced for an earring at one time.

"These are your papers, Luther," Fuentes said, handing McGill a bundle of documents. "Mr. Parrish may use his own passport. You and your family will be traveling under the name of Lester Brown. Your family may retain their given names. You will be posing as an importer from the Virgin Islands, until you get to Miami, of course. Valaczek knows who you are, but none of his crew does. We have contacted your friend, Wade Sumner, in Miami, as I suggested we might, Luther. He is ready to receive you at his home until you get settled. Also, we have persuaded him to receive our papers separately, when the *Maria Isabel* reaches Miami. He will come with his converted cutter at night and take the trunk off the ship, with your cooperation and that of Captain Valaczek, and deliver it to my cousin, Victorio Salazar, up the coast away from the eyes of the Customs people."

McGill raised his eyebrows. "I see."

Fuentes gestured toward Rueda. "Mr. Rueda here will leave the ship at that point, and accompany the trunk until it reaches my cousin."

All eyes went momentarily to the hard-faced Rueda.

"While aboard the ship, and in the two ports you'll enter en route," Fuentes went on, "Rueda will be watching for possible trouble directed at you or, of course, our papers. He will be armed, as I suppose Mr. Parrish will be." Fuentes cast a dubious look toward Parrish.

"I'll be armed," Parrish said.

Fuentes narrowed his dark eyes on Parrish for a moment. "I'm going to be frank with you, Mr. Parrish. I would have preferred for Luther to have taken along a second professional bodyguard."

Parrish shrugged. "That was Luther's choice. Not

mine."

Rueda now spoke up for the first time since the introductions. "Do you have any police experience, Mr. Parrish?" His voice was low and brittle, and he spoke slowly with great deliberation.

Parrish looked very much as he had at dinner the night before, except that his tie was a lighter one now, and he wore no handkerchief in his jacket pocket. The bruise on his cheek was still visible, and he could sense that Fuentes and Rueda were staring at it.

"I'm not a policeman, Rueda," he said evenly. "But I've had some experience with guns."

McGill spoke up quickly. "Jake was in the Special Forces in Asia. He was decorated personally for leading a devastating assault against the Viet Cong in the Mekong Delta."

Parrish gave McGill a hard look.

"I understand you also shot it out with some hill bandits when they attacked an Ameco car?" Fuentes said in a patronizing way.

Parrish saw the raging flames at the rubber camp, and heard the yells from inside the burning warehouse. A light perspiration popped out on his brow and upper lip. "That was pure television drama. They were never a real threat to us."

McGill gave Parrish a quick look.

"I hope you understand, Mr. Parrish," Rueda said in a studied voice, "that if trouble comes from Alvarez agents, there will be no opportunity for western-style draw-downs and battlefield bravado."

McGill frowned at Rueda, but Parrish regarded him impassively. "I doubt, also," he said without inflection, "that there will be much of a chance for ritualized, bully-boy-type executions."

Rueda's thin face clouded over. "Be careful whom you accuse, Mr. Parrish. You are still under Ecuadorian jurisdiction."

Fuentes made a face. "We're all aware of certain excesses of Biaza's secret police," he said easily. "But I can assure you that Mr. Rueda, gentlemen, was not privy to those excesses. As for your lack of experience, Mr. Parrish, I'm sure that if you will allow Mr. Rueda to guide you and advise you, and if you will not attempt to impair his own functioning, everything will go very well. I'm certain that once you're out of port, there will be no further danger to you."

"Jake will make every effort to cooperate with Mr. Rueda," McGill said quickly. "Isn't that right, Jake?"

"Oh, I wouldn't have it any other way," Parrish said.

The rest of that day was spent mostly in waiting. Ana became very jumpy, and McGill was short with Nita and Tony. Parrish stayed in his room and wished he had said no to McGill when he came to recruit him for this job. In mid-afternoon he went down to the hotel bar and bought a bottle of good gin, but when he got it up to the room, he could not bring himself to open it; he owed McGill sobriety. Also, sitting on his bed and staring at the unopened bottle, he found that he did not have the need for alcohol that he had had at Punto Segundo. He did not have the same emptiness inside him, gnawing at him day and night.

Nita was so excited about Parrish's joining them that she forgot her fears. Suddenly the crush she had had on Parrish as a sixteen-year-old seemed to be blossoming into something much more deep-seated. Whenever she was close to him, she felt all trembly inside and weak. It did not matter to her that he was over thirty and she was not yet twenty. She had been raised in a country where girls often married older men. In Nita's eyes, Parrish was just right for her, and she understood for the first time why the youths of Guayaquil had not interested her. They were not yet men—Parrish was.

Tony felt a camaraderie with Parrish that he had never felt with his own father, and a respect for him that

68

came close to hero-worship. Parrish was the kind of man Tony wanted to become—worldly, tough, competent. He had been very angry when his father had fired Parrish from Ameco. Now there would be a chance for the McGills to make it up to Parrish, to erase the errors of the past.

At twelve-thirty, a hired limousine arrived to take the McGills to the docks. The luggage, including the Fuentes trunk, went in a separate car. Parrish and Tony took a taxi there; they were dressed in work clothes, Parrish carrying a duffel. Rueda had already boarded when they arrived. Parrish and Tony went aboard first, then the porters carrying the trunks and luggage. McGill and the two women were the last to arrive, accompanied by Fuentes' aide. "Good God!" Nita murmured, as she stared at the *Maria Isabel*.

The freighter squatted heavily at dockside, its hull rust-streaked, its superstructure looking dark and menacing in the night. It was the smallest freighter McGill had ever seen in port, a relic of the past, stodgy and decrepit-looking. Barnacles clung to its sides at the water line, and an ugly odor of hot oil and garbage came from its decks.

"Oh, dear, Luther!" Ana said softly.

"I'm sure it will all look better to you when you get aboard," Esquinaldo told McGill. "Now you must hurry, please. There are spies everywhere."

McGill looked upward and saw Jake Parrish leaning on the gunwale near the gangplank. Parrish's presence reassured him. "Yes, of course," he said quietly.

At the top of the gangplank, Valaczek awaited them, looking big and salty in his uniform. He grinned widely. Behind him stood his only officer, a mulatto Haitian.

"Welcome aboard, *Mr. Brown*," Valaczek said loudly, winking at McGill. "Mrs. Brown. And I suppose this is your daughter. Mr. Dubois will show you to your accommodations. We'll be leaving very

69

shortly."

"Thank you, Captain," McGill said. He had not laid eyes on Valaczek previously—he was not impressed.

At the bottom of the gangplank, Raul Esquinaldo watched the McGills go safely aboard and sighed with relief. In only a half-hour, the greatest part of the danger would be over. Fuentes would be pleased. Esquinaldo, who had driven the limousine for the McGills, now climbed back into the long car and started the engine. He squinted up toward the deck of the freighter and could just make out McGill, his wife and daughter being led along a passageway by the first officer. Esquinaldo nodded his approval and pulled away.

The limousine traversed the long dock area, then made a right turn toward the street, a few hundred yards away. Esquinaldo was already thinking about his report to Fuentes that he would make upon his arrival back at the ministry when a car suddenly pulled out directly in front of him. Esquinaldo slammed on the brakes, the car skidding to a halt. His heart was now pummeling his chest, and a clammy feeling came into his palms as he saw two men get out of a black Fiat sedan. One of them came over to his window and looked in at him. He was a big, thick-set fellow with a perfectly bald head and a scar across his right eye. He was an Alvarista guerrilla who worked for Jesus Cuesta.

"Well, well," he said in a gravelly voice. "The Fuentes aide. Esquinaldo, isn't it?"

Esquinaldo swallowed hard.

"Let me introduce myself. I am called El Pardal . . .You know, the great spotted cat. The comparison has always escaped me. What are you doing down here at this time of night, Fuentes' lackey?"

Esquinaldo looked past him to the other man, a dark, hard-looking fellow who stood leaning against the other car. "I couldn't sleep," he lied. "I came to see what ships were in port."

Pardal frowned in an unnerving way. "You brought three people down here, two women and a man. They boarded the *Maria Isabel*. Who were they?"

Esquinaldo had considered bringing a gun with him but had not. He wished that he had been more cautious. "Oh, them. I just drove them down as a favor. A small Virgin Islands importer named Brown, and his wife and daughter. They wanted to get out of Guayaquil because of the trouble. I can't blame them."

The hard-looking Pardal studied Esquinaldo's face. "You're lying, Fuentes lackey," he said ominously.

Esquinaldo's face was suddenly etched with raw fear. "No," he said. "It's the truth!"

"Get out of the car," Pardal commanded him.

Esquinaldo licked dry lips. "But I'm telling you. . ."

"Get out of the car!"

Esquinaldo climbed out of the limousine numbly, his pulse pounding in his ears. When he got out on the pavement, he saw the razor-sharp stiletto in Pardal's right hand, its blade gleaming dully in the light from the street. Pardal searched Esquinaldo roughly with his free hand.

"The *Maria Isabel*. . .When is it sailing?"

"They. . .didn't tell me," Esquinaldo said. "I think perhaps tomorrow morning."

Pardal glowered into his face. "All right, let's go. Quickly. We want to ask you a few questions about all this, Fuentes lackey. Get in the other car. Now."

"Please," Esquinaldo pleaded. "I know nothing."

Pardal pushed the tip of the knife through Esquinaldo's jacket and shirt, breaking the skin beneath the clothing. He cried out softly, his eyes wide with fear.

"Now," Pardal repeated.

Esquinaldo moved off stiffly toward the other car.

Six

McGill and Ana stood in the middle of the cabin. It was about eight feet square, with a double bunk on one wall. Big asbestos-coated pipes ran through the room at head level, and there was a small, rusty sink on an end wall. Somebody had stacked two straight chairs against the other wall. The smell of ammonia and detergent soap hovered above the rank odor of oil and bilge-water.

McGill, seeing the look of despair on Ana's pretty face, put a hand on her shoulder. "It'll only be a few days, honey. Then we'll be in Miami, and all of this will be behind us."

Ana turned to him. "It's so small, Luther. Is it safe? I mean, seaworthy?"

McGill smiled tiredly. "It's been making this run up and down the west coast for some time now. I guess it must be more durable than it looks."

Just at that moment Nita appeared in the open doorway. She gave the cabin a sour look. "Mine and Tony's is just the same," she said, "except smaller. I guess they've put Jake and that Rueda fellow in a room that was used for storage."

"Has Tony come down yet?" McGill wondered.

"No, I think he's still on deck with Jake. Rueda is up there, too, supervising the storage of our extra luggage, including the Fuentes' trunk."

"Tony and the others can take that clothing off, now

that they're onboard," McGill said. "The crew knows they're not sailors. Valaczek told them that he got permission to carry three passengers, but had to sneak the others aboard because they're illegals. Tony is known to be one of the family, whereas Jake and Rueda are supposed to be businessmen on their way to Miami."

"Do you think they believe all that?" Ana wondered.

"I don't know," McGill admitted. "That Dubois was looking at us sidewise, I noticed. But as long as they don't know our real identity, I guess it doesn't matter much."

"Valaczek only has four crew besides Dubois," Nita said. "Can they really run this ship?"

McGill sighed heavily. "Look, I think we've just got to relax and presume that Valaczek knows what he's doing. Let's get our beds made and try to get some rest, shall we? We ought to clear the port by the time we're ready to pack it in."

"God, I have to go down the passageway to the john, just so I won't have to take my clothes off in front of Tony!" Nita complained. "What a disaster this trip is going to be!" However, she was very excited about Parrish's presence aboard the small ship.

"Go find your brother and tell him to get settled in," McGill told her.

Nita went back on deck and looked for Tony. She found the whole ship offensive. There were stacked crates of machinery parts on deck, and a big crane, and everything smelled of grease and machine oil. Gray paint flaked off bulkheads, and the decks were rusty under foot. The small crew was casting off lines now, and a couple of them, swarthy tough-looking men, eyed her as she passed. Parrish was still at the gunwale, watching the ship get ready to sail. Nita went over and stood beside him.

"I was looking for Tony," she said.

"I think he went below," Parrish told her.

"I can't say I like the looks of this crew," she added.

Parrish turned toward her. In the soft darkness she looked more a woman than she had in the daylight. Parrish had known she would grow up to be lovely, but he had not expected her spectacular beauty. "Don't be afraid, Nita. These are just tough men doing a tough job."

Nita met his eyes. "If you weren't here, I'd be petrified."

Parrish felt the stricture inside him again. "Don't short-change your father. . .or Tony. I'm. . .just an oil camp bum. Don't expect too much of me."

Nita stared at him in the soft light. "I don't believe that," she said.

Parrish turned and looked down at the dock. "Look, we're cast off. Now the tug will move us away."

Just as he finished that statement, the small ship edged forward almost unnoticeably, sliding away from the dock. They could hardly feel its movement.

"We're under way!" Nita said happily.

Parrish tried a grin. "In just minutes, we'll be downriver and into the open sea."

"Then you think we're safe now?" she asked him.

Parrish hesitated only a moment. "I can't imagine why not," he told her.

Idilio Alvarez stood ramrod-erect in the open military vehicle as it lurched to a halt. He wore a fatigue cap on his head and carried a Mauser 7.65 mm Parabellum automatic pistol in his right hand. With him in the vehicle were a driver, Council member Torres, and a soldier with a portable short-wave radio on his knees. In the distance could be heard the booming of light cannons and the crackling of rifle and automatic weapons fire. Alvarez had ordered a night offensive to penetrate into the city on its south side, and the fighting was going well. He glanced at his watch—it was 2:14

a.m.

"We're making some ground against them," he said with satisfaction. "Government troops don't like to fight at night."

"We caught them offguard," Torres offered, his bearded face looking somber, "but we must expect a counter-attack when they get organized. They will defend the capital vigorously because there is no place left to run."

"See if you can get General Perez," Alvarez told the radio man.

"Yes, sir." The fellow twisted some dials, and there was a pattering of static. "R Base One to R Base Two, R Base One to R Base Two, come in R Base Two."

There was an unintelligible exchange between the radio man and a voice on the other end; Perez was temporarily out of contact by radio. Alvarez swore.

"Try to get Cuesta in the city," he ordered. "Maybe he has observed movement of troops there."

Another try by the soldier with the radio, and then a voice on the other end.

"Cuesta here. Is that you, Idilio?"

Alvarez took the mike from the radio man, and spoke into it. "Yes, this is Idilio, Jesus. We're making some headway out here, but we're beginning to run into opposition. What have you seen from your end?"

Some more static. *". . .and there must be a division gathered at La Rotonda under Diaz. Maybe you ought to solidify your gains and dig in out there, Idilio."*

Alvarez grunted. "All right, Jesus. We'll be in touch later."

"Oh, incidentally, Idilio. One of my men saw some people board a freighter down at the docks. A family of three or possibly more. They were driven there by a Fuentes aide."

Alvarez frowned at the mike in his hand. "It wasn't Fuentes, was it?"

75

"We're sure not. Fuentes' wife is already gone."

"It doesn't have to be his wife, damn it! They might not be women at all! What action have you taken?"

Cuesta's voice was more subdued. "We've taken the aide into custody and have him here at our city base. He is being interrogated."

"Good," Alvarez said. "When does the ship sail?"

Cuesta's voice was even more subdued. "We've just finished checking it out, Idilio. It sailed just after one. It's on the open sea."

"Sonofabitch!" Alvarez growled. "Don't you see, this is a clever Fuentes trick! It could be anybody aboard that freighter! Even the Vice-President. And now the ship is gone. This is inexcusable, Jesus!"

When Cuesta spoke again, his voice was tougher. "There was no way we could have prevented this, Idilio. At least we have this fellow Esquinaldo. I think he will tell us who boarded the ship before we are finished with him."

"Be sure that he does, and then report to me immediately," Alvarez said. "Also, find out where the freighter is bound, and where it will stop en route." His voice was full of anger.

"Very well, Idilio."

"And double your men on duty at the waterfront," Alvarez added. "Immediately."

"Of course. It shall be done."

When Alvarez handed the mike back to his radio man, his face was clouded with frustration. "All right, driver," he said darkly. "Let's find our command post. This may turn out to be a long night."

Across town at that same moment, in the Ministry of Finance, Enrico Fuentes sat in his office and worried. He had expected Esquinaldo back within an hour of leaving, and there was still no word from him. Fuentes had called the port authorities and learned that the *Maria Isabel* had sailed on time. He glanced at the small

76

clock on his desk. He was becoming nervous; it was past 2:30. Where was Esquinaldo? He punched a button on the intercom and called in his secretary.

"No word yet from Esquinaldo?" Fuentes asked.

"No, none, Minister," the fellow replied. "Oh, I almost forgot. The guerrillas are staging an offensive tonight. They are fighting in the south suburbs of the city."

Fuentes' face changed. "Are you certain?"

"Yes, Minister. Alvarez is reportedly in charge, himself. Our troops are rallying, however, and are expected to throw the guerrillas back with much force."

"Where are they exactly?" Fuentes asked.

"They have crossed Avenida Loreto, Minister, and have dug in there."

"Good God!" Fuentes muttered.

"Is that bad, sir?" the secretary asked.

Fuentes eyed him acidly. "I think it will not take Alvarez a week to find us," he suggested. "His guerrillas, or Perez' troops, may be occupying this office in two or three days." He ran a hand through his thinning hair. "Maybe I should have taken McGill's advice. He suggested I leave on the *Maria Isabel* with him."

"The Vice-President says the capital will not fall," the sleepy secretary offered.

Fuentes gave him a sour look and rose from his desk. He began to pace back and forth, thinking. He had a lot to worry him, suddenly. "Let us hope he is right," he said. "The roads leading from the city to the east, I presume they're still held by government troops?"

"Oh, yes, sir. There is no rebel activity reported in that area."

Fuentes' hidden airstrip was located in a backwoods area east of Guayaquil. He had not made any last-minute arrangements with the pilot who would fly him out; there had not seemed any necessity, until this

77

moment.

"Try to get me the Vice-President on the phone," he ordered.

The fellow stared at him. "At this time of night, sir?"

Fuentes' face twisted up in quick anger. "I know what time it is, damn it! See if you can get him at his home!"

The secretary went to Fuentes' desk and made the call. "This is Minister Fuentes calling the Vice-President. Is he available?" A long pause, then a cupping of the receiver with the fellow's hand. "He says the Vice-President is receiving no calls, Minister."

Fuentes was outraged. "Repeat to him who is calling, damn it!"

"Do you understand that this is the Minister of Finance calling?" Another pause, and then he cradled the receiver. "He merely repeated the message, sir, and then hung up."

Fuentes' face was dark with anger. "Damn him! Damn all of them! There is no thought of real community effort! It is each man for himself!"

"Yes, sir."

Fuentes turned to the other man. "All right, go get some sleep, Roberto. But, first thing in the morning, I want you to contact a Mr. Moreno. I'll give you his number. If he is not at home, he can be reached through the National Pilots Association. I'll want to speak with him personally, and it's urgent. Do you understand?"

"Yes, Minister," the fellow replied.

"If they want to make it every man for himself," Fuentes said gruffly, "then that is the way it will be." He thought of the trunk he had sent with Luther McGill, and a feeling of grim satisfaction settled inside him.

"Yes, sir."

As the secretary turned to leave, Fuentes said, "If you hear from Esquinaldo, call me immediately."

"Yes, sir, I will."

Only a few blocks from the Ministry of Finance, in a small building near the waterfront, three men stood hovering over Raul Esquinaldo. One of the men was Jesus Cuesta, Alvarez' aide, and a second one was the cold-blooded El Pardal who had taken Esquinaldo into custody. The third man had accompanied Pardal when the latter had accosted Esquinaldo. His name was Juan Torreon, a recently recruited guerrilla who had spent half of his life, before the rebellion, in Ecuadorian prisons. He liked women, and one of his prison terms had been for rape.

The room, harshly lighted by a naked ceiling bulb, was littered with cardboard, paper and packing crates. Esquinaldo was tied to a chair with hemp ropes which cut into his wrists. His head hung down onto his chest, and his face and left ear were badly swollen and bruised. His right eye was swollen shut, and blood was caked on his mouth and chin.

Pardal stood directly before him, a wooden club in his thick hand, his bald head shining pink in the overhead light. Torreon stood on Esquinaldo's right, a curly-headed, brawny fellow who walked with a limp. Cuesta stood on Esquinaldo's left, glaring down at him with dark brittle eyes. Cuesta saw himself as a tough adventurer who deserved top leadership in the movement because he had the machismo to make things work.

"Now what do you say, you damned Biaza pig!" Cuesta said harshly to Esquinaldo. "Do you want Pardal here to get out his pliers? He can do interesting things to flesh and bone with that simple tool. Is that what you want next?"

Esquinaldo mumbled something.

"Eh?" Cuesta said, taking Esquinaldo by the hair and pulling his head upward. "What did you say?"

"All right," Esquinaldo mumbled. "Don't hit me

anymore."

"Who boarded the *Maria Isabel?*" Pardal asked in a hard voice. "And for what purpose?"

"An American. His name is Luther McGill."

Pardal and Cuesta exchanged looks. "I know that name," Cuesta said. "He's a rubber company executive, isn't he?"

"That's right," Esquinaldo choked out. "He boarded with his wife, son and daughter. They return to Miami with the ship."

Cuesta turned to Pardal again. "I remember now. McGill is a friend of Fuentes. His capitalist dollars kept people like Biaza in power. He is on Idilio's list."

Torreon grunted. "He will be very displeased, Jesus."

"That gringo cabron should have been brought before a people's court of justice," Pardal growled.

Cuesta leaned down and spoke directly into Esquinaldo's face. "Was that all of the party? Were there any others? Be careful that you tell the truth, traitor!"

"There were two others, bodyguards for the family. One is called Parrish. He used to be an employee of Ameco, McGill's company."

Cuesta snapped his fingers. "The scandal involving Nuñez' wife! Parrish was involved with her! A worse vulture than McGill! And the other man?"

"Pedro Rueda," Esquinaldo sighed. "A policeman."

"I know that name," Pardal said in the hard voice. "He was one of Biaza's goon squad."

"Ahh, what a nest of vipers!" Cuesta snarled. He turned from the bound man, reflecting on what he had learned. Torreon was right; Alverez would be extremely angry. He turned back to Esquinaldo. "This McGill has friends in Miami?"

Esquinaldo nodded. "A company man named Sumner will meet him there. . .Wade Sumner. . .a rich

80

executive with a Miami Beach house, three cars, and a yacht that is a converted Coast Guard cutter.'' Esquinaldo talked because talking was so much better than being beaten, and he couldn't take any more. "Sumner will take the trunk off the ship and deliver it to. . .''

He stopped short, realizing he had rambled much too far.

"What?" Cuesta said harshly. "What trunk? Deliver it to whom?"

"Oh, God," Esquinaldo groaned.

Pardal grabbed Esquinaldo by the hair again, and yanked his face upward, poising the club over him. "Keep talking, you damned beetle, or I'll crack your skull like a ripe coconut!"

"Fuentes sent a trunk with McGill to Miami," he said in a gasping, grating voice, as Pardal held his head upward. "To be delivered to Victorio Salazar."

"Damn!" Cuesta hissed out. "Another Biaza pus-bag!"

"This begins to take on serious proportions, Jesus," Torreon said quietly.

Cuesta spoke quietly into Esquinaldo's face. "Now, you insect. What is in the trunk that Fuentes sent with McGill and which is to be received by Salazar in Miami?"

Esquinaldo felt a new, numbing fear. "I don't honestly know. Fuentes said there are papers. . .government files. . .That is all I know."

"Papers, heh?" Cuesta said, his voice tight with restrained emotion. "Filthy lies, maybe, about the guerrilla leaders? False titles and claims to lands and businesses? Memos and correspondences that would reveal criminal guilt of present officials if viewed by a people's court? What else is in this steamer trunk, son-of-a-pig?"

"Fuentes did not discuss the contents of the trunk

81

with me," Esquinaldo said honestly. "Except that it is only papers and files. I am telling you the entire truth. You must believe me!"

"I think that is all he can give us," Pardal said.

Cuesta turned and looked into the thin face, with its swollen, blood-caked flesh. On the floor at Esquinaldo's feet were his spectacles, shattered beyond repair. Cuesta shrugged his shoulders eloquently, and sighed heavily. "All right. I'll be out in the car when you've finished."

Pardal nodded. Cuesta turned and left the room, Torreon following after him.

"No, wait!" Esquinaldo called after Cuesta. "I've told you everything! Everything!"

Cuesta and Torreon climbed into the black Fiat and waited. There was a muffled cry from inside the building. Then, a moment later, Pardal came out, cleaning the blade of his stiletto on a handkerchief. He pocketed the knife and dropped the handkerchief into a trash can.

He got into the car beside Cuesta, his bald head glistening with sweat. "Let's go," he said.

Seven

Wade Sumner worked feverishly on the girl. His hands roughly mauled her naked breasts, while his mouth angrily devoured hers as he moved and moved on her, probing and straining, seeking the hot vortex of her passion.

"Oh, God!" Accompanied by a soft, throaty outcry.

An acceleration of flesh inflaming flesh, Sumner grunting, gasping out suppressed sounds of anticipation.

"Easy." Breathlessly. *"Make it last. . .darling."*

But it was too late. There was a mutual and spasmodic contracting between them, a stricture of muscles and arching of backs, the girl's cries rising into the darkness of the yacht's cabin.

Finally Sumner collapsed on her, still joined warmly, enjoying the after-intimacy.

"God, Wade. It's so good with you."

He touched her lips with his again, but less zealously. "I've missed you all week. But Bette has had me hopping, damn it. And then there was that Salazar."

Susan Benedict, the woman whom Sumner had been bedding for almost a year, moved her hips under him and made a sound in her throat. "Who's Salazar?"

Sumner caught himself. "Oh. Just a potential buyer of Ameco products, honey." He kissed her again, and she wriggled her bottom.

"Mmm," she breathed.

He grinned slightly. "I can't, baby. I'd like to, but I can't."

"Darn," she pouted.

"Give me a rest," he said. "Maybe later."

"I'll remind you."

He rolled onto his side beside her. The *Sea Witch* rocked slightly under them, and he liked the feel of it. He traced a circle around her right nipple. She was a ripe, richly curved girl in her late twenties—Sumner had a grown daughter almost her age—with dark blond hair and a pretty unremarkable face. She worked for a subordinate of Sumner, but had begun flirting with Sumner almost from her first day at Ameco. Now it was getting serious.

"I'm going to tell Bette any day now. It's just a matter of finding the right time. She knows, anyway. She's been dropping little accusations. I just can't stand to be around her anymore. Pretty soon it will be just you and me, honey."

"Let's get married in Las Vegas," she said. "I love to play the machines."

Sumner glanced toward her. "Well. There'll be plenty of time to talk about things like that," he said.

"You are going to marry me, aren't you, Wade?" she said quietly, turning to meet his gaze.

"Hey. Didn't I tell you that you're the only one for me?"

She hesitated, then smiled a slow smile. "Yes. You did."

"After I get McGill situated here, and the house is mine again, I'll find an opportune time to talk with Bette. But between now and then, it will get pretty hectic with four other people in the house. I even have to go out and meet the freighter." He remembered the visit by Salazar and the young punk with the gun. "Say, since I have to get the engines tuned, maybe you and I could

84

have one last afternoon on the boat before I'm up to my neck with McGills. Bette wouldn't know the difference. I'll tell her I'm taking the *Sea Witch* out to clean the engines."

Susan smiled, her hand falling between his thighs. "That's a great idea, honey. We can go up the coast and find some secluded cove and just make like rabbits all afternoon."

Sumner grinned. "Is that all you think about?"

"What else is there?" she said.

He touched her face lightly. "Let's see. . .this is June 15, and McGill is due here on the night of the 20th. The 18th is a Sunday. What do you think?"

"I think it sounds perfect," she told him.

"We'll take all day to go up the coast. There's a place called Jenkins' Cove that ought to give us privacy, and it has a white beach."

She smiled. "It will be an afternoon to remember," she said.

It was late morning, and Enrico Fuentes had just arrived back at his office after only a few hours of sleep. On his drive to the Ministry, there had been troops everywhere, armored cars and even cannons in the streets. Out in the south suburbs, it was reported that buildings were burning and streets were blocked with rubble. The Alvaristas now held a large area of that part of the city, but fighting had tapered off with daylight.

As soon as Fuentes arrived in his reception office, Roberto met him with a sober face. "Ah, Minister. I've been waiting to speak with you, sir. It's about Esquinaldo."

Fuentes saw the look in the fellow's eyes, and something grabbed at his insides. "Come into my office, Roberto."

They went inside the private office together, and Fuentes took his suit jacket off and threw it onto a chair, then heaved himself into the swivel chair behind his desk. Roberto stood tensely in front of the desk, waiting.

"All right," Fuentes said, looking five years older than he had twenty-four hours earlier. "What about Esquinaldo?"

"A body was found early this morning on the waterfront, Minister," the secretary said quietly. "The police say it is Raul Esquinaldo."

Fuentes slammed his fist onto the desk, making Roberto jump slightly. "Sonofabitch!" Fuentes hissed out.

"I'm very sorry, Minister," the secretary said. "Esquinaldo was my friend, also."

Fuentes looked up at him. "What happened?" he asked, not really wanting to know.

"He must have been intercepted while leaving the dock area," Roberto told him. "The limousine was found not far from the dock where the *Maria Isabel* was tied up. The keys were still in its ignition."

"And Esquinaldo?" Fuentes said.

"There is a small storage building about a half-mile from there. Esquinaldo was found there by a longshoreman. He had been tied to a straight chair, beaten, and then killed. . .stabbed just once, under the chin."

A shudder passed through Fuentes. They all worried about death, now. In the beginning, when Alvarez had merely had the capacity to harass military outposts in the jungle, the Guayaquil politicos had all laughed at his audacity, nobody taking him seriously. but now, the mere mention of Alvarez' name was enough to leave most Guayaquil big-wigs in a cold sweat, those who still remained in the city.

"Those cowardly bastards!" Fuentes grated out. "Why did they have to kill him?"

"The police thought you might be able to shed some light on that, Minister," Roberto said.

Had Esquinaldo told all, before they killed him? It was possible. "Have you located the pilot, Moreno?" Fuentes asked.

Roberto nodded. "I got hold of him just before you got here. He said he would be at this number for the rest of the morning." He reached into a pocket, withdrew a slip of paper, and handed it across the desk to Fuentes.

"All right, Roberto. I'll call him back myself. Please keep yourself available through the day."

"Of course, Minister."

When Roberto had gone, Fuentes made the call himself to Moreno at his home.

"Moreno here."

"Moreno, it is Fuentes."

"Ah, Fuentes! How does it go with you this morning? Did you hear the news about the fighting last night?"

"I heard," Fuentes said grimly.

"Alvarez was smart to recruit Perez and Linares to his cause. The question is, will he be able to control them if he takes power, huh?"

"What do you think, Moreno? Are we going to hold?"

A short pause on the other end. *"I really don't know. I don't think anybody does. But my guess is that the capital will fall. . .within the next few days, possibly."*

"Our troops have no confidence now," Fuentes said grimly. "Since Biaza ran like a rabbit. It's a goddamn national disgrace, Moreno. Next, our generals will be running."

When Moreno spoke again, his voice was very quiet. *"Fuentas, I was sworn to secrecy about this, but I think you ought to know. The Vice-President flew out of here this morning on my plane."*

Fuentes was incredulous. "What?"

"It's true. He rented my plane and hired a special pilot."

Fuentes was staring at the phone as if it had been

87

transformed into a viper. "I don't believe it!"

"You must. He's in Iquitos already. The word is that he took quite a lot of currency with him. Of course, it may be worthless soon."

"That dirty cabron! Doesn't he know where that leaves the rest of us! If this gets out to the troops, they'll just give up. What the hell are they fighting for? This plays right into Alvarez' hands!"

"I know, Fuentes," Moreno said. *"You don't have to worry about the plane, though. It will be back here tonight. At our hidden base."*

Fuentes quieted down some. "What about the roads? Are they going to stay open?"

"They should, for another few days. That's where our troops are massed and fighting the hardest. But if I were you, I wouldn't wait until the date we chose. You never know when the situation will change."

"That's just why I called you," Fuentes said. "Other cabinet members and many congressmen are packing up, getting ready to run. I don't intend to be the last one out."

"Then you're ready to fly out?"

"I will be, tomorrow. I just have to do some last-minute packing and close up my house."

"You'll be going to Iquitos, as planned?" Moreno asked.

Fuentes was silent for a long moment. Then: "No. I want you to fly me to Bogota."

"Bogota? But your wife is in Peru."

"My wife is in good hands," Fuentes said. "I intend to go on to Miami from Colombia. I have business there that must be completed before I join the rabbits in exile."

"Well. . .of course, Bogota is a much longer flight. I might have to re-fuel somewhere."

"If you're talking about danger, don't worry. I have friends there. If it's money, tell me what it will cost."

Moreno paused for a calculation. *"It will be double the fee to Peru."*

"That seems like a very high price," Fuentes said acidly.

"How do you measure the value of an escape from terror?"

Fuentes sighed. "I'll have the money, don't worry. Can we go tomorrow night?"

"Let's see. I've got business tomorrow night. The plane will be in use."

Fuentes was nettled. "In use? What use could it have that is as important as ours?"

"The same kind," Moreno said levelly.

"You're flying somebody else out?" In a shocked voice.

"Does that surprise you?" Moreno said.

"Who is it that you fly out ahead of me?"

"I can't say. As it is with you, the arrangement is on a strictly confidential basis."

"I'll pay you more than him, whoever he is," Fuentes said in a hard voice. "I'll pay you three times the Peru fee."

"That's very generous. But I've made a deal. You wouldn't want me to welch on ours, would you?"

"Damn!" Fuentes growled.

"We can go two nights from now," Moreno said firmly.

"Where and at what time?" he asked in a grim tone.

"I'll pick you up at your house. It's part of the service. I know the best routes to the airstrip. We won't want to leave until at least mid-evening, for security. Why don't I pick you up at, say, nine?"

"All right. Nine at my house."

"Don't pack more than two average-size bags. We want to keep the weight at a minimum. I'll see you at nine, then, on Saturday night."

"I'll be there," Fuentes said bitterly.

It was early afternoon when Jesus Cuesta finally got to see Alvarez privately at their new headquarters, a schoolhouse in the south suburbs. He had held court with his leaders and generals that morning, discussing strategy for continued offensive thrusts through the next couple of days. Alvaristas were capturing more and more weapons from the surrendering and retreating government troops, weapons that were to be used against the defenders of the capital. Local citizens were welcoming the guerrillas with open arms now, not so much because they saw Alvarez as the savior of the common man, but because he appeared to be winning the battle for power.

Alvarez was surprisingly calm after being apprised about the *Maria Isabel* situation. He ordered Cuesta to bring in four of Cuesta's best men—soldiers of the rebellion who could get a job done.

"I don't think I understand, Idilio," Cuesto told him.

"Just bring them here, and I'll tell you what I have in mind," Alvarez replied to him.

In late afternoon, Cuesta returned with four men. Two of them were the men who had been directly involved in the interrogation of Esquinaldo—El Pardal, the killer and Torreon, the rapist. The two other men whom Cuesta brought with him were Francisco Morales and a newcomer called Valdez. Morales had joined the Alvaristas two years previously, had worked his way up to the unofficial rank of sergeant, and was an excellent soldier. He had served once in the regular army and had earned respect there, too. Valdez, a young, cocky ex-athlete who knew little about the reform movement or Alvarez, had a criminal record and had joined the Alvaristas to loot and pillage.

On that hot June afternoon, Alvarez watched the men file in behind Cuesta, the five looking grim and tough.

Alvarez sat behind the school principal's desk, his feet up on a corner, scratching a pencil through his thick beard. Cuesta seated the four men but remained standing near Alvarez.

"I believe you have met Pardal, Chairman," Cuesta began the meeting. He never addressed Alvarez by his first name in front of the common soldiers. "He and Torreon have been assisting me at the waterfront."

Alvarez nodded without speaking, looking formidable behind his boots and beard.

"They took Esquinaldo into custody," Cuesta added.

Alvarez continued stroking his beard with the pencil. "The two of you observed the McGills go aboard the freighter?"

"That is right, Chairman," Pardal answered.

"You should have attempted to detain them," Alvarez said evenly.

Pardal's face was expressionless, but Torreon's revealed discomfit. "We did not recognize Esquinaldo until the family was already boarding the ship," he said.

Alvarez studied Torreon's face without replying to the explanation.

"There was no opportunity, Chairman," Cuesta said carefully, not wanting to rouse Alvarez' anger. "There were longshoremen about, and the ship's crew."

Alvarez again said nothing.

"This third man is Morales, a valuable soldier in the reformation," Cuesta went on. "He was at Loja when it fell, and helped defeat government troops at the municipal building."

"I know Morales," Alvarez said. "Good to see you here, Morales."

"It is my privilege and pleasure, Chairman," Morales replied. A man in his mid-thirties, he looked like a back country farmer, with his brown skin and black eyes. His thick hands had obviously seen hard physical work, and his square face showed lines of fatigue etched by years

91

of poverty and deprivation.

Alvarez had already noted the arrogant manner of the fourth man, Valdez. He was young, with a shock of thick dark hair, and fair-skinned. His face wore a perpetual sardonic grin that had begun to irritate Alvarez.

"And you?" Alvarez said to him. "Who are you, soldier?"

Valdez grinned easily. "I am Valdez." He noticeably omitted addressing Alvarez by his title. "I have killed over one hundred of the enemy."

Cuesta and the others looked toward him, Cuesta scowling slightly.

"How many were women and children?" Alvarez asked levelly.

The grin slid off Valdez' face. "Who counts?" he said.

"Valdez, when the Chairman. . ."

But Alvarez put a hand up to stop Cuesta. He held Valdez' gaze with a cool one now. "Didn't I see you with R company last night in the business district, looting the stores there?"

Valdez shrugged. "Perhaps. I was there."

"You're surely aware of my directive against looting?" Alvarez went on, almost courteously.

Valdez raised his dark eyebrows. "Every soldier is entitled to a certain amount of contraband as the spoils of war, yes?" He tried a grin again.

"Chairman, I didn't realize," Cuesta apologized.

Valdez gave him a dark look. "I don't understand the difficulty. Everybody in the ranks confiscates from the enemy. Surely you must know that. . .Chairman."

Alvarez' face was suddenly taut with a controlled anger. He took his Mauser automatic from a desk drawer and laid it on the desk. He looked at Torreon who had spoken up so audaciously in defense of his and Pardal's actions at the waterfront.

"You, Torreon, are quick to defend failure. Are you

also quick to follow all orders of your superiors in the movement. . .giving your loyalty without question?"

Torreon narrowed his eyes on Alvarez. "Yes, of course, Chairman."

Alvarez nodded. "Come and take this gun, Torreon."

Everybody looked curious, including Cuesta. Torreon came and took the Luger-type pistol from the desk. Valdez leaned forward slightly.

"Now kill Valdez with it."

Torreon's face exhibited surprise. Cuesta stared at Valdez who, in sudden shock, rose from his chair. "Is this some kind of joke?" he asked gruffly.

Torreon held Alvarez' gaze for a moment. Then, he turned and aimed the gun at Valdez. Valdez' eyes widened briefly. "Jesus and Mary! No, wait! This is all crazy! I did not mean. . ."

The gun exploded loudly in the room. Lifted onto his toes, Valdez danced backwards, crashing into his chair and knocking it over, smacking the wall behind him, arms flung outward, jaw hung open. When he finally slid to the floor, he left a crimson smear on the white-washed wall. He had been hit center-chest.

Torreon examined the gun casually, turning it over in his hand. "It shoots well, Chairman, but I can improve the slide action, if you'd like for me to work on it."

One of Valdez' legs spasmodically drummed the floor and then he was still. Morales had risen from his chair, and now stared grimly at the dead man. Pardal had not moved. He grunted a hard laugh deep in his throat, looking at the lifeless Valdez. In the next moment, the door crashed open and two armed guards rushed in, guns drawn.

"It is all right," Alvarez told them quickly. "We have just exterminated a vermin. Take him out, please."

It took only a moment to drag the body from the room. Cuesta slowly wiped his mouth. No one spoke.

93

Alvarez struck a match and held the flame to a very thin cigarillo. Then he sat back and put his feet on the desk, looking somber.

"Four of you will be sufficient," he said.

Cuesta picked up the chair, knocked over by Valdez in his death plunge, and sat down. "For what, Chairman?"

Alvarez met his curious look. "I have had quite enough of this goddam Fuentes. He is as bad as Biaza, maybe worse. Now he hires a rich American friend to smuggle government papers and God knows what else out of the country. I am fed up with Enrico Fuentes."

"He is a traitor to the dignity of all good Ecuadorians," Cuesta said, mouthing Alvarez doctrine.

Alvarez sucked on the cigarillo. "I want Fuentes," he said. "I want to prevent his escape from Guayaquil."

"At this point," Cuesta said, running a finger along his black mustache, his hard eyes serious, "there is no way to prevent an official exodus from the capital to the east. But, we are gaining ground, as you know, in that area all the time. Also, there is little chance of anyone reaching the border by land. With a little luck, we will be able to round up escapees in the countryside."

"Put some agents on the government buildings, if you can get them close enough," Alvarez told him, "and appoint a subordinate to supervise the operation. You will not be here."

Cuesta frowned. "No?"

"You are going after Luther McGill," Alvarez said. "You and your three men here."

Cuesta's face showed surprise. "Go after him?"

"I have done some checking on the *Maria Isabel*. It will stop at Panama City before passing through the Canal." He puffed on the brown cigarillo. "It will also stop at Port au Prince, but that government is unfriendly to us, and it would be too dangerous to try to fly you in there."

94

"You want us to go to Panama?" Cuesta said.

"The freighter is due to arrive at Panama City tonight," Alvarez said. "We have a plane that can fly you to Neiva later today, and there are regular flights from there to Bogota. The freighter is expected to be in Panama City for two days. You should be there by late tomorrow."

'You can get us papers before we leave today?" Cuesta asked.

"I have someone already working on it," Alvarez said.

"You wish for us to intercept the freighter at Panama City?" Morales spoke up now.

Alvarez nodded. "The captain, a fellow named Valaczek, will be taking on freight there, offering excellent opportunity for the McGills to go ashore and stretch their legs."

"You want us to detain the McGills?" the fellow Morales said.

Alvarez held his open gaze. "The trunk that Fuentes sent with them is of the first importance," he said. "That means you'll have to board the vessel at dockside. Remember, there are only two officers and four sailors aboard, and some of them may be ashore at any given time. And, of course, the fellow Rueda might stay aboard to guard the trunk. I want that trunk. I don't want it to fall into the hands of Panamanian customs."

Cuesta nodded. "I know a way," he said.

"In the port, you might hijack a small boat," Alvarez went on. "That should not be difficult for you, Jesus."

Cuesta smiled.

"You will open the trunk, put its contents into smaller bags, and bring the bags back here," Alvarez said.

Now the ugly-looking Pardal spoke up. "What about McGill?" he asked.

Alvarez let out a long breath. "As I said, you may

find him on shore or on the ship. When you do. . . execute him. . .as well as Rueda and the Parrish fellow, if the opportunity arises." He paused. "Also, learn what McGill knows about Victorio Salazar in Miami, his whereabouts and so forth, before you kill him."

"And McGill's family?" Torreon said.

Alvarez studied the end of his cigarillo for a long moment. "An example must be made. . .yes."

A silence fell over them.

"Avoid killing the crew, if you can," Alvarez added.

"We will try to keep the incident as quiet as is possible," Cuesta promised.

"That is important," Alvarez told him. "If authorities in Panama become involved in an *aborted* operation, the incident will be taken up by newspapers everywhere. At this particular moment in time, we do not need adverse publicity."

"We understand perfectly," Cuesta said. "Where will we land the boat on our return, Chairman?"

"You will put in at Santa Elena. There will be a contingent of troops there to meet you."

Morales shuffled his feet, his thick hands clasped before him. "I must say that I regret the orders concerning the women, Chairman."

Pardal turned and gave Morales a curious look. A pensive expression crossed Torreon's hard face. Alvarez took the cigarillo from his mouth. "I do, also, Morales."

Morales nodded uncertainly.

"Go to Panama," Alvarez said deliberately, "and do what you have to do." He looked at Cuesta. "Don't come back until your mission has been successfully completed."

"We would not wish to do otherwise, Chairman."

Eight

The *Maria Isabel* was on its way up the coast, past Punta Galera and Tumaco and Buenaventura. It was early evening. In less than three hours the freighter would pull into the harbor at Panama City.

The ship's few passengers had adjusted to the grim routine aboard the rusty old tub. They had had three meals aboard already, sharing the questionable fare with Valaczek and his mate, Dubois. In between the meals there was nothing to do. Time was spent reading, sleeping, and talking; the McGills could not do much of the latter, fearful that one of the crew might overhear something confidential.

Nita was quick to place herself beside Parrish at meals, and had begun flirting with him openly, embarrassing Parrish considerably. The scandal, three years previous, made him an undesirable suitor in the eyes of McGill and Ana. So, Parrish tried to ignore Nita's charming advances, but Nita was not an easy girl to ignore. Her physical beauty was stunning, and it was both flattering and physically unnerving to have her so interested.

Rueda ate with them, but spoke little. He was always going below deck where the big luggage and the Fuentes trunk were stored. He treated the family, particularly Parrish, more like adversaries than allies, and he always seemed to be just within listening range when any two members of the family were together, watching them from the corner of his eye.

"I don't like him," Parrish told Tony that evening on deck, as they stood at the rail watching the sun set across the Pacific. Their hair blew in a sea breeze. It had cooled down considerably, and both wore sweaters. Tony was pleased that he could have some time alone with his friend.

"Rueda?" Tony said, glancing toward Rueda briefly. The Fuentes hireling stood at the stern, leaning on some crates, looking toward the bridge.

Parrish nodded. "Fuentes didn't send him to protect you. His only interest is in that damned trunk."

"He wouldn't win any personality contests," Tony joked. "I've never seen such a sober-puss. The guy must take cranky pills."

"I'd like to have been hiding in a closet when he got his instructions from Fuentes," Parrish said pensively.

"I guess if we didn't have you, we'd be on our own," Tony said to him.

The sun poured slowly into the sea, its molten color lining the horizon.

"When it comes down to it," Parrish finally said, "you're always on your own. Don't ever forget that."

Tony glanced at him, his hair moving in the wind. "When Dad needed you, he wasn't alone."

Parrish turned from the dying sun to look into Tony's eyes. "I told you before, and I want you to listen this time, that was blown out of all proportion. On another day, it might have come out differently. I. . .might have frozen. . .or gone to jelly."

"Oh, hell, Jake," Tony said.

Parrish looked away. "Don't ever depend on anybody but yourself. Don't ever count on somebody else. We. . .can't be responsible for each other. It's tough enough just surviving, yourself."

"You don't believe that," Tony said lightly.

Parrish turned back to him. "I do believe it," he said.

Tony decided to change the subject. "Did you bring a gun with you?"

Parrish made a face. "Luther furnished one. A Sterling .380 PPL."

"But you don't carry it, do you?"

"No. It's for trouble, Tony. I haven't seen any hint of any, have you?"

"Just Rueda. His jacket came open once, and I got a look at what he packs. It's a Belgian Centennial .44, I think. He could hunt elephants with it."

"Rueda is supposed to be on our side, remember."

"It was you who said you didn't like him," Tony said.

Parrish grunted. "That doesn't mean anything. I think I've probably just joined a club with a wide membership."

They stood there staring westward. The sun slipped below the horizon, and, for several minutes, the sky revealed its inflamed wound, then it was covered over by night.

"Nita can't seem to keep away from you," Tony said. He was grinning slightly, his brown eyes looking out to sea.

Parrish turned and gave him a narrow look. "We're old friends. . .like you and me."

"No, it's more than that," Tony said definitely. "She's steaming up her undies for you. You've got her all heated up, buddy."

Parrish scowled slightly. "I like your directness."

Tony shrugged. "I'm enjoying it. And you could do worse, you know. Nita looks pretty good in a bikini."

Parrish sighed. "Let's drop it, what do you say?"

"Sure," Tony said, stealing a look at him.

"I think I'll go below and have a look at a magazine," Parrish said. He clapped Tony on the arm. "See you later."

"Okay, Jake," Tony said, subdued.

Just as Parrish reached his and Rueda's room, he

99

spotted the sailor who had been assigned as a make-shift steward for the passengers, an unkempt-looking, burly fellow who spoke no English and was a native of Colombia. Parrish, feeling very tense, stopped the fellow and asked if there was any liquor aboard.

"A little, sir. We all have our own private stuff."

"Can you sell me something?" Parrish asked him.

"What were you interested in?"

"Anything," Parrish said.

The fellow's eyes narrowed slightly. "I have an extra bottle of rum, but I'll have to charge you top price."

"I'll take it," Parrish said, not even bothering to ask what the sailor would charge him.

Five minutes later the fellow was at Parrish's door with the bottle. Parrish paid him, lay down on his cot, and opened the bottle. Maybe, if he got drunk enough, he thought, he would stay out until he got to Miami. His good intentions at the hotel in Guayaquil were gone. He owed Luther McGill nothing.

The door opened, and Pedro Rueda came in. Parrish turned and stared blankly at him, as Rueda's eyes focused on the bottle in Parrish's hand.

"I didn't know there was a ship's bar."

"There isn't." In a slurred voice, "I made this in the captain's bath-tub. The main ingredient is coffee beans. Did you know you can make booze from almost any agricultural product, Rueda?"

Rueda went to his cot, and took his shirt off. He had worn the shirt outside his trousers, and it had hidden from view the Centennial revolver that was now visible in his waistband. "It sounds as if you have already ingested a considerable quantity of this agricultural product."

Parrish's eyebrows went up. He was propped against a bulkhead at the head of the cot, the bottle standing on his chest. "Who's keeping track? I know it isn't gone yet. How about a swig, Rueda? With some of this in you, you might not need that cannon.''

Rueda had pulled on a clean shirt and was buttoning it, the gun no longer showing. He was on his way to see McGill. ''I notice you no longer wear yours,'' he said, his intelligent eyes opaque with mild anger. His thin face looked pale in the dim light of the cabin, and Parrish could just make out the hole in his ear-lobe that gave Rueda a piratical look. ''Did you lose it already, perhaps?''

''It's around somewhere,'' Parrish grunted out, ''where it won't hurt anybody.''

Rueda stared at Parrish grimly. ''Maybe that is just as well,'' he said. Then he turned to leave.

''Don't get your finger caught in that trigger guard,'' Parrish called after him. ''You might shoot something off that your love life can't do without.'' He laughed. ''Have you ever had a love life, Rueda?''

Rueda hesitated for a moment, then left without further comment.

Out in the passageway, he stood still, frowning back toward the door. From the beginning he had disliked the idea of sharing quarters with Parrish, but, now, the situation was becoming worse.

A few moments later, Rueda knocked on the door of McGill's cabin. McGill had arranged to meet with Rueda, at Rueda's suggestion, so that Rueda might make a brief report to him on security. Ana had absented herself from the cabin, visiting Nita in Nita and Tony's cabin.

''Ah, Rueda,'' McGill said, when he opened the door. ''Come in, please.''

Rueda and McGill sat on two straight chairs, facing each other.

''I've just spoken with Captain Valaczek,'' McGill told Rueda. ''He seems a good sort. His language is rough, but he acts courteous enough to the women. He says we'll be in port by eleven tonight. We can all go

101

ashore tomorrow, if we want to.''

Rueda blew out his thin cheeks. "I don't know if that would be advisable. Somebody should stay aboard with the Fuentes trunk, and that someone should be me. That leaves you without a bodyguard, unless you count Parrish.''

McGill did not miss the slur against Parrish. "But I'll ask Parrish to come. Valaczek might be in port for two days. Surely it would be good for all of us to go ashore and get off this rusty tub for a few hours.''

"Remember, your papers are false ones. Also, if Alvarez by some chance got wind of our sailing, he could have somebody waiting for us at Panama. You'd be safer aboard ship. But, of course, that's your decision to make.''

McGill pursed his lips. "Yes," he said thoughtfully.

"I've circulated among the crew," Rueda went on. "They seem an ordinary sort. I don't see any of them as Alvarez agents. Dubois watches us a lot, and I think he is trying to figure out who we really are. Of course, Valaczek may well have told him by now. If so, there probably would be more danger to the trunk than to you and your family.''

McGill eyed Rueda narrowly. "You seem very concerned about the trunk, Rueda.''

Rueda put on as innocent a look as he could manage. "It is part of my responsibility. My concern, of course, is for all of you.''

McGill was trying to figure Rueda out. His eyes dropped to the bulge under Rueda's shirt. "Since you have no suspicions regarding the crew, maybe it isn't necessary to wear that on board." He gestured toward Rueda's waist.

Rueda glanced downward, and when he looked up, his eyes were glassy. "Your man Parrish seems to have the same feeling. . .without checking the security on shipboard in any way.''

"Jake doesn't like guns," McGill said, "but he knows how to use them."

"Since you have only one man you can trust on board," Rueda said acidly, "I would think you'd be happy to have him armed."

McGill decided to take up the gauntlet thrown at Parrish. "How do you mean?" he said.

"I mean that your man Parrish is an incompetent drunk who is no good to anyone," Rueda said in a low, hard voice. "I just came from our cabin. He is so drunk that he cannot talk straight. He must have bought a bottle from one of the crew."

McGill looked past Rueda for a moment, remembering the bottles he had seen beside Parrish's cot at Punto Segundo.

"Jake can keep it under control, I assure you," McGill said lamely.

"I do not think so," Rueda told him. "I think you ought to disarm him. He cannot be relied upon—he cannot be trusted."

McGill held Rueda's level gaze. "Jake Parrish is a friend, Rueda. I trust him as I've trusted few men in my life. He'll keep the gun I gave him, and the fee I paid him to accompany us. And that's the end of it."

Rueda shook his head slowly. "Very well, Mr. McGill. It's your family that's involved. In any event, I strongly suggest that you try to separate him from his liquor. He could become a problem."

"If he does," McGill said evenly, "it's a problem I'll handle, Rueda."

"As you say," Rueda told him.

After Rueda had left, McGill went down the passageway to Parrish's cabin, knowing that Rueda had gone up on deck. When he knocked on the door, he heard Parrish's slurred voice yell for him to enter. Parrish was still propped on his cot, just as Rueda had left him. The liquor bottle was almost empty.

"Rueda said I'd find you here," McGill said.

"Oh, Luther. What brings you down to the cattle pens?" His handsome face was blank-looking, and a lock of dark hair had fallen onto his forehead.

McGill sat on the edge of Rueda's cot. "I see you bought yourself some happy time."

Parrish patted the bottle. "It's nature's own medicine, old sport," he said. "You want to share the warmth?"

McGill nodded and took the bottle, swigging a small amount of it down. It tasted good. He handed it back to Parrish. "You must have paid plenty for that."

"I paid the poor bastard in sucres," Parrish said. "They're probably worthless by now."

McGill grinned. "Jake, are you all right?"

Parrish frowned toward him. "All right? What the hell do you mean, all right? Don't I look all right?"

"You know what I mean. I hope your bad luck in Ecuador didn't get to you. You never used to have much of a taste for booze."

"Oh, Christ," Parrish muttered. "I think I feel a lecture coming on."

"No lecture. But I hate to see you hitting the bottle so hard, Jake. For your own sake. And then, of course, we do need you."

Parrish squinted at him. "Oh, is that it? You're afraid I won't be ready, my guns blazing, if Valaczek decides to steal Fuentes' trunk and dump you overboard?"

"Jake, you know what. . ."

"Hell, I'll give you your money's worth!" Parrish said. He got off the cot, put the bottle on a shelf, and went staggering to a duffel bag in a corner. Fumbling in it for a moment, he came up with the short-muzzled PPL automatic. He turned back to McGill.

"There's the damn gun." He stuck it awkwardly into his waistband and it almost fell out. "Right out in sight, ready to scare off muggers or guerrilla spies. Does that make you feel more secure, Luther?"

McGill rose from the cot. "It would make me feel better if you had a better opinion of yourself, old friend," he said quietly.

Parrish stared at him for a long moment, then sat down heavily on the cot. "I'm tired, Luther. I'm very tired. I'd like to get a little rest. . ."

McGill nodded. "Sure, Jake. I'll see you at breakfast tomorrow morning."

"Maybe," Parrish told him.

McGill left. Parrish didn't move; he was concentrating on feeling sorry for himself. He looked at the bottle, but McGill had taken away his thirst.

He stood up, grabbed the bottle, and left the cabin, clumsily making his way up a companionway to the main deck.

It was very dark on deck, and there was a cool breeze. Parrish walked aft where two sailors were rigging a deck crane for action in port. Parrish nodded to them, and then leaned over the gunwale. He took a last swig, made a face, and heaved the bottle into the sea.

He heard Valaczek's voice. "All right, boys, bear a hand on that winch. The day isn't over just because you've made sunset. We'll be mooring at anchor before you know it, and you'll still have the stink of the bilge on you."

"Aye, Captain."

"Get the gratings off those forward hatches, and coil those hawsers up there. Then stand by for making port."

Another mumbled acknowledgment. Parrish heard Valaczek come up behind him. "By Jesus, if it isn't Mr. Parrish." He clapped a big hand onto Parrish's shoulder. "You look a bit under the weather there, lad."

Parrish turned and focused on him, feeling a little

better. "Captain. I just came topside to see if this derelict was still making way."

"Oh, she'll go the route a couple of times yet," Valaczek said easily. "You a little queasy, are you?"

Parrish made a face. "It's not the sea. Just some cheap hooch I put down on top of that swabby fare you gave us for dinner."

"You don't like the food aboard?" Valaczek said. "Maybe you should have booked the Cunard."

"Now why didn't I think of that?" Parrish said.

Valaczek leaned on the rail beside him, big and rough-looking in his sea uniform with its peaked cap. His gray hair fluttered below the brim of the cap, and his small lined eyes studied Parrish's face closely.

"What are you really doing here, Parrish?"

Parrish turned and met his narrow gaze.

"You don't look like the bodyguard type to me. Now Rueda is different. He even smells like a cop. But you . . .Why the hell did McGill bring you along?"

Parrish stared out to sea. "I'll be damned if I know."

Valaczek continued to appraise him. "Maybe he wants to get something going between you and that good-looking daughter, eh? She's got the heat for you, hasn't she?"

Parrish turned to him, feeling much more sober. "Nita is an old friend, Captain. I've known her since she was a kid. I wouldn't waste time conjecturing about the relationship between me and the McGills, if I were you. You might end up in Acapulco instead of Panama."

Valaczek laughed harshly. "Well, it's your business. But I'd keep one eye on that Rueda, while you're waltzing the princess McGill."

Parrish frowned at him. "Why do you say that?"

"Because one of my men saw him going through your duffel earlier today."

"Damn."

"I thought you two were supposed to be on the same side of something?"

Parrish grunted. "We are," he said.

Valaczek grinned at him. "I'd almost forgotten how entertaining it can be with passengers aboard," he said.

Parrish scanned Valaczek's square face, but the captain had already turned away and was heading back toward his crew, his broad back stiff against the sea breeze.

Nine

It was a bright, sunny morning, and the *Maria Isabel* was docked at the smelly waterfront of old Panama City. Large ships were lined up along the dock and pier area, loading and unloading cargo, a few dropping off or picking up passengers. Down the waterfront a few hundred yards sat a luxury liner that had just come through the Canal, out of service, headed for Los Angeles to be repaired.

In the cramped mess room of the *Maria Isabel*, Captain Valaczek was holding forth in particularly good spirits that morning. Valaczek sat at the head of a long wooden table, First Officer Jacques Dubois at the other end. The McGills, Parrish and Rueda sat along the short length of the table: Parrish, Nita and Tony on Valaczek's left; McGill, Ana and Rueda on his right. The four-man crew would use the same facilities in two shifts, after the room had been vacated by Valaczek and his passengers.

The mess cabin was white-painted but the paint was marred and scratched. The cabin bulkhead on one wall bore shelves of dusty canned goods that had overflowed the pantry. In one corner stood an oil drum with some sticky substance on its top that the women had to maneuver around for fear of soiling their clothing. The table itself was polished, and a low railing around its edge kept the dishes from sliding off in bad weather.

Before them were eggs, toast and thick black coffee. There was sugar but no milk. Valaczek picked up his coffee mug and smiled broadly.

"There's nothing like a hearty breakfast to start the day off right, by Jesus. Don't you agree, Mr. Brown?"

McGill looked scrubbed and fresh that morning. He had lost most of his appetite on that first day out, but now he felt like eating again. "Yes, I do," he told Valaczek. "I don't suppose you'd happen to have a little fresh fruit aboard, Captain?"

"We don't have the facilities to carry such things," Valaczek said, rather abruptly, but still smiling. "How are you doing, Mrs. Brown? Would you like some more coffee?"

"Not just now, thank you," Ana told him.

"I'll take some," Reuda said quietly.

"Of course, Mr. Rueda," Dubois said in his creole accent. He moved a pot over to Rueda, and Rueda poured himself a second cup of coffee without acknowledging DuBois' help. "Something else for you, Miss Brown, or the young mister?" Dubois asked.

Nita and Tony both declined. "I don't want to be stuffed, walking around in town," Nita said, anticipating going ashore with a great deal of pleasure.

"Have you decided to do some shopping, Mother?" Nita asked Ana brightly. Nita was dressed in a sheer, lemon-hued dress with a low neckline, and her hair was drawn into a French twist at the back of her head. She looked as if she were going to be photographed for a magazine cover.

"I'm just going to a couple of waterfront shops to buy some toiletry items, dear," Ana told her. "If you want to see more of the town, maybe Jake wouldn't mind escorting you."

Parrish had been staring into his coffee. He had no eggs on his plate, just toast, and he had eaten little of that. He had a hangover and a thick tongue.

"Oh. . .Yeah, sure," he said, figuring it was part of the job he had undertaken. Nita could not go into the city alone.

"I think Mr. Parrish needs a little hair off the dog that bit him," Valaczek grinned broadly.

Rueda grunted, eyeing Parrish sidewise from his end of the table.

"Jake's all right," McGill said. "A little exercise this morning will do him a world of good."

"Oh, I'm so glad you're going, Jake!" Nita smiled. "I want to walk along Avenida Alfaro to the Presidential Palace, and then go look for some silk on the Avenida Central."

Parrish nodded without turning to her. "Sounds great," he lied.

Valaczek laughed quietly in his throat, Parrish ignoring him.

"I'm not feeling so terrific," Tony said. He, too, had only eaten toast. He was still getting his sea legs. "I think I'll pass it up this morning and just rest here."

Valaczek looked down the table to Rueda. "And you, Mr. Rueda? I'll bet you'll stay here too, won't you?"

Rueda gave him a look. "As a matter of fact, yes. Do you have any objection?"

"None at all," Valaczek grinned. "I think you're the kind who would rather look around the ship than go into town, that's all."

Rueda studied Valaczek's face, but it was unreadable. Parrish quickly glanced at Valaczek, then looked at Rueda. Rueda met Parrish's gaze for a brief moment, then looked back down at his plate.

The sound of the crew beginning to unload cargo with the big crane could be heard below. Valaczek listened for a moment, then went on.

"We'll be unloaded by mid-afternoon, and then the length of our stay will depend on an importer I'll be talking with this morning. I had expected to stay through tomorrow, to take on some linen goods, but now there's some doubt as to whether that cargo is ready for us. So we might sail early, maybe even late tonight. That means you ought to all be back by dinner-time. If you don't intend to have dinner aboard, let me know before you go ashore."

"Will an early leaving here put us in Miami sooner?" McGill wondered, thinking about Wade Sumner and his rendezvous with the ship.

Valaczek knew exactly what he meant. "No, it won't, Mr. Brown," he replied easily. "We'll just add the time at Port au Prince. I'll take on some extra cargo there."

They were through eating. McGill and Ana rose. "Well, if you'll excuse us, Captain. I guess we'll get ready to debark."

Valaczek rose, and Dubois, and then all of them, one by one. "Mr. Dubois will sign you off as you leave," Valaczek told them. He cast a concerned look at McGill. "Please be careful in town, Mr. Brown. The water, for instance, may not be safe for drinking."

"We'll take the usual precautions," McGill replied.

They filed out of the cabin. Parrish waited until last, following Rueda out onto the passageway. "Rueda."

Rueda turned and looked back at Parrish. He could see the bulge under Rueda's shirt where the Centennial .44 rested. All the others had moved off now, except for Dubois who was out of earshot inside the mess cabin.

"What is it?" Rueda asked him, in a hard voice. "I don't have any liquor to sell you, if that's what you want."

Parrish held his look with a cold one. "I'm going to make this short and sweet, Rueda. Keep away from my stuff."

Rueda raised his eyebrows in a look of mock surprise. "Your stuff? I don't understand."

"You went through my duffel yesterday," Parrish said flatly.

111

"Who says this?" Rueda replied cautiously.

"An eye-witness," Parrish told him. "Just keep out of my gear, goddamn it. . .and the McGills' gear."

"You don't know what you are talking about, Parrish," Rueda said arrogantly. "You must ·have dreamed this up in a drunken state."

"I'm not drunk now, by God, and I'm warning you."

Rueda laughed softly. "Is that a threat, then?"

"Take it how you like it," Parrish said.

"A man who does not even carry a gun should not go around talking so loudly in accusing words," Rueda said meaningfully. "He could have a·bad accident some dark night on deck, talking and talking when he should be watching where he is going."

Parrish glanced at the bulge under Rueda's shirt, and wondered if he would have the guts to go against Rueda, or if he'd have the guts to take a stand against anything. "Just keep away from my stuff," he finally said, walking past Rueda quickly.

On his way to their quarters, Parrish realized that Rueda had blatantly threatened him. If Parrish got in his way, Rueda was telling him, Rueda would handle the situation with his gun. Rueda neither feared nor respected Parrish. The same went for McGill. Rueda's gun was really in charge.

McGill, Ana, Nita and Parrish left the ship together. Valaczek had to notify the Panamanian immigration people, and the four were obliged to check through with the officials before leaving the dock area. There was no problem with their papers, and they were soon released into the city. McGill and Ana walked to a small shopping area near the waterfront, Nita and Parrish accompanying them for a short while.

Actually, Parrish was as glad to be off the ship as Nita. It was a pleasant morning, and there was a flavor of colonial Spain in the town. They walked along a broad boulevard to the Presidential Palace, and then made a turn toward Avenida Central. Nita was exuberant about seeing the city. She smiled and joked and talked Parrish's ear off. He found that he liked it. In fact, he liked Nita. She was not just beautiful to look at; she was a vivacious witty girl, a girl with substance. Unlike most young women who took to modeling, she did not see it as a career. She wanted marriage and a family. She liked flamenco music, pre-Columbian history, and she was a handball expert as well as an accomplished swimmer and diver.

Nita took Parrish into one shop after another along Avenida Central, buying pieces of silk and a couple of scarfs. At noon, Parrish took her to the Dorado Restaurant, on the corner of Calle Colombia just off the broad Via España. They ordered *mariscos* and *arroz marinera* and a dry white wine. Nita was delighted. They did not talk much during the meal, but when they were finished, and the waiter had brought Parrish an after-dinner aperitif, Nita engaged Parrish in conversation.

"I don't see any dark-eyed men peering at us from behind the potted palms. I guess Fuentes' concern about Alvaristas was unfounded."

Parrish returned her smile. "We're not in Miami yet. I guess it won't hurt to be cautious until we get there."

"I've had so much fun this morning, Jake," she said happily. "It's been a long time since I've enjoyed myself so much."

Parrish nodded. "I've enjoyed it, too, Nita. I guess I've always liked being around you. . .and Tony, of course."

Nita looked down at her plate for a moment. "What will you do when this is over, Jake?"

Parrish shrugged. "I don't really know. I guess I'm still thinking of all of this as the end of something, rather than a beginning. I haven't thought ahead very far."

"We'll be going to New York, at least for a while. I'll probably do some modeling there. The agency has offered me more work."

"I can see why," Parrish said. "You must be damned photogenic, Nita."

She looked down again. "It's been special. . .this time with you. I don't think I knew how special it would be. I've. . .never felt this before."

Parrish looked into her blue eyes with their large, open, inviting look. "You've forgotten, Nita," he said, "how it used to be. You used to play me a wicked game of tennis, remember? You were always telling me jokes from school, and getting the punch lines balled up. We had a great time together."

Nita was shaking her head, though. "I remember all of that. When you kissed me on the cheek, I felt like doing cartwheels. I would have gone to China with you, no questions asked. But this is different."

Parrish was beginning to wish he had not gotten into this conversation. "Nita. . ."

"I find that I'm very fond of you, Jake. Not like a schoolgirl but like a woman."

"Jesus, Nita." He was suddenly embarrassed.

"I know I've only been around you for a few days. But remember, there's all that time from before. That counts, Jake. It didn't mean anything then, but it does now. I've known a hundred boys and men since then, and I've come to know what I like. Ask Ana."

Parrish looked into her lovely face. "I'm not the guy you knew three years ago, honey. I've changed, even if it doesn't show. You don't know me anymore. I'm a hell of a lot more cynical about the world than I was then. I don't have any purpose now, any direction. Don't involve yourself too deeply with me, Nita. We're not just separated by years, but by what has and hasn't happened to us."

Nita leaned closer to him, and he could smell the

sweet scent of her. "Look at me, Jake. This isn't the same girl you knew three years ago, either. I was a kid then. Now I'm a woman. I'm no longer flighty, giggly, scatterbrained. . .virginal." She averted her eyes momentarily. "Don't keep seeing me as the kid you used to push into the swimming pool and help with algebra. Give us a chance, Jake."

Parrish stared hard at her.

"You do like me, Jake. I can tell. As a woman, I mean, not as a friend from the old days. If I hadn't seen that in your eyes, I wouldn't be talking to you this way."

Parrish rubbed a hand across his chin, and looked away. "All right, Nita. I wouldn't say this to Luther, but yes, you do turn me on. All the way on. You did from the first moment I saw you sitting in the dining room at the Humboldt. And, yes, I think you're a special woman. A hell of a lot of fun to be with, so much so that I'm beginning to feel like some lascivious uncle who can't be trusted with the children." He turned back to her. "But don't think I intend to make anything of that, Nita, or take advantage of you by sneaking you into bed."

Nita smiled slightly at the last part.

"That's all it would take to make me lose the last of whatever vestige of respect I may still have for myself," he added.

Nita was still smiling. "You wanted to kiss me on deck last night, didn't you?"

Parrish hesitated. "Yes."

"I wish you had," she told him.

Parrish looked at her. She was more woman than most men ever got a chance to get close to. Suddenly he wanted her so much that it made him ache.

"Don't spoil what could be between us, Jake," she said soberly, "just because I'm Luther McGill's little girl. You're not my uncle, you're not old enough. You 'don't have to feel guilty because you're attracted to me. If you feel something ought to happen between us. . . let it.''

Parrish wanted to grab her to him, smother her with kisses, feel those rich curves against him. He had never wanted a woman so much in his life. He swallowed hard and stood up.

"I think we'd better get back, Nita," he said quietly.

Nita rose, filling the room with her lovely presence. Two men at nearby tables turned to stare openly at her. "All right," she said. "You're the guide today, Jake."

The sun had not yet set that day, when the jet set down at Belisario Porras Airport with four somber men aboard: Jesus Cuesta and his three Alvarista agents. They had no trouble at customs, and within an hour were checked in at a small grubby hotel in the older section of Panama City. But they wasted no time at the hotel. They were out on the street in ten minutes, and within another hour, Cuesta had managed to purchase four weapons—three throwaway revolvers and a Bowie-type knife for Pardal.

It was mid-evening when they took a taxi to the dark waterfront. They had to locate the *Maria Isabel*, apprehend the McGills and the trunk, and finish the job as Alvarez had ordered. Cuesta had decided that, since they had to get aboard on some pretext to locate and steal the trunk, it would be best to also dispose of the McGills and their bodyguards on board, hopefully out of sight of the crew and Valaczek. But first he had to find the freighter's location. Step One led him to the Port Authority.

"Which ship is it, the *Maria* what?" A bespectacled fellow peered up at Cuesta from behind a counter piled with papers.

Cuesta sighed impatiently. "The *Maria Isabel*. out of Valparaiso, Chile. A Captain Valaczek commanding."

The clerk looked down a list on a clipboard. *"Maria Isabel.* . .When would she have arrived in port?"

Cuesta was frustrated. "Yesterday or early today. She's to be here at least today and tomorrow, moving cargo. Perhaps I may have a look at the register, yes?"

The clerk glanced up at him, then looked back down at the paper. *"Pacific Queen.* . .*Seaward.* . .Ah, here . . .The *Maria Isabel."*

Cuesta released a long breath.

"You're right. She arrived late yesterday. Last port of call, Guayaquil, yes?"

"Yes," Cuesta said abruptly. "Where can I find the ship? At which dock is she tied up?"

The clerk ran a finger across the page. Above him, a ceiling fan moved slowly. "That would be Pier F, docking space three."

"And which direction would that be?" Cuesta asked.

But the man's face had drawn into a slight frown. "Wait a moment. You say the ship was to be in port through tomorrow?"

Cuesta's stomach tightened up. "Yes, that's right."

"My record here shows that she's sailing just about now. For Port au Prince."

Cuesta's face clouded over. "What are you talking about? My information says she is here another day!"

The clerk shrugged tiredly. "I only know what the record tells me, mister. Maybe the ship has not yet sailed. Pier F is just down the line about a hundred yards. If you hurry, you might be able to. . ."

But Cuesta was already gone. Out in the big room, he hurried over to his men. Pardal was paring his nails with a clipper, Morales sitting stoically on a bench near a woman with three children, and Torreon reading a newspaper. Cuesta came up to them a little breathless.

"Pardal! Come with me! You two stay put right here!"

"What is it?" Torreon said.

"I'll tell you shortly," Cuesta said. Then he was off, hurrying through a service door out onto the dock area, Pardal close behind.

Pier F was not far, as the clerk had said. Cuesta ran in a frenzy of tension now, Pardal trying to keep up with him. They came to the docking space three, it was empty.

Cuesta looked at the designation on the piling three different times, then stared at the surrounding ships, "It's not here," he kept saying. "It's not here!"

"Sonofabitch," Pardal growled in a low voice.

A longshoreman came along the pier and stopped beside them. "Looking for the *Maria Isabel?*"

Cuesta turned to the slim, muscular fellow. "That's right."

"She sailed just a half-hour ago. She's probably just clearing the harbor about now."

Cuesta's eyes were filled with rage suddenly. "Goddamn it! I don't believe it! What happened? She was supposed to be here at least another day!"

"I guess she didn't pick up the cargo she was supposed to," the longshoreman told him. "Listen, you can probably still reach the ship by radio, if you have to speak with the captain."

Cuesta was numb with shock. "Uh. Yes, I'll consider that," he said.

The longshoreman moved on, and Pardal went and leaned against a piling. "Alvarez will not like this," he said.

Cuesta looked at him sidewise. "Come on," he said tightly. "We have to do some heavy thinking."

Cuesta hardly spoke to the others after advising them of the new, unforeseen situation. The four flagged a cab and were driven to a cantina in the waterfront area, not far from their hotel. Cuesta found a table at the rear of the place, away from the other customers, and ordered a bottle of Mexican mezcal. They all poured themselves a glass and swigged it down before anybody spoke of their problem.

"Sonofabitch," Pardal finally commented.

"This is miserable luck, Jesus," Morales said, his peasant's face sober and straight-lined.

The curly-headed Torreon made a sound in his throat. "Alvarez will line us up against a wall and set a firing squad on us."

Cuesta poured himself a second drink. "If you will remember, gentlemen, the chairman advised us not to return until we had fulfilled our mission."

"But surely," Morales said, "there is no possibility of carrying out the chairman's orders now. As he himself pointed out, we would not be welcome in Haiti. We would undoubtedly be recognized by Duvalier's tonton macoutes and arrested. Such a venture would be fruitless."

"We could always wait for McGill in Miami," Pardal suggested.

Cuesta shook his head slowly. "We could lose the trunk to Salazar if we did that. And the McGills would not be easy to get to with Salazar's people around."

"Then it seems obvious that we must go back and face Alvarez with a failed mission," Torreon offered.

A silence fell over the table. They watched Cuesta's face as he stared at his glass of mezcal, and they waited.

Finally, he said: "Maybe there is another way."

Pardal and Torreon exchanged glances. "What way, Jesus?" Torreon asked.

Cuesta looked up at him. "We could intercept the *Maria Isabel* at sea," he said.

Morales frowned hard. "At sea?" he said incredulously.

Cuesta raised dark eyebrows, his mustachioed face brighter now. "Why not? There would be no authorities or police to deal with. Only Valaczek and his crew. We would execute the traitors, grab the trunk, and make our departure. Actually, it is better than doing it in port.''

Torreon made a face. "Excuse me for mentioning it, Jesus. But we have no means to intercept a ship at sea. Even if we had a boat of some kind, the captain would not heave to and let us board, just because we asked him to. Freighters do not stop in mid-ocean."

"They do along the Florida Straits and the Keys," Cuesta said to him. "U.S. Coast Guard cutters stop them all the time to search for illegal drugs. Small freighters just like the *Maria Isabel.*"

"But we are not the American Coast Guard," Morales reasoned. "Is that not a significant defect in your proposal?"

Cuesta met Morales' sober look. "With a little luck, we could be the Coast Guard for an hour or so."

Now they were all frowning quizzically. "Jesus," Pardal said in his low voice. "How could we manage such a magical trick?"

Cuesta looked past him. "Because there is a Coast Guard cutter that just may be available to us," he said more to himself than to them. "Wade Sumner, the fellow who is meeting McGill, owns a yacht that is a converted cutter."

Torreon's rough handsome face brightened. "What an interesting situation!"

Pardal and Morales were still frowning. "What do you propose, Jesus?" Morales asked.

"I propose flying to Miami tonight, first of all," Cuesta said evenly. "Our papers should work there."

"Oh, God," Torreon groaned. He was very tired.

"My plan is not a complex one," Cuesta went on. "In Miami we locate Sumner and his yacht, steal the yacht, restore its official Coast Guard markings, and sail it out into the gulfstream where we intercept the *Maria Isabel* as it leaves the Caribbean and heads north along the Florida Keys to Miami. Dressed in white uniforms, we hail the ship, stop it, and board it. When finished, we return to Santa Elena in the yacht."

Morales rubbed a hand across his square Indian face. "You say it is not complex."

Cuesta was excited now. "Taking Sumner's yacht should be no problem. What pleasure to use this conspirator's own vessel against him and McGill."

"But we have so little time," Torreon said. "The ship is due to arrive in Miami on June 20. It may get there sooner, now."

"Valaczek will probably give himself more time in Haiti," Cuesta said. "We'll check on its progress in Miami."

"But disguising the boat," Pardal said, the scar across his eye showing in the oblique light from the bar. "And finding uniforms."

"I have some ideas," Cuesta told them. "I know there may be difficulties. But would you rather go home and tell Alvarez that we have failed?"

There was no reply to that question. In a moment, Torreon said, "To steal Sumner's boat, we must have its keys, or else get involved with the ignition system. It would be easier, I think, if Sumner were aboard."

"I agree," Cuesta said.

"Then Sumner would have to be taken care of, too," Pardal said evenly.

Cuesta shrugged. "I suggest that would please the chairman very much," he replied with a grin.

Ten

It was Saturday the seventeenth.

Wade Sumner had just arrived home from his downtown Miami office where he had confirmed with Susan Benedict their sail on his yacht the following afternoon.

Sumner did not find his wife in the kitchen helping their Cuban cook fix the midday meal, as he had expected. "Where is the senora?" he asked the portly woman.

"She not cook today," the cook answered him. "I think I see her in bedroom, mister. You check and see."

Sumner did find Bette in the bedroom. She was sitting at a writing table, still dressed in her peignoir. She glanced at him when he entered the bright, airy room with its louvered French doors that gave onto manicured grounds, but then looked away without greeting him.

"I thought you'd be up and around," he said.

She looked tired, and washed out. "I am up," she said. "I'm just not around."

"What's the matter?" he asked her. "You seem. . . out of sorts."

Bette turned to him, and he thought she looked haggard. She had lost all her youth and no longer appealed to him physically.

"I am out of sorts," she said. "I got a call from a friend this morning, while you were away. She saw you

122

at Wolfie's for lunch a couple of days ago.''

Sumner, tall and distinguished-looking in a light-hued summer suit, raised his long eyebrows. ''So?''

''So, she said you were with Susan Benedict.''

Sumner sighed, inside. ''Oh, I see. Your friends are spying on me now, is that it?''

''I knew it was her,'' Bette said in a hard voice. ''I knew it was her all along. There have been signs, Wade. Undeniable signs.''

''Susan works where I do,'' Sumner said heavily. ''I often have lunch with people who work at Ameco.''

''Do you kiss them goodbye. . .on the mouth?'' Bette asked bitterly.

Sumner sat on the edge of the bed. The friend had seen too much. They were beginning to be indiscreet. ''All right,'' he said. ''No, I don't kiss everybody I have lunch with. Susan is special to me, if you want to hear me say it.''

''You're laying her!'' Bette said loudly, her face twisted up in sudden anger. ''You're screwing her every chance you get, goddamn you!''

''I'm. . .in love with Susan,'' he heard himself saying. ''I don't know how it happened, frankly. I had no control over it.''

''You had control over the fornication!'' Bette said, her voice shaking slightly. ''We've been married for twenty-five years, for God's sake! You have grown children! What do you think Marta would say if she knew you were acting like some hyped-up teenager! What would your superiors at Ameco say?''

Sumner gave her a look. ''I'm sorry, Bette. I didn't want it to come out like this. I value what we had between us. But that's gone, now. You've said so yourself. I'll give you a generous settlement. You can start a new life, like I'm doing. All I want is a quiet divorce with no trouble. I think, after all this time, that we can be civilized to each other.''

Bette turned away from him, crying. *"Civilized.* So that's the way you want it. You don't want any trouble because of what we've meant to each other. Damn you, Wade! Oh, damn you!"

His face lengthened slightly. "On the other hand," he said easily, "it doesn't have to be civilized. My lawyer says that if I get this before the right judge, I could cut you loose with very little."

She looked up at him, fear in her face.

"You would, wouldn't you? You'd do that to me, after all these years together?"

"I can be what I have to be, and do what I have to do, to give myself a life again," he said.

"You used to. . .buy me little presents. You used to call me darling, and whisper things into my ear."

"Oh, for Christ's sake, Bette."

"You used to be. . .nice," she added. She looked up at him. "What happened to you, Wade? You've become a different person since they gave you the vice-presidency. I remember how disappointed Luther McGill was when you fired his top man. . .A fellow named Parrish, wasn't it? You could have saved that fellow's job, Wade. But you figured you'd impress the people in New York by blowing the thing up. . .flying down there and firing him."

"I'm having Luther into my house," Sumner said levelly. "I'm meeting that goddam freighter to accommodate an arrangement of McGill. I don't think that's being such a bastard."

"It's only to ease what's left of your damned conscience." She turned away from him, facing the writing desk. "Well, I'm not going to just fade away gracefully, Wade, like the last rose of some wished-away summer of yours. I won't let you cast me off so effortlessly. If you want a divorce, you'll have one. But the rest of the world will know what you are when it's finished."

Sumner narrowed his eyes on her. "I thought you'd

124

be like this. You never did have any class, Bette. I often wonder what impelled me to marry you."

She faced him, her eyes red and watery. "That's one of the nicest compliments I've received recently," she said in a hard voice.

"I'll be discussing this with you again when you're in a better mood. In the meantime, do you think we might act just somewhat normally toward each other when the McGills arrive?"

There was complete dejection written across her tired face. "I'm not promising anything, Wade," she said. "I'm not promising a goddamn thing."

In Guayaquil, the fighting had increased again in its ferocity. The entire southern district of the city, within a mile of downtown, was in rebel hands. Dead government soldiers lay rotting in the sun because troops could not reach them. Buildings burned day and night. A radio station had been taken, and periodic announcements were now being broadcast, informing the populace that the city was about to fall and all resistance should cease immediately. Roads were open to the east, and the remaining officials of the Biaza government were evacuating, seeking a place to hide.

In late morning, Enrico Fuentes took his luggage and drove to the Ministry, intending to ask Moreno to pick him up there in the early evening. Upon arrival, he dismissed most of the Ministry employees, telling them to return home and look after their personal affairs. A few had already stopped coming to work, worried about the Alvaristas and disgruntled because other governmental agencies had already closed their doors.

Fuentes immediately called Moreno. The pilot said he would meet Fuentes at the Ministry, and that everything was ready for Fuentes' escape flight. When Fuentes hung up, he felt jittery. This was going to be a big day for him, a very important one in his life. He could feel it. He must keep calm and make as few mistakes as possible.

In early afternoon, Moreno arrived at the airstrip, which was hidden away in a wooded area east of the city, to do some light maintenance work on the plane. It was a medium-sized Cessna, with two engines and extra gas tanks for longer flights. It sat beside a shack at the west end of a clearing where a long asphalted runway had been constructed years before. A narrow dirt road led into the area, a road that once serviced a now-abandoned banana plantation.

Only Moreno and an Indian named Jorge were at the airstrip that afternoon. Moreno had a ladder up at the engine of the plane, and he was adjusting the cowling. Jorge, a skinny, older fellow with caramel-hued skin, had brought Moreno his tools from the shack, and now was making up some tortas for lunch.

After he had been there about an hour, and the Indian Jorge was about to invite him to halt his work for something to eat, Jorge looked out through the shack's open doorway, past the plane and Moreno, his eyes narrowing. He came out of the shack, held his hand up to shade his eyes, and squinted.

"Mister Moreno," he called to the pilot.

"All right, I'll be there in a moment, Jorge."

"No, it is not the food, mister. I think there are men in the trees at the far end of the field."

Moreno, on the ladder, turned quickly to look. He squinted, too. Then he saw them. Fatigue-clothed men carrying rifles moved along the perimeter of the clearing toward the shack.

"Jesus and Mary," he mumbled.

"What is it, patron?" Jorge wondered.

Moreno clambered down from the ladder, and drew a Brazilian automatic pistol from his belt. "I think it's Alvaristas, Jorge! Go get the rifle!"

Jorge swallowed hard, and ran toward the shack. In

that moment, a shot rang out from the trees, and another. They missed Jorge narrowly, chipping wood on the shack near him. He jumped, and stopped.

"The rifle!" Moreno yelled.

Jorge ran into the shack, as Moreno fired twice toward the figures that were coming closer now. A small military vehicle appeared on the road near the clearing, and four burly guerrillas piled out of it. Two of them carried automatic weapons.

Moreno frantically threw the ladder to one side. He had two choices: he could try to escape in the small car that sat behind the shack; or he could attempt to fly the Cessna out. He chose to save the plane.

Jorge returned with the rifle. There was a burst of automatic fire. They were closing in. Moreno turned to the Indian. "Keep me covered while I start the engines! Then come and get into the plane! We'll try to fly out!"

Jorge nodded, continuing to return fire. Moreno climbed into the Cessna, bullets flying around him. He started the port engine, and it whined into life, then roared in his ears. A chunk of hot lead busted the window beside his head, narrowly missing him. He ducked, his stocky figure hunched in the cockpit, his Spaniard's face damp with sweat. The other engine revved up and doubled the noise coming from the plane.

"Come on, Jorge!" he yelled. "Climb in!"

The Indian fired off a round toward the trees, and a guerrilla yelled and went down. Then he was running for the plane. A hot slug hit him in the left side of his head, blowing his right ear off, throwing him to the ground. The rifle went flying. The Indian jumped and jerked for a moment, his limbs flailing. Moreno turned and stared hard for a split-instant. Then he gunned the engines and moved the Cessna forward. It started down the bumpy runway, gathering speed.

"Come on, goddam it!" Moreno breathed. "Come on!"

A bullet smacked him in the left arm. He yelled, and the plane swerved as he grabbed at his arm. His fingers came away with blood on them. Pain rocketed up and down the length of the arm which had become virtually useless to him. He got the Cessna going straight again, pulled back on the wheel, and the plane was airborne.

But now the guerrillas were out on the clearing only fifty yards away, firing at him. The plane gained some altitude as it approached the far end of the runway. Moreno got a glimpse of a guerrilla firing an automatic rifle at the plane, just below him, and then there was a bright flash of yellow as the port engine burst into flame.

"Oh, no!" Moreno muttered numbly.

He tried to control the plane, but it started spiralling downward, over the treetops at the end of the runway, then nosing down toward the thicker woods beyond, black smoke trailing out from its engine. Moreno saw the trees rise up at him, and knew he was crashing. In the next instant there was a violent wrenching of his body as the Cessna hit, and a splintering of wood and glass as the aircraft plunged through leafy branches to smash at the hard ground. Moreno crashed against the controls and the windshield.

Fire began to engulf the plane. Already the heat was unbearable. He was trapped in it and there was nothing he could do to save himself. He heard, somewhere in the distance beyond the fire, men shouting as they ran toward him. Smoke clogged his lungs, and he coughed up blood. The heat sent him spiralling down and down, into a dark emptiness from which he knew there was no return.

His part in the struggle for survival was finished.

Fuentes never learned of Moreno's death or the loss of the plane. By late afternoon the fighting became so fierce in and around Guayaquil that he began to worry about being able to leave the city. He called Moreno's home again, but got no answer. That did not concern him because he figured Moreno was out at the air field with the plane.

He sat around his office for another hour, trying to decide what to do. Then he locked up his office and sneaked out a side door of the Ministry, saying nothing to anybody in the building. His bags were already in the trunk of his car. At exactly 6:15 he got in his car, pulled out of the parking lot at the Ministry and headed east on Avenida Nueve de Octubre.

The streets were deserted, except for an occasional military vehicle. Fuentes drove carefully, not knowing what to expect, hoping for the best. There was no sound of fighting to the east, so he figured everything was all right. But he knew that the capital would fall within the next day or two, no matter how desperately the Biaza generals fought. The men under them had lost heart, and in their heads, the capital already belonged to Alvarez.

It was out in the suburbs, just as Fuentes was leaving the city, that he ran into the roadblock. Figuring it was just a routine checkpoint, he pulled up to the soldier at the barrier with little concern.

The soldier saluted him. "Sir. I'm sorry, but you can't drive beyond this point."

Something constricted inside Fuentes. "I'm Enrico Fuentes, soldier, Minister of Finance." He took a card from his pocket. "I have authorization to pass freely from sector to sector."

But the soldier shook his head. "You don't understand, sir. There's fighting up ahead. It's not safe for you. There are mortars and cannons being fired. Listen."

Fuentes did listen, and heard the crumping of mortars in the near distance, and the occasional crackling of small arms. He looked into the soldier's face with an ashen one. "But there are surely roads open to the east. I have business outside the city, you see. How can I get out toward Alausi?"

"Sir, I'm sorry to tell you that the guerrillas have encircled the city, just in the past few hours. There are no roads open to the east now. There is heavy fighting in all sectors to the east here, and guerrillas are everywhere. To attempt to drive eastward, sir, would be suicidal. You would be in enemy territory in two miles. Maybe it is less than that, now. There is a possibility that capital may fall tonight. We cannot hold out much longer."

Fuentes swallowed hard. "How about to the north?" he said. "Can I get out of the city to the north?"

"I'm afraid it's worse there, Minister. My advice is to go to your office or home and stay there until you find out what this day brings us. And pray to God that by some miracle we are able to save the capital."

Fuentes felt his heart lurch inside him. "All right, soldier. Thanks for your help."

"May God help you, Minister."

Fuentes turned the car around in a daze. It was still unbelievable that he had waited too long, that he could not get to the airstrip now. He drove two blocks, then pulled over to the curb and sat there with the engine running.

There was no place to run, no place to hide. Alvarez would seek him out remorselessly, and arrest him, or worse. All Biaza officials would be arrested or killed on sight, and Fuentes was one of the highest of them.

Fuentes put the car in gear again, and pulled away from the curb, turning left at the next corner. He drove several blocks off the big boulevard to a narrow side street that paralleled it, and turned left again, heading east once more. He drove slowly down the street, squinting ahead. There was no roadblock up there. He passed corners and side streets, and saw nothing. Up ahead, he heard the booming of mortars again. He kept going. He passed a newly-made crater in the street, with rubble lying around. At an intersection, he glimpsed an army vehicle racing east. He kept going. A mortar shell exploded fifty yards ahead of him.

Fuentes wheeled the car up onto the narrow sidewalk, and it slid to a halt. The explosion had spidered the windshield, and flattened his right front tire. He got out and looked down the street. Three guerrillas came out of a building only thirty yards away, and one saw Fuentes immediately.

"Hey, there is a brave defender!" Hard laughter. "Look, he must be somebody important! See the fancy suit!"

A second guerrilla raised a rifle and fired at Fuentes. The slug caromed off his car, missing him but scaring him badly. Seeing an open doorway in a building near him, he turned and ran inside, as the guerrillas came after him.

Inside, Fuentes found himself in a small office building. As Fuentes frantically ran down a corridor, he heard the sound of running footsteps outside on the street. He ducked into a room.

There was nothing in it, nothing to hide behind, no window to leave by. "Oh, Jesus!" Fuentes muttered. "Oh, God!" He turned and hurried back out into the corridor.

"There!" A thick voice. A resounding crack of gunfire. Fuentes felt hot searing pain rip through his side and chest. He slammed against the wall, mouth gaping, eyes wide. "Oh, God!" he repeated, more quietly, and with more urgency, as he slid down the wall. The three guerrillas came and stood over him.

"You were right. He's somebody all right. Look at that stickpin, the shoes."

"He won't need them now." Fuentes could see one of them aim a pistol at his head.

131

"Wait!" Another voice from the front of the building. More footsteps, and then an officer was standing over him. It was Idilio Alvarez.

He scowled down at Fuentes. Fuentes felt a shudder pass through him, and he was seeing blackness at the edge of his field of vision.

"Sonofabitch," Alvarez muttered.

Fuentes felt his strength ebbing. "Mr. . .Chairman," he said.

Alvarez looked at the guerrillas. "Who shot this man?"

The one with the pistol spoke up with a grin. "I did, Chairman."

Alvarez drew the Mauser on his hip, aimed it casually at the guerrilla with the pistol, and fired. The gun exploded loudly in the corridor, and the guerrilla went running in reverse down the length of it, a hole in his chest from front to spine. When he hit the floor on his back, he was already dead. Alvarez holstered the gun and turned to the two guerrillas. "Leave me alone here for a moment."

Alvarez knelt beside Fuentes. "Well, Minister. Needless to say, I'm sorry about this. I wanted to try you before a people's court."

Fuentes was relaxed now. He felt no pain, only a light-headedness. "A left-handed apology is better than none, Alvarez," he grated out.

"Frankly, I thought I'd lost you. But then I suppose you underestimated our strength, eh? As you have from the beginning."

"I suppose I did," Fuentes admitted thickly. The blackness edged in on him, and then eased back.

"You should have gone with the Vice-President. Or did you know he was leaving?"

Fuentes eyed him without replying.

"Ah, so that's it. You looked up from your complacency, a couple of days ago, and found that you were

132

alone. Well, they won't know about your frustration, your panic. Biaza die-hards will regard you as a kind of hero. Ironic, isn't it?"

Fuentes gave him another look. A feeling of unease was spreading through him like hot water. It was death, he knew it now. He was a dead man, sitting there, talking to Alvarez, plugging the hole in his side.

"This Luther McGill," Alvarez now said in a different voice. "What kind of conspiracy have you concocted with him? Is he to lead a counter-rebellion from Miami in partnership with that corrupt cousin of yours?" He blew cigar smoke into Fuentes' face.

Fuentes turned partially away, gasping. He was surprised to learn that Alvarez knew about McGill. "I merely helped him get. . .his family out of Ecuador."

"Ah, really?" Alvarez said through the cigar smoke and the thick beard. "Then what was in the trunk you sent with him, and why did you send a man to guard it?"

Fuentes stared at him, impressed with his intelligence system. "The trunk? It is nothing important to you. A few papers from the Ministry." He coughed an ugly, grating cough. "A few files we wanted to preserve."

Alvarez leaned down very close to his face. "I don't believe you, Biaza swine!"

Fuentes held his gaze. "Believe me or not. . .damn you. You can hardly. . .threaten me now, can you?"

Alvarez grinned. "I don't have to, Minister. I have sent some men after McGill, you see. When they catch up with him, they will get the whole truth from him, and kill him. And they will retrieve your trunk and its contents. . .whatever they are."

Fuentes was going fast. "Possibly," he grated out. "But my man Rueda has instructions to destroy the contents of the trunk at the slightest sign of trouble. And to execute McGill before allowing him to fall into your hands."

Alvarez took the cigar from his mouth. "Very clever, Fuentes. Very thorough. You sent the right man for the job, too. But I don't think my man Cuesta will give your man Rueda a chance to do anything but unsuccessfully defend himself, Minister. Then we will have your trunk and McGill. Then we can also put that Biaza boot-licker out of business."

Fuentes gasped raggedly. It gave him some small satisfaction, even in death, to think that Alvarez' boasts were probably just that, and that he would never lay a hand on that well-packed trunk, containing a bigger surprise than even Alvarez imagined.

"We will see, Mr. Chairman," Fuentes choked out, his face suddenly gone gray. "We will see."

In the next moment, Fuentes' heavy-lidded eyes widened dramatically, as if he had just had a look at grisly Death himself, and then he stiffened and went lifeless, his eyes still staring past Alvarez.

Alvarez knelt there for a long moment. Then he rose, stuck the cigar into his mouth, turned and left the building without looking back.

His officers needed him now.

He wanted to be at their fore when they rolled into downtown Guayaquil.

Raising their voices in glorious victory.

Eleven

The *Maria Isabel* had arrived at Port au Prince, Haiti. The freighter docked at that sultry port just after two p.m.

Captain Valaczek and First Officer Dubois both went ashore that afternoon. Dubois stayed until evening, visiting relatives in the north suburb of the city. No passengers went ashore except for Jake Parrish and Nita McGill.

McGill, Ana and Rueda ate with Valaczek in the mess cabin. Valaczek related a couple of sea stories, and McGill listened appreciatively. Rueda, with little to say, eyed Valaczek soberly through the stories. When the meal was finished, McGill and Ana strolled on deck for a short time, feeling more relaxed now that they were in the Caribbean and nearer their destination. Tony was up on deck, too, after having had only a sandwich in his cabin. He told McGill and Ana that he wished he had gone ashore with Parrish and Nita. Tony remained on deck, staring at the grimy waterfront view of Port au Prince, after McGill and Ana had retired to their cabin at dusk. The black-skinned longshoremen, who had helped unload some cargo earlier, were gone now, as were two of the four-man crew.

Down in their cabin, Ana sat in a straight chair and sewed a small repair on a skirt, while McGill was lying on his upper bunk, reading an old magazine that

Valaczek had given him. The light was poor, though, and McGill lost interest. He dropped the magazine and looked down at his wife.

"Well, Ana. We'll leave here day after tomorrow. That will put us in Miami on the twentieth, a Tuesday. I told you it wouldn't be long. Guayaquil seems like some awful nightmare now."

"I wish Rueda were not aboard," Ana confessed. "He is not a pleasant man."

"Well, we might have needed him. Fuentes was just trying to keep the danger to a minimum."

"To the trunk, or to us?" Ana said, smiling sourly. She put the sewing down and leaned back on the chair. She looked tired and a little pale.

McGill nodded. "Jake has the same feeling, I think, that Rueda is aboard to protect the trunk."

"He exhibits no interest in us at all. He's one of the coldest men I've ever met."

"His personality shouldn't matter to us, I guess, if he's good at what he does."

Ana got up and walked over to McGill, leaning on the bunk where he lay propped against a bulkhead. "I wonder what's in that trunk," she said.

McGill narrowed his blue eyes on his Ecuadorian wife. "Why Fuentes told us what's in it. Papers. Documents. Things that would be important to a government in exile." He paused. "Don't you believe it?"

"It seems awfully large for a few important papers. I half expect a dead body to fall out when they open it in Miami."

McGill grunted out a short laugh. "This isn't a Michael Caine movie, Ana. I'd guess that the trunk contains very mundane files and documents, just like Fuentes said. In the real world, very rarely do corpses fall out of closets or steamer trunks. Nor, for that matter, do Alvaristas materialize out of nowhere to do

136

us harm. We were all a little tense back there in Guayaquil, including Fuentes. You can't help getting paranoid, with rebel troops moving in on you.''

"Well," Ana said. "The trunk doesn't have to contain a corpse, of course. It could be stuffed with guns and ammuntion or sucres.''

McGill shook his head. "Guns won't do Fuentes or Biaza any good in Florida, Ana. As for sucres, their value may be almost worthless for a long while to come, because of what's happening in Guayaquil.''

"I wonder if Rueda has seen the contents of the trunk," Ana said, pensively.

"I doubt it very much, and Rueda is probably just as curious as you are.''

She smiled tiredly. "Jake doesn't like Rueda, does he?''

"I guess not. It's a mutual thing, I think. Rueda thinks I was foolish for bringing Jake along.''

"Were you?" Ana said.

McGill hunched his shoulders. "I don't know. I'm glad he's here, though.''

"So am I," Ana said, looking past him now. "And so, I believe, is our daughter.''

McGill studied Ana's somber face. "Do you think she's getting too serious about him?''

"She likes him a lot, Luther. And she has a mind of her own. I just hope she goes slowly. We . . . don't really know Jake anymore.''

McGill touched her face with his hand. "Nita is a woman, Ana. She has good judgment. Let's not worry about her too much. Okay?''

Ana smiled. "Okay," she said quietly.

About a half-hour later, McGill left the cabin and went up on deck to get some night air. Tony was talking with the sailor on duty, and McGill joined them for a couple of minutes. Tony was questioning the fellow about his life at sea. McGill walked down the deck to the bridge, looking for Valaczek, but did not find him there. Coming back, he found Rueda leaning over the rail, staring toward the dark city.

"Well, Rueda," McGill said, as he stopped beside the slim, hard-looking policeman, "I see you needed some air, too."

Rueda turned to him. "Mr. McGill." He smiled stiffly, a rarity for Rueda. "I was just reminiscing. When I was a young man, I lived in Haiti for almost a year." That was the first fact about himself that Rueda had disclosed to anyone aboard.

"Why, I didn't know that, Rueda," McGill said to him.

"It's a filthy place," Rueda said, grimacing. "Run by black men who have no principles at all."

McGill frowned. "Really?"

"They have no morals, the blacks," Rueda pronounced. "You must know; you have many in your country."

McGill shrugged. "I'm afraid I've never found them that way, myself."

Rueda held McGill's frank gaze. "I see that Parrish is ashore with your daughter."

McGill scowled slightly. "I didn't know you were keeping such close tabs on us, Rueda."

"I'm a policeman. It's my job."

"Yes," McGill said doubtfully.

"I wonder," Rueda said, "whether Parrish is the kind of man I'd want my daughter to be out with. . . if I had a daughter."

Now McGill was frowning. "I'm delighted that Jake Parrish is spending some time with Nita. They've enjoyed each other's company for years."

Rueda smiled in a way that infuriated McGill. "I understand that you were forced to terminate Parrish's employment at one time."

McGill made a face. "Fuentes shouldn't have told

138

you that."

"It is important, Mr. McGill, that I know as much as possible about everyone aboard this ship, particularly those who have come aboard armed. You must understand that."

"Jake is one of us," McGill said harshly. "You don't have to treat him as an enemy."

"Oh, I don't," Rueda said evenly. "But, he is an unknown factor in this mission, Mr. McGill. You have not seen him for three years. You think you know his motivations for coming along with you, but do you? He could be more than a drunk. He could be a thief or an enemy agent. I'm only suggesting these as possibilites, of course."

"What is all this leading up to, Rueda," McGill asked, barely suppressing his anger, "if anything?"

"Well," Rueda said, "you've already indicated your unwillingness to disarm him, and I accept that as an added burden on my shoulders. But, the least you cán do is speak to him about keeping in the background. I saw him meddling with the luggage today."

McGill held Rueda's brittle look. "Meddling?"

"Yes, he was in the storage compartment with your luggage and the Fuentes trunk. . .allegedly checking on their security."

"So what?" McGill said.

"I don't want him in there," Rueda said flatly.

McGill was astounded at Rueda's manner. "*You* don't want him in there? Goddamn it, Rueda. I'll remind you that that trunk you worry so much about is part of *my* luggage, put in my custody by Enrico Fuentes. If Parrish wants to check on that luggage, I think that's a matter between him and me, by God!"

Rueda's face was stony. "You are mistaken, Mr. McGill." He rested his right hand lightly on the bulge under his flowered sport shirt. "The Fuentes trunk is my responsibility, mine alone. As long as it is with your luggage, that entire cache of bags and trunks is off-limits to everyone aboard, including Parrish. . .and you.''

McGill's face crimsoned. "Why. . .this is outrageous! Are you warning me away from my own baggage, for Christ's sake?''

"You will have no need of that baggage until you get to Miami,'' Rueda said easily. "I suggest that you don't make an issue of this, Mr. McGill, merely on principle.''

McGill did not know what to say. He knew he ought to tell Rueda to go to hell, that he would do as he wished with his baggage and Fuentes' trunk, but he was afraid of Rueda, afraid for his family, afraid for himself.

"By God, I'll go ashore tomorrow and try to call Enrico Fuentes in Guayaquil! I'm sure he'll be interested that you're treating us like police suspects!''

"It is Fuentes who recommended this policy toward the stored luggage,'' Rueda said smugly. "But if you can locate him, I have no objection to your making such a call.''

"Objection!" McGill said hoarsely. "Objection, you say! Do you think I would give a good goddamn whether you had an objection?''

Rueda smiled crookedly at McGill, then turned and casually walked away, his hands clasped behind his back.

McGill stared after him. It was foolish to become upset with Rueda, the end of the voyage being so near. Parrish had been right about the man—he was in no way a member of their small fraternity. And McGill was sure that, in fact, Rueda had received his instructions from Fuentes.

McGill glanced down the deck. Tony was still talking with the sailor at the gangplank. Jacques Dubois was coming aboard, acting as if he had had a couple of drinks, speaking a bit more loudly than usual, and

140

joking at length with Tony and the crewman.

McGill sighed heavily and headed for the companion-way to the cabin deck. He would forget Rueda for the moment. As the freighter got closer and closer to Florida, Rueda became less and less important in McGill's life. When they arrived in Miami, he would be able to laugh Rueda off as the last bad joke of a dramatic comedy of errors.

Down in the captain's cabin Valaczek was adding a couple of invoices when Dubois knocked on the door. Valaczek invited him in, and Dubois sat down beside Valaczek's small desk.

"I saw Mr. Brown up on deck," Dubois said in his French-creole accent. "He looked disturbed about something."

Valaczek, bare-headed and tired-looking, leaned back on his chair. "He probably thinks his daughter should be back by now. She's with that Parrish guy again." He grinned harshly.

Dubois laughed in his throat. "She is some female, eh? I could forgive the sea for a year of troubles, for just one hour in a soft bed with that one."

"Give me the woman Ana, myself," Valaczek grunted out. "An hour with that sexed-up kid could kill a man my age."

Dubois laughed breezily. "Maybe you are right, Captain."

"Did you find out about that load of cane?"

Dubois nodded. "It will be here tomorrow afternoon. We can have it aboard by dark, but we'll have to pay Sunday wages. We'll take the other cargo on Monday morning, and sail late that day or early Tuesday, which-ever you prefer."

"Might as well wait until early Tuesday. That ought to put us in Miami late the same day, with good seas. If we get there too soon, I'll have to anchor out until that

141

yacht meets us, anyway."

Dubois was frowning slightly when Valaczek looked up at him. Valaczek had not intended to mention Sumner's pick-up of the Fuentes trunk, for Salazar.

"What yacht?" Dubois asked.

Valaczek took a deep breath. "It probably doesn't matter if you know now, since we're almost there. The fellow we call Brown is carrying something for Enrico Fuentes, and a friend is coming, while we're at anchor, to take it off the ship."

Dubois leaned forward on his chair. "So, our passengers are friends of a big Guayaquil politico. Who is this Mr. Brown, anyway?"

"You wouldn't know the name," Valaczek said. "He's a rubber company executive that doesn't want to stick around Ecuador to see what Alvarez thinks of him. Rueda and Parrish are aboard to protect our Mr. Brown and his special cargo."

Dubois' face brightened. "The security trunk. . .the one with the locks. That's it, isn't it? The Fuentes cargo."

Valaczek hesitated, then nodded. "All of this is confidential, Dubois. You can't let our passengers know that you know. And you can't say anything to any of the crew. Not even after we leave here and put to sea."

Dubois shrugged. "Of course." He sat there a moment. "What is in this Fuentes trunk?"

Valaczek expected the question. "I don't know. Fuentes suggested government papers, but you never know."

A slow smile crossed Dubois' mulatto face. "Interesting situation, Captain."

"Oh?" Valaczek said.

"Well, what I mean is, Fuentes may be captured or dead by now. There are rumors here that Guayaquil has fallen."

"I'm sure Fuentes managed to extricate himself from

142

that, if it's true," Valaczek said.

"But if, hypothetically, he did not," Dubois said, "Fuentes' instructions to you and Brown are meaningless, for all practical purposes."

Valaczek sat there silent.

"We could be taking a very potentially valuable cargo to a man who no longer has connections in Guayaquil," Dubois mused, staring at the ceiling of the cabin. "I think it is an interesting situation."

"Government papers, if that's what the trunk contains, would have little value in terms of money," Valaczek reasoned.

Dubois smiled. "On the contrary, Captain. Depending on what they are, they might have great monetary value to certain parties. . .Alvarez, for example."

Valaczek frowned, his square face somber.

"Depending on what the papers contain," Dubois repeated.

"Well," Valaczek said pensively. "Since the trunk is not ours to open, I suppose we'll never know the answer to that one."

Dubois allowed a small grin to move his mouth. "I suppose not, Captain," he said carefully.

At the Oloffsen Hotel in Port au Prince, Jake Parrish and Nita were just finishing their meal in the open-air dining room. Often called the Gingerbread Palace, the Oloffsen was an old wood-constructed colonial hotel, with fancy balustrades decorating its long facade and lush tropical foliage crouching in profusion about its foundations. In the dining room, big ceiling fans moved the heavy air, and potted plants vied with guests for available floor space. There were only two other couples sharing the dining facilities with Parrish and Nita; it was off-season in Haiti. An hour ago, there had been a brief rainshower that made the foliage steam in the dusk and had cut the electricity for a short time. Now, the lights were on and the fans were working. The meal had been a delicious Creole dish recommended by the management.

"I love this place," Nita told Parrish, as a young black waiter came and took their plates. "It's been the watering hole for artists, journalists and novelists. Haiti would not be Haiti without the Oloffsen."

Parrish wrinkled his nose. "It smells," he said, "like old wood and. . .maybe like the jungle."

"Exactly," Nita agreed. She had not mentioned her feelings to Parrish again, and she was more poised in his presence. "I smell jasmine from the garden."

Parrish smiled. He was wearing a white shirt that he had purchased at the Iron Market on their way to the hotel. "It's nice," he told her.

"It's like a Maugham novel," she said. "None of it seems real. . .it's too romantic."

Parrish looked into her blue eyes with the big dark pupils, and her chiseled lovely face. Suddenly, he wanted Nita very much. "I know what you mean." He laid some bills on the table. "Would you like to take a walk around before we catch a taxi back to the water-front?"

Nita smiled, averting her eyes for a moment. "I'd like to show you more of the hotel, if you don't mind. There's a nice view from the upper verandas, even at night."

Parrish nodded. "That sounds like a nice idea," he said.

They walked out onto the long porch and climbed a stairway to a higher level where there were special suites and rooms that overlooked the pool and garden. The suites had been named after celebrities who had stayed at the hotel.

"There's the John Gielgud Suite," Nita said, as they strolled along the upper porch. "I understand there's a

James Jones Cottage down below somewhere."

"Impressive," Parrish admitted.

They crossed a catwalk to a section where smaller units were located, still overlooking the grounds and the city. The many lights of Port au Prince sparkled through the treetops, the black harbor barely visible.

"This one is open," Nita said. "Let's take a look."

She entered a small room and switched on a light. It was a narrow, two-level room, with a bed on one wall, a dressing table and chair on the other, and a spartan kitchen in the raised portion beyond the bed. There were gay curtains at a window and bright pillows on the bed.

"Nice," Parrish said.

"Do you really like it?" Nita asked him.

Parrish could not take it any longer. He reached out for Nita and pulled her young, richly-curved body to him, and then they were kissing. He did not intend for it to be a passionate kiss, but it was. When it was finished, they both stood there breathless.

"Good God!" she murmured.

"I shouldn't have done that," he said, breathing shallowly.

"Remember what I said, Jake. Forget who I am. Show me how you really feel about me."

Parrish gently touched her face with his hand. "I think we'd better vacate the room for some paying customer."

"The room is paid for," she said.

Parrish studied her flushed face. "Paid for?"

"Yes. I rented it for the evening. . .just in case."

Parrish swallowed hard.

"I spoke to the manager while you were at the bar." She was not looking at him. "I. . .hope you don't mind."

Parrish let his eyes travel over Nita, and suddenly he was all afire inside. "God, Nita. I. . .don't know."

"We can be back to the ship by ten," she said.

"Nobody will worry about us."

He hesitated, then moved to the open doorway. He intended to leave. But when he got there, the scent of jasmine came to him, and a breeze fluttered the curtain at the window.

He turned back to Nita, and switched off the light. Nita began to tremble. He closed the door and came over to her. "I can't do it. I can't walk away from you."

"I'm glad," she whispered.

Parrish took her in his arms and kissed her. Nita was inflamed by the touch of him. His hands were on her breasts and hips. She was breathing heavily when he broke away.

"Oh, Jake!"

He went to the bed, pulled the cover down, and removed the fluffy pillows. When he turned back to her, she was almost nude. All of her clothing, except for a tiny pair of panties hugging her hips, lay on a chair beside her. Parrish sucked in his breath almost inaudibly. Her body was as beautiful as her face. He had never seen such physical perfection in a woman. There was a strip of lightness across her breasts underneath the sheer cloth at her hips.

"Goddamn!" he muttered.

Nita walked over to him and helped him undress. He could not keep his hands off her. In moments he was nude, and he slipped the last piece of cloth down over her hips. Then they were on the bed, Nita's hotness nestled against him, their mouths making love, Parrish's hand working on the dark place between her thighs. Small, lovely sounds issued from the depths of her throat as he caressed her. A mental flash of a sixteen-year-old with pigtails came to him for a half-moment, but he forced it out of his head. There was a torrid joining, with Nita's eyes widening in quick surprise, then the hot reaching, the fiery touching, and the exquisite sweetness of it. There were several throaty cries from Nita as it was finishing, and the strained arching of their backs in the closeness of the dark room, the scent of her natural perfume as lovely as the jasmine's.

They did not speak for a long time. Parrish touched her mouth with his, gently. They were still joined, and he could not bring himself to separate from her. Finally, he rolled onto his back beside her.

"It was. . .beautiful," her voice came to him in the darkness. A breeze caressed their bodies.

He touched her face lightly. "God, Nita. What have I done?"

"Expressed affection, I hope," she said.

"That isn't an excuse," he said heavily.

"What other one is there?" she wondered.

Parrish looked over at her lovely face.

"Are you sorry?" she said. "Would you rather I hadn't brought you up here?"

"I've never enjoyed myself more," he admitted.

"Then don't think about anything else," she told him. "Nothing else is important."

"I wish to hell I could myself believe that."

She kissed his lips again. "I'll make you believe it," she whispered to him.

Parrish sighed in the darkness.

Twelve

Miami, that Sunday morning, was hot and quiet.

There was almost no traffic along Biscayne Boulevard, and the beaches were deserted. June was a bad month for tourists.

Jesus Cuesta was ready to make his move. On the previous evening, he had taken El Pardal and gone out to Wade Sumner's place. They stealthily boarded the *Sea Witch,* hoping to find keys—there weren't any. Pardal had made a try at crossing wires, but did not know enough about the boat's ignition system. What Cuesta did discover, though, was that Sumner probably intended to take the boat out on Sunday; there was extra gasoline aboard and food. So Cuesta decided to try to take the yacht while Sumner had it out.

"It is better," Pardal assured him with a grin.

Now, on Sunday morning, Cuesta waited in a fleabag downtown hotel. He and Pardal shared a room, while Morales and Torreon shared a second one down the hall. Morales and Torreon, however, were already gone from the hotel on an assignment by Cuesta. Across the room from Cuesta, Pardal sat in an old chair, the cotton stuffing creeping out of the upholstery, and read a copy of the Spanish language newspaper, *Diario Las Americas.*

Cuesta glanced at his watch. "They have had more than enough time," he complained. "We should have heard from them by now."

Pardal did not look up from the paper. "It is early. We will hear shortly, Jesus."

Cuesta stared at the phone, as if to do so might make it ring. The two guerrillas had been gone for two hours, since seven. It was not a long drive to Sumner's place. Why hadn't they called by now? He turned away from the phone, and it rang.

Cuesta turned back quickly and picked up the receiver. "Yes?"

"Morales here, Jesus. I'm calling from a pay phone near the Sumner place."

"Well?" Cuesta said impatiently.

"Sumner took the boat out about twenty minutes ago. He went alone, without his wife, so you can talk to her directly."

"Are you sure he was alone?"

"We saw no one else aboard. He was heading in the direction of the nearest marina. He might be picking up someone there."

Cuesta grunted. "All right. Get back over here immediately."

"We'll be back as soon as we can get there," Morales said.

Cuesta hung up the receiver, but did not release his hold on it. He turned to Pardal who had dropped the paper to his lap. "Sumner has taken the boat out. Morales thinks the wife may be there alone."

Pardal nodded. "That should be good."

Cuesta referred to a number that he had written on a pad, and then dialed Sumner's house phone. He heard it ring three times. Then Bette Sumner's voice came on the other end.

"Yes?" Curt and unfriendly.

"Is this Mrs. Sumner?" Cuesta asked her in accented English.

A short pause. *"Yes, it is. Who's this?"*

149

"Mrs. Sumner, this is a friend of Victorio Salazar."

"*Who?*" the tired voice came.

"Victorio Salazar. You remember, the fellow who is interested in the arrival of Luther McGill aboard the *Maria Isabel.*"

"*Oh, yes. You're Mr. Salazar's friend?*" Dully.

"Yes, that's right. I want to speak with your husband, Mrs. Sumner, if he is there at the moment."

"*You missed him. He just left on the boat.*"

"Oh, I see. What a shame! I must pass on some information to him immediately, about Mr. McGill."

"*Are the McGills all right?*"

"Oh, yes. This has to do with Mr. Sumner meeting Mr. McGill when the freighter arrives here," Cuesta said nicely.

"*Well, you can leave a message if you'd like.*"

"I would much enjoy doing so, but I have my orders only to speak with Mr. Sumner himself."

"*Then you'll have to call back,*" Bette Sumner said sourly.

"Mrs. Sumner, may I ask where your husband is going on his boat? Maybe we can get in touch with him somehow."

A grunted laugh. "*Wade doesn't tell me anything nowadays, didn't your Mr. Salazar know that?*" A pause. "*He said something about getting the boat in good running order to meet Luther. He was stopping at the North Beach Marina, I think. Probably to pick up that damnable woman!*" Another pause, longer. "*Maybe you can catch him there, Mr. . .*"

"Garcia," Cuesta lied quickly.

"*Yes,*" she said. "*Wade also mentioned sailing up the coast on a test run, maybe as far as Jenkins' Cove. That's all I can tell you, Mr. Garcia.*"

"You have been very helpful, Mrs. Sumner," Cuesta said graciously.

After he hung up, Cuesta had a smug look on his

face. "Well, we have a beginning point. And it looks like today is our day. Sumner is taking the yacht up the coast, and he mentioned a specific destination, despite his wife's apparent distrust of his leisure activities. When Morales and Torreon get back here, we'll drive up to Jenkins' Cove. I think we'll find the *Sea Witch* there."

Ed Pardal grinned harshly. "That gives us something to look forward to on this quiet Sunday," he said.

The capital of Ecuador had fallen to rebel forces on Saturday night. Government troops had surrendered to the Alvaristas in droves during the last hours, and one government general had committed suicide. Buildings burned, and cars were overturned, and Alvaristas swarmed the streets. Now, on the morning after the big victory, Idilio Alvarez held court in the spacious office of the president at the Government Palace. He received his generals, and noted the detainment of Biaza supporters as they were reported to him. All such men were thrown into the local jail to await trial for treason, unless an *accident* occurred during the arrests. Alvarez wanted them to survive, however. He wanted a nest of snakes to show the world, before he stepped on them.

But Alvarez was having his troubles. The defected generals, Perez and Linares had been difficult to control through the last few days of the fighting. Alvarez had heard a rumor that the two ex-Biaza militarists thought that he, Alvarez, was too idealistic, too concerned with reform programs to effectively take control of the new government. They cared little about trials, or showing the world the righteousness of the reform coup. They wanted things, as a matter of fact, pretty much as they had been under Biaza—except that they saw themselves in charge.

Torres stood before the massive presidential desk that dark, gloomy morning, and discussed the matter briefly

151

with Alvarez. Alvarez hunched forward, looking tired. Behind him were unfurled the Ecuadorian flag and the banner of the new reform movement.

"I'm telling you, Idilio," Torres was saying to Alvarez, leaning on the desk for emphasis, "now that these two have served their purpose, they must be taken into custody, just as if they were opposing generals, which they are. In fact, the military leaders who opposed us to the end are probably more trustworthy then Perez and Linares."

Alvarez stared at Torres with fatigue-smudged eyes. "Bring me real evidence of treason, Torres," Alvarez told him, "and I'll act. But until that time, I have many problems of government to solve which must have priority."

Torres stood there scowling, as if Alvarez had reprimanded him rather than merely disagreed about policy. Torres took all of this very seriously. If Alvarez was in trouble, so was he. "I understand the difficulty, Idilio. But if there were a move against you, it would be immediate, before you consolidated your power. The matter must be handled now."

Alvarez sighed audibly. "Come to me tonight, Torres. Bring with you anyone you think can help us resolve this problem, and we'll discuss it. All right?"

Torres smiled slightly. "All right, Chairman."

"And now, go find these people for me." He gave Torres a list of names. "Subordinates in the Biaza government who had little to do with policy, and who allege sudden loyalty to our government. We're going to need people to help us run the machinery of government."

Torres took the list. "Yes, of course."

"I want them all here in this office at eight tomorrow."

"I'll see to it, Idilio."

On Torres' way out, he passed an aide coming into

the room, carrying a message for Alvarez. The fellow was dressed in battle fatigues, like Alvarez and Torres, and carried a pistol on his hip. He came up to Alvarez and saluted him smartly.

"Yes, Eduardo. What is it?"

"This message has come from Panama, Chairman, through Colombia. A wire from Jesus Cuesta, I believe."

Alvarez' face brightened slightly as he took the wire and read it. It was in code, from Cuesta in Panama City, and it told how he had missed the *Maria Isabel*. Alvarez' face darkened again. The message went on to say that Cuesta had not given up and intended to intercept the ship at another location.

Alvarez crumpled the paper in his fist. "That blundering fool!" he growled. "He did not even say what his plan is. He probably does not have one."

"Yes, Chairman," the aide said quietly.

"I should have settled for the trunk, anyway," Alvarez said to himself. "The McGills are no longer important to us. Cuesta will probably bungle the job on them and cause an international incident, for God's sake. If I could retract the order for their executions, I would. But there is no way to get in touch with that incompetent sonofabitch."

"Would the Chairman like to try a message to Panama City?" the aide wondered.

Alvarez shook his bearded head. "No, he won't be there. The matter is out of my hands at this point. That will be all, Eduardo."

"Yes, Chairman."

When Alvarez was alone again, he rose and walked to the big windows. Outside, a crowd had gathered and was beginning to chant pro-reform slogans and *"Viva Alvarez!"* The movement had been a popular one, as Alvarez had thought it would be. Now he owed the people new hope. He would keep power to himself for a while, but it would be a benevolent power, with the promise of elections when order was restored. He would not allow the reform to degenerate into a military junta, no matter what men like Perez and Linares wanted. He was certain he could handle them, as he had done all through the rebellion. But if Torres proved that they were a real danger to him, he would follow the Council's recommendations.

Alvarez heard the door open behind him. When he turned to look, there stood General Perez just inside the room. He was flanked by two of his colonels, men who had come over to Alvarez with him.

"Mr. Chairman," Perez greeted Alvarez pleasantly. He was slightly shorter than the men who stood beside him, and stocky, his swarthy face creased with a hard grin.

Alvarez' eyes narrowed slightly when he saw the two colonels with Perez. Alvarez always saw his generals in private, and it was a presumption to bring two subordinates with him.

"Perez," Alvarez said, returning to a position just beside the long presidential desk. He glanced beyond Perez to see if his two guards were outside, but Perez closed the door. Alvarez had given his guards strict orders to admit only one visitor at a time, except by permission from Alvarez himself. "What brings you here this dark morning?"

The stiff-backed colonels remained near the door, but Perez came over to the desk. He usually had a cigar sticking out of his mouth, but he did not at that moment. That surprised Alvarez, and made him realize that Perez considered the visit very important, despite his casual manner.

"Have you seen the mob outside, Chairman?" Perez said.

Alvarez nodded. "Yes, I just went to the windows. They are wholeheartedly with us, I'd say. Wouldn't you?"

Perez stood there arrogantly. "For now, yes. But if you do not make good on all your promises, within a few days they will be throwing bricks at the building."

Alvarez frowned.

"A couple of days ago, Chairman, you refused to honor my request to reach further down into governmental ranks for our arrests."

Alvarez was further surprised, by Perez' sudden aggressiveness toward him. "That's right," he said. "Most of these clerks and technicians are not enemies of the movement."

"How can we know who are enemies, and who not, until we have interrogated them?" Perez said forcefully.

Alvarez glanced at the two stern-faced colonels and frowned more deeply, looking tough behind his beard. "Is that why you have come here this morning, Perez? To raise that issue again? I'm sorry, but I can't spare the time now."

But Perez went on, almost as if Alvarez had not spoken. "Just last evening, you also refused to hear a suggestion by my colleague, General Linares, that we should use summary executions for highly placed Biaza officials, rather than go through formal hearings which would allow these criminals to voice their reactionary philosophies."

Alvarez was angry, suddenly. "That matter, too, is closed, Perez. I thought I made that quite clear last evening."

Perez smiled cynically. "Yes, you did. But I wanted to feel out your conviction on these matters this morning."

"My conviction is strong," Alvarez stated. He looked past Perez again. "How did the three of you get in here, by the way?"

Perez' smile widened, making his fleshy face only uglier. "I had a squad of men with me, Chairman. They

155

convinced your guards of the propriety of our visit with you.''

Now Alvarez' face showed hot anger, but there was also fear deep in his gut. "You overpowered my guards?''

Perez dropped the smile like a rubber mask. In the same instant, he drew a .45 calibre Mexican Obregon automatic, a gun many officers of the regular army used as a service pistol. "Idilio Alvarez, I charge you with treason against the movement, by weakening its resolve to succeed, and by your fraternization with Biaza enemies of the people.''

Alvarez was shocked. Torres had been right—Perez and Linares should have been taken into custody at the moment they evidenced insubordination, or at the latest, when their usefulness was past. He was breathing heavily now, his face crimsoned.

"You sonofabitch! You dare call me, Idilio Alvarez, a traitor to the reform cause! You who came to us for personal gain, because we were winning! You who have no feeling for or understanding of the goals of the Reform Council, and who. . .''

But Alvarez was not allowed to finish his accusations. He was thrown bodily onto the desk by the impact of the bullet from the .45 automatic. Slowly, he slid to the floor, leaving blood markings on the white papers lying on the Presidential desk. There was a large hole in his middle chest.

Perez went and stood over him, aiming the gun at Alvarez' head. But he could see that the first shot was fatal. Perez turned and stalked from the room, his colonels silently following him.

A few minutes later, Torres stormed into the room, having discovered the two dead guards outside the presidential suite. Torres knew, before seeing Alvarez, what had happened. He rushed over to the inert figure on the floor. Alvarez' eyes opened and tried to focus on Torres.

"You. . .warned me, old friend."

"My God! Was it Perez?" Torres asked.

Alvarez nodded. "The rebellion has failed. Because of me. . .the rebellion has failed."

"It is not your fault, Idilio. You've always given a man the benefit of the doubt. But I knew these cobardes for what they are."

"They will be after. . .the rest of the Council. Get out of here, old friend. Get out of Ecuador. You can begin again. . .from elsewhere."

"I'll get you help," Torres said thickly.

"No, there's. . .no time." A ribbon of red appeared at the corner of his mouth. He was as ashen-faced as an Inca mummy in the Quito museum. He saw, now, that the movement had been so naive. You could not change a world with a half-dozen believers—especially when you had to become like the enemy in order to beat him at his own game. Alvarez had become like Biaza. He had become ruthless in his attempt to gain reform. Men like Luther McGill were not his enemy. The Perezes of the world were the real enemy, and always would be.

"Do me a small favor, Torres," he gritted out.

"Anything, Idilio."

"Say a small prayer. . .for Luther McGill and his family."

Torres' brow furrowed. "That's it?"

Alvarez nodded. "Maybe it will lighten. . .my burden."

"If you wish it, Chairman."

"I have too many sins to be forgiven," Alvarez muttered in a hollow, odd-sounding voice.

"Please lie quietly," Torres said to him.

But in that moment, Alvarez' eyes winced in ugly pain, and then went lifeless.

Torres hurried from the room, his promise to Alvarez already forgotten. Not a religious man, Torres had not taken Alvarez' last wish seriously. But, even if he had

157

been, he would have found it difficult to pray for the gringo who had so far escaped Ecuadorian justice.

If the McGills wanted deliverance from Jesus Cuesta, they would have to do their own praying.

It would probably not help them, anyway.

The *Sea Witch* sat alone in one of the several inlets at Jenkins' Cove, bobbing lightly on the surface of the calm water. Brilliant sun struck the sea, turning it into an undulating carpet of cut gemstones. Gulls lazily wheeled overhead, pirouetting against a cobalt sky. Subtropical vegetation fringed the shoreline, deep-green and exotic. It was a perfect summer afternoon.

Onboard the yacht, Susan Benedict knelt beside a bunk in the sleeping quarters, wearing only a tiny bikini on her tanned body, and made oral love to Wade Sumner. Sumner lay nude on the bunk. Susan had just pulled his swim suit down over his legs, and now caressed him expertly with her mouth.

"Oh. . .God, Susan!"

She paused and met his gaze. "Every day will be like this. . .when you move out of that house. I promise you."

She took him to her again, and Sumner's eyes glazed over. "Oh, Jesus!" he gasped.

Susan had been good in bed from the very beginning, but she had only recently shown him her oral skills. It was part of an acceleration on her part, a stepped-up campaign to wrest him completely from his wife, and he knew it.

"I've never done this before," she had told him on the first occasion. "I may not be any good at it."

But that was probably the greatest misstatement of the century, Sumner concluded, lying there under her sexual attack.

"Oh, Christ!" he panted.

Susan released him, smiling, and rose beside the

bunk. Reaching behind her back, she undid the small bra and let it fall to the floor. Then she slid the bottom down over her hips and thighs, and stepped out of it.

Sumner looked her over. She was all woman. She was everything Bette had once been, and more. She was a new beginning for him, and not just physically.

She had climbed onto the bunk and was sitting astride him now. He reached for her breasts and cupped them in his hands. She was so firm, so smooth, so young. She guided them to union, making a nice sound in her throat when it was accomplished.

"Mmmm, that's nice," Susan breathed.

"Yes." Muttered.

There was the sound of a boat engine nearby, but neither one of them paid any attention to it. Susan moved her hips, slowly and enticingly.

"Just relax," she told him, "and let me make it happen."

They had copulated this way once before, and Sumner liked it. She was more athletic than he, and performed with more abandon. Also, he liked the view, with her breasts hanging in beautiful arcs above him, her face upturned, her long throat exposed in a sensual way.

Sumner was grinning. "You're in charge, Captain," he said.

The boat sound had stopped now, the engine no longer audible. They forgot about it, as Susan moved and moved on him, making him reach for her, more and more urgently.

"Ohhh," she announced throatily, as the tempo increased.

There was a bumping sound at the bow of the boat. Sumner found himself listening for a moment, but then he could not keep his mind on it.

To the left of Sumner's head was an open port hole. Now, as climax neared, Sumner felt a shadow fall partially across his face, and a quick movement caught his eye. He turned just slightly as climax came for both of them, and saw the ugly head of El Pardal grinning at him through the aperture.

But Sumner was in spasm and could not find his voice. Susan strained and thrust on him, and his eyes widened in uncontrollable pleasure and shock as he saw the muzzle of a gun appear in the round window. Sumner opened his mouth to protest, but in the next moment, the gun exploded. The shot hit Sumner in the left cheek and spattered the back of his head onto the pillow.

A short abrupt scream issued from Susan's throat, and then a very long piercing one as she pulled herself loose from the jerking and twitching body of Wade Sumner, stumbling off the bunk, staring in horror at Padral's face in the open porthole.

But now there were sounds above, on deck, and in the next moment she heard steps on the stairway down. She turned just in time to see Torreon come and stand in the open doorway.

Pardal's knife in hand, Torreon looked Susan over carefully, a grin slowly crawling over his hard face.

"Well, well," he said in his throat.

Morales was up on deck examining the boat. Cuesta came up behind Torreon, shouldered his way past him, and entered the cabin. He stared at the naked and curvaceous Susan cowering against a bunk, trying pathetically to hide her nudity. He glanced from her to Wade Sumner.

"Her, too," Cuesta ordered.

Susan made a whimpering sound in her closed mouth. She was trembling all over. "No, please," she muttered drily. "Don't kill me. Please don't kill me."

Torreon grinned. "Maybe we can work something out," he said.

Cuesta frowned at him.

"The boat must be prepared. There is plenty of time. I will enjoy myself."

Cuesta did not want any dissension at this early stage. He needed Torreon. "When you're finished, come up above and lend a hand."

When he turned to leave, Pardal was there, leering at Susan. "I, too, will be up there shortly," he said.

Cuesta held his gaze for a moment, then nodded. "Just don't cause me any trouble."

A moment later Susan was alone with Torreon and Pardal.

While the boat was being inspected by Cuesta and Morales, Susan was raped twice by Torreon and once by Pardal, and then stabbed to death.

The *Sea Witch* moved out of the inlet in late afternoon, heading south. In some secluded place the yacht would be rigged to resemble its original conformation.

Then they would meet the *Maria Isabel*.

Thirteen

Captain Valaczek had taken more cargo aboard then he had planned. He decided to stay docked in Port au Prince until Tuesday morning when the ship's anchor would be raised and the *Maria Isabel* escorted from port by an attending tug.

It was a hot Monday afternoon. The harbor was as calm as death, the water as still as a sheet of molten steel.

Jake Parrish had propped himself in a sitting position on his bunk, near a port hole, and was carefully cleaning the Sterling .380 PPL that Luther McGill had given him. He did not know why he suddenly was taking more interest in the gun, but when he had left Nita at her cabin less than an hour ago, he had thought of the stubby automatic and was seized by an unexpected urge to clean it, to make certain it was ready for use.

Since his intimacy with Nita at the Oloffsen Hotel, Parrish was feeling even more guilt than previously; he was taking McGill's money and posing as something he was not. To make love to McGill's daughter, even with as much affection as Parrish felt for her, while otherwise defrauding McGill had been an unconscionable act. He had gone to her that afternoon in order to tell her that what had happened at the hotel could not happen again, but Tony had been there, and he had been unable to speak privately with her.

Now, Parrish cleaned the small thick-barreled gun, wishing the voyage were over. When they all arrived in Miami, he would tell Nita good-bye, and put as much distance between himself and her as possible. That was the only moral thing to do, if he still had the capacity to act morally. He stopped cleaning the gun and stared at the end wall. The thought of saying farewell to Nita left a surprising emptiness inside of him. It made him angry to think that he was falling in love with her; in his wildest imagination, how could he think of himself as a mate for Nita. She deserved better. He could not help wondering how things might have worked out if he still had been working for Ameco. He might have felt free to court her, despite the age difference. He might not have been drawn into that affair with another man's wife. He would have been promoted and become Nita's prosperous husband, a member of the family.

He would have arrived at this point in his life without hating himself.

A knock on the cabin door roused Parrish from his thoughts. He looked up. "Come in."

The door opened and one of the crew stepped in. He was the thick-set fellow who had sold Parrish the bottle of liquor. He closed the door behind him and held up an unopened bottle of gin. "Senor Parrish. I have something else for you. You like gin, too, yes?" A crafty smile.

Parrish shook his head. "No, no more booze, thanks. I don't want to be too drunk to get ashore when we hit civilization."

The burly sailor came over and stood beside Parrish's bunk. "You don't like your cabin mate much, do you?"

Parrish frowned slightly. "Rueda? Not much, no."

"I am the one who found him going through your duffel," the sailor grinned.

Parrish nodded. "I know."

The sailor went and leaned against the nearby wall. "I

163

know more about this Rueda. . .from a mate of mine.''

"Oh?" Parrish said.

"If you don't want to buy any gin, maybe you'd like to purchase some information."

Parrish narrowed his brown eyes on the burly fellow. "What makes you think I'd pay good money to learn about Rueda?"

The fellow shrugged his thick shoulders. "I just think so. It might be important to you." He eyed the gun Parrish had laid on the bunk.

"How much would you want for this information?" Parrish asked.

"Well. . .First, I will tell you what I am not supposed to know. Neither you nor Rueda are businessmen. You came aboard to watch over Mr. Brown. Is it not true?"

"Maybe," Parrish said.

"Or possibly you guard something Mr. Brown brought aboard? I think maybe you watch over Mr. Brown, and Rueda watches over something else. . . and you."

"Is that all of it?" Parrish said impatiently.

"Oh, no. Now we come to the part that I sell. . . for twenty American dollars."

At least, Parrish thought, the demand was reasonable. But he was certain this Colombian would know nothing about Rueda that he did not already know. "Make it ten," he said.

"It's a deal," the sailor told him.

Parrish pulled out an American bill and gave it to the other man. He took it and stuffed it into his shirt pocket.

"Rueda was with Biaza's secret police," he then said.

Parrish sighed. "I know that."

The sailor looked toward the door for a moment, conspiratorially. "Do you also know," he said, turning back to Parrish, "that he was Biaza's special executioner?"

Parrish frowned. "Executioner? You mean he was involved in the killing of political prisoners at Loja?"

The sailor was shaking his head sidewise. "No, no. You misunderstand me. My friend says he graduated from that and became a private assassin under Biaza for a short time. It is suspected that he murdered as many as five of Biaza's political enemies, a couple of years ago, when Biaza began fearing an uprising, like the one that is occurring at this moment in his country. Rueda was a salaried murderer, Senor. It is a fact, I assure you."

Parrish sat there staring past the burly man. The information was news to him, even though it did not surprise him. Rueda looked like the kind of man who could kill for hire.

"I think you did not know this, heh?" the sailor was saying.

"No," Parrish admitted. "Is there anything else?"

"No, but if I learn anything, I will come to you again."

Parrish nodded, and the sailor left with Parrish's ten dollars.

At that same moment, McGill had just arrived in the wheelhouse to ask Valaczek about sailing time on the following morning. He had left Ana below to nap, if possible, in the stuffy cabin. He had found Valaczek alone in the bridge, plotting a course on a chart lying on a small table. McGill had put his question, and Valaczek had answered it. Valaczek now faced McGill, leaning on the table, his grizzled head bare, his uniform jacket lying nearby on the wheel, his shirtsleeves rolled up.

"Can I get you a beer?" he asked McGill.

McGill shook his head. He, too, was in shirtsleeves and sweating profusely. "No, thanks, Captain. I had one just a few minutes ago. Are you sure we can't leave this furnace before tomorrow morning? It might be cooler at sea."

"Oh, it will be. But we can't leave early, my boy.

Cargo and equipment have to be secured this evening. It will probably cool off some when the sun is down."

McGill sighed, looking wilted. "Well. . .I'm beginning to wish this was all over. I can't wait till we get to Miami where we can live like human beings again." He shot a look at Valaczek. "No offense, Captain."

"I understand, Mr. McGill. I can assure you it will be somewhat easier for us, too, when our ship is back to normal." He eyed McGill sidewise. "Have you heard the rumor that Guayaquil has fallen to rebel troops?"

McGill scowled. "Let's hope that's all it is. . .a rumor." He thought of Fuentes possibly caught in Alvarez' closing net.

"Maybe our mutual friend, Fuentes, is in trouble now," Valaczek continued in a congenial tone.

"Enrico had an escape plan," McGill said.

"Yes, I was telling my officer, Dubois, that Fuentes could take care of himself."

McGill deepened the scowl. "Why were you discussing Enrico Fuentes with Dubois?"

Valaczek was grinning easily. "My, my. . .You are suspicious, Mr. McGill."

McGill held Valaczek's open gaze tentatively.

"I haven't revealed your real identity to Dubois," Valaczek said. "We were just discussing Ecuadorian politics, and it occurred to me, thinking about it all by myself, that an interesting situation may be cropping up."

"Situation?" McGill said. "What kind of situation?"

Valaczek lifted his thick spidery eyebrows. "I know this may sound ridiculous, but both Fuentes and his arch-enemy Alvarez could be dead now, both of them killed during the fierce fighting in Guayaquil. Wouldn't that be a crazy situation?"

"It seems absurd to conjecture about it," McGill said in sudden irritation.

Valaczek continued more slowly. "I'm not an expert on law, but I can't help wonder where that would leave you. . .or me, for that matter, if Fuentes were dead."

"Leave me?" McGill said rather loudly. "I don't follow you."

"Well, let me explain. Would you be under an obligation to carry out Fuentes' instructions concerning his property, if he were dead."

McGill colored slightly. "I take it you're referring to the trunk, Captain?"

Valaczek nodded. "Exactly."

McGill moved closer to Valaczek and scowled into the captain's face. "In the first place, what you propose is unlikely ever to come to pass, Captain. But, in the second place, if something did happen to Enrico Fuentes, I would deliver the cargo to his cousin at Miami as I had been asked to do. . .with your help, of course."

Valaczek merely grinned at McGill.

"Does that answer your hypothetical question?" McGill asked hostilely.

Valaczek rubbed a hand across his square chin. "I suppose Fuentes confided to you what was in the trunk?" he said.

"He told me the same thing he told you. There are government papers in the trunk." It seemed as if, suddenly, everybody was interested in the Fuentes trunk. That surprised him, since he had not given it a second thought since it had come aboard.

Valaczek had been scrutinizing McGill's face closely. "Well, yes, that's what Fuentes told me. I just wondered whether he might not have given you more details."

"None at all," McGill replied curtly, beginning to worry a little about Valaczek and his officer, Dubois.

"Then it seems to me that you ought to be as curious as I am about its contents," Valaczek said casually.

McGill scowled again. "I don't give a damn about what's in Fuentes' trunk because it's none of my business, Captain," he said stiffly. "My only concern is that the trunk reaches its destination safely. If I were you, I'd remember that Jake Parrish and Mr. Rueda have the same concern."

Valaczek's face sobered for the first time. "I'm no pirate, Mr. McGill. I was just passing the time of day."

"I presume dinner will be served aboard again tonight, Captain?"

"As usual," Valaczek said tautly.

"Good, I'll be looking forward to the cuisine," McGill said sourly. Then he turned and left the wheelhouse and the bridge, wishing more strongly than ever that this voyage would end. He longed to get on with his new life in the States.

McGill walked to the fore section of the deck. Some longshoremen and crew were still unloading crates. He stood and watched them for a few minutes, then moved into the shade at midships, leaning against a bulkhead near the companionway to the cabin deck below. He lit a cigarette and began to think about what lay ahead for him in the States. He knew that he was finished with the company; Ameco had not done well the past couple of years, and people in New York had quit talking about how great a manager McGill was. He would not be offered a comparable job in Miami or New York—he would be pushed out to pasture, and McGill would go peaceably. He might buy a little business of some kind, if he could salvage the capital from Ecuador. Something that would keep him busy. Maybe Tony would join him. Father and son. *Like hell,* McGill thought. Tony was too independent to work with his father. Maybe McGill could get him into the foreign service. Maybe, maybe, maybe. That was what his future was, at this point. It scared McGill.

McGill had been standing there for almost a half-hour when Jake Parrish came up through the companionway. Parrish walked over to him.

"Oh, hi, Jake," McGill grinned weakly. "Come up for some air?"

Parrish nodded. "My God, it's still down there. I thought there might be a breeze on deck, but I don't feel one."

"No, I think it's as bad up here as below," McGill said. "I just talked to Valaczek; he says we'll be here until tomorrow. So, I guess we're stuck in this until then."

"How is Valaczek? He seemed to be in a foul mood earlier, on deck."

"Oh, he was quite congenial. He began asking me questions about the Fuentes trunk," McGill told him, eyeing him for his reaction.

Parrish frowned. "Hmmm. Well, I suppose that's natural."

"He wondered what I would do if Fuentes were killed by Alvaristas. What goddam nerve!"

"He hasn't heard anything, has he?" Parrish wondered.

"I don't think so. But he's convinced that Guayaquil has already fallen."

Parrish leaned on the bulkhead beside McGill. "I heard something about Rueda. From a crewman. He says Rueda was a hit man for Biaza."

"Rueda. . .a hired killer?"

"That's right. There's no way of knowing if the story is true, of course."

"You couldn't tell me anything about Rueda that I wouldn't believe," McGill said flatly. "Unless you said he's the good fairy."

Parrish smiled.

"Rueda told me to keep away from the baggage room," McGill said pensively. Until that moment he had kept that exchange with Rueda confidential, even

169

from Ana. "He warned us all away from it."

"Oh?" Parrish said.

"He made it clear that he was in charge of Fuentes' trunk. I don't give a damn, frankly, but his manner has been insufferable."

"He's dangerous, Luther," Parrish said quietly.

McGill held Parrish's sober gaze. Parrish finally looked away, out over the gunwale of the ship, toward the city.

"Assuming there are papers in that trunk that are important to the Biaza people," he said slowly, "what do you think Rueda would do to keep those papers from falling into the hands of Alvarista agents?"

McGill shrugged. "Why, destroy them, I guess."

Parrish nodded. "Exactly." He turned to McGill. "How much of Fuentes' and Biaza's business do you know, Luther?"

McGill raised his light eyebrows. "Why, not much. Fuentes has discussed a few ministry deals with me that I suppose Alvarez would like to know about."

"What do you know about his cousin, Victorio Salazar?"

McGill looked at him. "Salazar? Oh, I know where to get in touch with him, a little about who his people are in Miami. . .that sort of thing." His voice trailed off, and he stared past Parrish.

Parrish nodded. "So you fall into the same category as important government documents," he said carefully.

McGill swallowed hard. "I hadn't really thought much about that, Jake."

"It may be that Rueda would protect you vigorously, as he would the trunk, up until the moment he thought he had lost you. And then. . ."

McGill stared bleakly at Parrish.

"I didn't mean to scare you," Parrish told him. "And I wouldn't say that to anyone but you. But, if

170

Rueda is a hit man, he would be an ideal bodyguard to send on such a mission, with instructions to see that neither you nor the trunk fall into enemy hands.''

McGill nodded. "I see what you mean, Jake.''

Parrish sighed slightly. "Of course, we're almost to Florida, now. The chance of trouble has been greatly reduced. Once we've cleared port, even if Alvarez has somehow learned about you and the trunk, I think we'll be pretty safe.''

"I wish you'd carry that PPL, anyway," McGill said. "It would make the rest of the trip a whole lot more comfortable for me.''

Parrish hesitated only briefly. "All right, Luther. But there's something I've got to tell you.''

McGill studied Parrish's serious, handsome face. "What is it, Jake?''

Parrish avoided McGill's gaze. "I've joined you on this trip home under fraudulent circumstances, Luther. I'm. . .not the man you knew when I left Ameco.''

"Oh, hell, Jake. I know you've had hard times, and that you got to drinking.''

"No, I'm not talking about that." Parrish had begun to sweat lightly on his upper lip. "There was a rubber camp fire, Luther. I had a shot at saving three laborers trapped in the flames. I. . .froze, Luther. I let them die.''

The words hung in the still air.

"So you see, I can't be trusted to protect you and your family from Alvaristas, or Rueda, or anybody else. In a confrontation with Rueda the other day, I let him back me down. That's the way it would be if trouble came, Luther. Whether I'm carrying your PPL or not.''

McGill absorbed all of this. Finally he spoke, "I'm sorry about the fire thing, Jake.''

"I'm returning your money when we get to Miami," Parrish told him. "I guess I was getting even with you for the separation from Ameco, Luther. I had no right.

I've placed all of you in great danger by filling a job you could have given to a more competent man.''

"Jake, for God's sake," McGill said heavily. "We all can react badly under certain circumstances. I did, when I let Wade Sumner fire you. Maybe fire has a special horror for you. Maybe you instinctively knew that the attempt would be useless. You have to put what happened there that day into perspective."

Parrish was shaking his head. "No, you've got it wrong, Luther. I'd lost something inside me, something that's gone forever. I didn't care enough about *myself* to act. And nothing has changed since then."

McGill put his hand on Parrish's shoulder. "Well, I may have a lot of shortcomings, Jake, but I know men. I put my money on you, and that's where I want it to stay. I don't want to hear any more talk about returning your fee in Miami."

"I'm feeling pretty rotten about all this, Luther." He wanted to tell McGill about Nita, about their feelings for one another, but he could not bring himself to do it. "Apologize to Ana for me."

"Ana won't know anything about what you've said to me here," McGill told him. "Or anybody else. I'm going to forget we had this conversation, and I suggest you do the same. Put all that behind you, Jake. You went through a bad period, and now you're beyond it. That's the way to look at it."

"Sure, Luther. But don't say I didn't warn you." Then he brusquely turned and walked away.

Fourteen

The *Maria Isabel* sailed for Florida the following morning. By noon, the freighter was passing through the Windward Passage and heading along the northern coast of Cuba toward the Florida Straits. A breeze sprang up as soon as the ship turned west, and the temperature aboard dropped to a comfortable level.

Parrish was glad to be gone from Port au Prince because he figured that was the last likely place for trouble. He was staying away from Nita now; he was afraid of further intimacy between them. Nita had noticed his aloofness and was hurt by it, even though she had thought that she understood Parrish's motivation.

Rueda kept entirely to himself, except at meals, and nobody cared. He was not a pleasant man to be around. Even the crew kept away from him. Parrish still had to sleep in the same cabin with him, but they hardly ever spoke. The morning of their sailing, Rueda saw Parrish stick the small automatic into his pocket; Rueda smiled but made no comment. Even that irritated Parrish.

In early afternoon, Dubois came to Valaczek on the bridge to report that they were making good time so far. When the technical exchange was over, Dubois returned to the subject of the Fuentes trunk.

"He is outside the baggage compartment half the time, this Rueda," Dubois said. "He is a little paranoid

173

about this trunk, I think.''

Valaczek, handling the wheel—himself, turned to Dubois. ''Our Mr. Brown is pretty touchy about it, too. I talked with him a little, at Port au Prince.''

''And all this for a few papers?'' Dubois wondered.

Valaczek stared through the long glass windshield to where the bow of the ship cut the sea in a white swath. The engines throbbed below him, and the smells of machine oil and exhaust came to him, carried by the sea breeze across the rusty deck of the freighter.

''It does seem odd,'' Valaczek agreed. ''Did you hear anything about Guayaquil last night?''

''No, no further news. But my relative in the city assured me that Alvarez now controls Ecuador. He heard it from a friend who has a short-wave radio.''

''I wish I knew what had happened to Enrico Fuentes,'' Valaczek said, more to himself than to Dubois.

''He may be under arrest now, and in an Alvarez-run jail,'' Dubois offered.

''Or worse,'' Valaczek said.

Dubois rubbed his chin. ''I would like to get a look inside that piece of baggage,'' he said pensively.

Valaczek glanced over at his first officer. ''Well, of course, we're the law on this ship. If we wanted to look in that trunk or any other piece of luggage, we'd have the right to do so.''

Dubois' creole face brightened. ''Does that mean I have permission to make a small search?'' he suggested. ''At an appropriate moment, of course?''

Valaczek hesitated. ''There are locks on that trunk that might stymie an expert. Do you know anything about locks, Dubois?''

Dubois grinned. ''I've never seen one I couldn't open, Captain, given a few minutes to play with it.''

''That's all you might have. Rueda is there at the storage compartment regularly.''

"I would be very careful," Dubois insisted.

"Well," Valaczek said slowly. "Take a pistol from our gun rack. Wait until Rueda is occupied elsewhere. If you get it open, take nothing from it. Just report directly back to me."

Dubois was grinning. "Part of my duties, Captain, are to see that the luggage is riding well and is safe. We are, after all, ultimately responsible for the baggage, more so than Rueda, as long as it is on this ship, Captain."

"Agreed," Valaczek said. "But if you are seen actually unlocking the trunk, Dubois, you're on your own. I'll deny we ever had this conversation."

Dubois nodded. "I understand, Captain."

The trouble was, Rueda was being more and more protective of the Fuentes trunk. He spent a large share of the afternoon within sight of the baggage compartment which was located forward on the main deck. It was a place where Valaczek usually stored special cargo, especially valuable freight or perishable items. It had a metal door with a big padlock on it, and the padlock was always kept locked.

Dubois went about his duties as usual that afternoon, passing the baggage compartment every so often, but Rueda was always nearby, reading a magazine or trying to pick up a station on a portable radio.

Finally, during the hottest part of the day, as the freighter approached the Florida Keys, Rueda went down to his cabin for a rest.

Within moments of his departure from the main deck, Dubois went quickly to storage, unlocked the big padlock, and opened the compartment. After snapping on the naked bulb on a bulkhead near him, he closed the door behind him and looked around.

The Fuentes trunk was just where the crew had put it. It stood against the back wall of the small room, with Luther McGill's big luggage all around it. The trunk was the size of an ordinary steamer trunk, but it was made completely out of a light aluminum alloy. Two large built-in locks adorned its front, and there was a similar lock with extra-strong, extra-long hinges on each side. Dubois thought it appeared impregnable. But it was not, not to an expert like Dubois. He had been a locksmith at one time in his life, and he had never forgotten his trade.

The trunk stood on end. Very carefully, Dubois tipped it over so that it sat on its bottom, the lid up. He was sweating in the close confines of the compartment. He knelt down and examined a lock on the front of the trunk; it required a special key. In fact, each of the locks required a different key.

Dubois took a ring of keys and lock-picks from his trouser pocket, and sorted through them. He inserted a device into the first lock, turned it, and heard tumblers move inside. But the lock did not spring open. He chose another pick and inserted it. Sweat popped out on his forehead, and he was becoming short of breath. Again, the pick failed. But Dubois thought that now he had the right pick in mind. He selected a third one and held it up to the light to examine its conformation.

There was a slight sound outside the door.

Still kneeling, Dubois jammed the ring of keys into his pocket. In the same instant, the door slammed open.

Pedro Rueda stood there in the bright opening, a scowl on his hard face, his .44 revolver aimed at Dubois' chest.

"What the hell are you doing here?" he said in deliberate Spanish.

Dubois rose slowly, expecting the gun to go off at any moment. He composed himself, and when he replied, his manner was fairly casual.

"Doing here?" he said. "I might ask the same of you, Rueda."

"You know what I'm talking about," Rueda said in a

176

harsh tone. "What are you doing in here with the Fuentes trunk?"

"Fuentes trunk?" Dubois said innocently. "Ah, is this one not Mr. Brown's then?"

"You know damned well it isn't!" Rueda said loudly. "Valaczek has told you, hasn't he? He couldn't keep his mouth shut!"

Dubois put on a look of outrage. "I don't know what you're talking about, sir. This is our responsibility, this ship, after all. I merely came in here to check out the baggage, to see that it is safe and secure. That, too, is my responsibility."

"This baggage is my responsibility!" Rueda said, coming up close to Dubois. "That was agreed with Valaczek, and you damned well know it!" He grabbed Dubois' shirt front and slammed him against the nearby bulkhead. "Now tell me, you black bastard! What were you doing with Fuentes' trunk? Trying to open it up? What did you have in mind, heh? Theft, perhaps?"

Dubois looked into the barrel of the .44, and perspired even more heavily. "You misunderstand," he gasped out. "I was merely checking the trunk, along with the others, to make sure the crew had not tampered with anything. It's part of my duties aboard. You can check with Valaczek!"

Rueda yanked a .38 Smith & Wesson revolver from Dubois' waistband, releasing his shirt front. He examined the weapon, a gun in each hand now. "So. You came prepared for trouble, too!"

Dubois swallowed back his fear. "It is unlawful to disarm an officer of a legally registered vessel at sea, Rueda. I must insist that you return my revolver."

Rueda now held Dubois' own gun up against his cheek. "I think that rule is mitigated if the officer is discovered looting from his own passengers! Wouldn't you agree? Perhaps it would not be completely unjustified if such an officer were shot dead in the act?

Heh?''

Dubois sweated and said nothing, expecting the revolver to go off and blow the side of his face off. Rueda finally lowered the gun, jammed his own into his waistband, and opened the cylinder of the Smith & Wesson, dumping the cartridges onto the floor. They clattered like fragments of Dubois' shattered courage. Rueda smirked and stuck the gun back into Dubois' trousers.

"Now," Rueda said. He reached into Dubois' pocket and pulled out the key ring. Dubois started to object, but decided against it. "So this is what you use, heh?" Rueda stuck the keys and lock-picks into his own pocket.

"You can't have those," Dubois objected. "I need them for my daily duties."

Rueda drew his own gun again, showing its muzzle to Dubois. "You're lucky you're still alive, black man. Don't press your luck. Now go tell Valaczek that if I catch you in here again, or anybody else aboard, I'll shoot first and ask questions of the corpse. Do you understand me?"

Dubois stood stiff against the wall. "No part of this ship is off-limits to her officers, Rueda. Valaczek won't like this."

"Tell him that if he wants to make an issue of it, I'll press charges against you in Miami for attempted looting of passengers' baggage," Rueda growled at him. "Now, which key locks this compartment?"

Rueda hesitated a moment. "The long steel one."

"All right, get out of here. And stay out until we get to Miami."

Dubois left without further protest. Rueda locked up the compartment and kept Dubois' keys. He did not go to Valaczek. He did not care to defend his actions. When Dubois arrived back at the bridge and reported what had happened, Valaczek was very angry.

"That sonofabitch! Get my scatter-gun, Dubois! I'll show that greaser who's in charge aboard this goddamn freighter!"

But Dubois calmed him down. "We don't want a shoot-out, Captain, especially with these illegal passengers aboard. It could mean our licenses."

"That sonofabitch!" Valaczek fumed.

"He'd have your man Brown and Parrish on his side," Dubois added. "As much as they both dislike him, they are very protective of the trunk, also."

"I am tempted to lock the bastard in his cabin until we get to Miami," Valaczek muttered. "And unload the Fuentes trunk there without him. That would cool his heels some, the sonofabitch. I've got two other keys to that compartment. I could lock him up and take all day to inspect that frigging trunk, if I wanted to."

But Dubois was subdued by his confrontation with Rueda, and was not about to encourage Valaczek. "We don't want any trouble, Captain. I'd have had a hell of a time getting the trunk open, anyway. It is like a portable safe. Let Rueda have the keys for now, we don't need them. If I have to go into the compartment, I'll go, and to hell with Rueda."

"This evening, before we get to Miami, maybe we'll change the padlock on that compartment door. I've got another one that looks just like it, you know."

Dubois narrowed his dark eyes on the captain. "What for?"

Valaczek grinned slightly. "If that sonofabitch is so damned excited about keeping that trunk from inspection, there might be something in there worth our taking a look at. Like you suggested. So maybe we ought to take control of the trunk. Permanently."

Dubois felt excitement prickle through him. "But, Rueda! And the others!"

"Rueda won't spend all night on deck. Like I said, we'll catch him in his cabin and lock him in there."

"How would you ever let him out? He has a gun and is good with it. He might shoot one of us."

"I wouldn't let him out," Valaczek said deliberately. "Not until we could drag him out feet first, and throw him into the sea."

Dubois licked at his full lips. He had not thought through the implications of opening the trunk. Now, this all seemed rather extreme to him. "But this Brown. . ."

"His name is McGill," Valaczek said evenly.

Dubois nodded. "All right, this McGill. And Parrish. They, too, expect to supervise the delivery of the trunk to Fuentes' man in Miami."

"We don't have to worry about Parrish; he's no fighter," Valaczek said. "And McGill knows we're bringing the trunk ashore illegally. Who will he complain to, if I tell him to go ashore without the trunk? The police? The immigration people or customs?"

"I see your point," Dubois said uncertainly. He thought of Rueda, starving and thirsting and finally rotting in the locked cabin. Nobody would make a fuss about him, either. Salazar might not even know he was aboard.

"Once back home, McGill won't give Fuentes' trunk a further thought, believe me." He grinned toward Dubois. "Well, what do you think? This was all your idea, you know, to find out what's in the trunk."

Dubois rubbed a hand across his face. Valaczek was talking about murdering Rueda, there was no nicer way to put it. Dubois did not consider himself a killer.

"Let me think about it, Captain," he said quietly.

Valaczek eyed him narrowly. "All right. But not for too long, first officer, or the opportunity for us will be gone."

A couple of hours later as the sun slipped lower in the

western sky, the freighter made its way up past the Florida Keys toward the mainland of Florida, on the outer reaches of the infamous Bermuda Triangle. Dubois had not returned to Valaczek yet. Rueda had taken a chair and set it outside the baggage compartment, planting himself in it, and announcing to Valaczek and Dubois that he would tolerate no more undue interest in the Fuentes trunk. He had gone to McGill to warn him about Dubois, not because he felt any obligation to keep either McGill or Parrish apprised of occurrences, but because he wanted McGill on his side if there was trouble with Valaczek. McGill had been taking a shower when Rueda appeared at McGill's cabin door, and Ana told him that she would send McGill up on deck to see him as soon as McGill was dressed.

Tony had had a long talk with Parrish that afternoon. He had observed Rueda and Parrish that morning when the two men had met briefly on deck. Rueda had warned Parrish to keep out of the way at Miami when Sumner came to take the trunk off the ship, and Parrish had seemed to defer to Rueda. That bothered Tony. The old Parrish would have told Rueda to go to hell. He broached the subject with Parrish during their afternoon talk, and Parrish finally told Tony what he had already told Nita—that he was not the same man they had known earlier.

Now, as Parrish returned to his cabin in order to freshen up before the early evening meal, Nita saw him and aked if she could come in. Reluctantly, Parrish admitted her.

Nita looked particularly lovely that afternoon. Her hair was up on top of her head, and she was wearing a bra-less T-shirt and shorts, with sandals on her tanned feet. Parrish hungered for her.

"You've been avoiding me, Jake," she accused him, when she had closed the door behind them.

Parrish glanced at the closed door. "Yes, Nita. I

181

have.''

"I thought we had all that out," she said, her blue eyes smiling at him.

Parrish looked from her lovely face to the stretched-tight T-shirt, and something in his groin moved. "You ought to leave, Nita. I don't want any more trouble aboard than I already have. If·Luther knew you were in here. . .''

"He knows I'm a big girl now," Nita said softly. "What is it with you, Jake? Why are you so afraid of us?''

"I told you. I don't want this to get out of hand. I don't want us to get emotionally involved, Nita.''

"Don't you think it's a little late for that?'' She came over to him, put her arms up over his broad shoulders, and melted all her curves against him. Parrish found that his throat was suddenly dry.

"Nita. . .'' he protested.

But then she had touched her full lips to his, and they were kissing. It had an urgency that surprised both of them. Parrish's hands went almost automatically to her rich curves as his mouth explored hers hungrily. Finally, he pushed her away, breathing raggedly.

"Jesus H. Christ!'' he murmured.

Nita was breathing hard, her breasts rising and falling. "God, Jake. Don't turn me away.''

"It isn't right," Parrish said shallowly. "It just isn't right.''

Nita came back up against him and leaned her dark-tousled head on his chest. "Don't you understand, Jake? I'm in love with you, damn it!''

Parrish looked down at her. "Oh, God, Nita.'' He wanted to tell her how much he was in love with her, how much he ached to have her, but he could not trust himself to do so. He could not be sure what he would do when she reacted to his confession of love.

"It's the same with you, isn't it?'' she asked. "Say it,

Jake. Say it is."

"Jesus, Nita. Don't do this to us. Please!"

"I know you love me, I know it!" she said with quiet urgency. "Why won't you admit it? Why won't you let it all happen? It would be beautiful, Jake. I'd make it beautiful for you."

Parrish stood there, holding her, trying not to let her move him, physically. "When you get to New York, there will be all kinds of men clamoring after you. Believe me. You'll have your pick, honey."

"I don't want my pick, Jake. I want you."

"God. Don't say that."

"I will say it. It's you I want. It's always been you I wanted. I didn't understand my feelings when I was younger. Now I do."

Parrish gently pushed her away from him. "I've got to go take a shower, Nita."

"I'll take one with you," she offered.

He grinned weakly. "I'll see you at dinner."

"Damn it, Jake!"

Parrish stood there, hoping she would leave before he let something happen again.

"Maybe I should go to my father and tell him what happened in Port au Prince," she said angrily. "That would get it all out in the open, and maybe you'd quit acting like a. . .defrocked priest, for God's sake!"

"If you want to do that, Nita, I won't stop you."

She turned away from him. "Oh, hell, Jake!"

Parrish went over and touched her arms lightly. "I want what's best for you, honey. You have to believe that."

When she turned back toward him, her blue eyes were moist. "Sure," she said.

"Oh, Christ."

"It's all right. I'll be okay." She wiped at her eye. "I'll see you at dinner."

Parrish nodded, and then Nita left the cabin.

183

After she was gone, Parrish stood there for a long moment, then went and slammed his fist against the wall. "Damn!" he hissed out. "Damn, damn, damn!"

It was only a few minutes later that McGill went up on deck to find Rueda. The sun was close to the horizon now, and turning color spectacularly. The ship was making good headway. On the port side, off in the near distance, could be seen the chain of keys that stretched from the mainland to Key West, low flat greenery that appeared to float several feet off the surface of the sea. Dubois was down below somewhere, seeing to some duties in the engine room, but Valaczek was up at the gunwale on the bridge, overseeing his three crewmen who were *making sunset*, preparing the vessel for darkness. The fourth crew member was in the galley.

"Oh, there you are, Rueda," McGill greeted the executioner who was sitting in front of the baggage compartment. McGill leaned against the bulkhead beside Rueda, noting that Valaczek was staring at them from the bridge.

Rueda glanced toward Valaczek, too. He did not mind that the captain saw him speaking privately with McGill. In fact, he rather liked the idea.

"What can I do for you?" McGill asked him curtly.

Fuentes turned to McGill. "There has been an attempt made against Enrico Fuentes' baggage," he said flatly. The gun bulged conspicuously under his shirt.

McGill frowned. "An attempt? To steal it, you mean?"

"To open it and steal from it," Rueda said. "I caught the first officer red-handed this afternoon. He was trying to unlock the trunk with a lock-pick."

McGill deepened his frown. "My God! Are you sure that's what he was doing?"

Rueda regarded him contemptuously. "It is my business to be sure. He intended to break into the trunk. I have the evidence.''

''Well, have you gone to the captain?'' McGill asked excitedly.

''No, I have not gone to the captain. I suspect the captain sent him here,'' Rueda said.

''But, if this is true, it's an outrage!'' McGill insisted. ''I'll go speak to Valaczek immediately. He's up there on the bridge.''

But Rueda stopped him. ''What will that prove, Mr. McGill? Do you think he will admit a conspiracy to steal from us? I told Dubois that if I caught him inside this compartment again, I would kill him. I think he got the message. I think also that Valaczek did.''

McGill did not like it that Rueda had presumed to handle the matter himself. He looked toward Valaczek, but Valaczek was staring out to sea. ''Well, I think we should confront him,'' McGill said.

''Late tonight or early tomorrow morning we will arrive at Miami,'' Rueda told him imperiously, ''and your friend Wade Sumner will come to take the trunk away to Victorio Salazar. Until then, I will make quite certain that nobody tampers with the baggage.''

He saw Jake Parrish emerge from the nearby companionway, and wished Parrish had been with him when Rueda had told his story. ''Here's Jake, maybe you'd better tell him.''

Rueda scowled at him. ''You tell him, Mr. McGill, if you think he ought to know.''

McGill glared at Rueda for a moment, then turned and walked over to Parrish who was standing at the rail. Parrish's hair was wet-combed from his shower. He wore a sport shirt, and in the back pocket of the slacks reposed the Sterling automatic which he was carrying to appease McGill. McGill saw the shape of it as he came up to Parrish.

''Oh, Luther. I think we've raised a vessel out there.

Looks like a Coast Guard cutter." A white boat could be seen on the horizon.

McGill stared out toward the boat. "Could be, Jake." He looked down at the water. "Rueda says that Dubois was nosing around our stored baggage earlier."

Parrish glanced toward him. "Oh?"

"Rueda threatened Dubois but didn't go to Valaczek. He tells me there's no point at this stage. I don't know."

Parrish grunted. "Better let it rest, Luther. Rueda is paranoid, anyway. He might have been seeing what he wanted to see. He loves to throw his weight around."

The small boat was coming closer now. One of the three sailors on deck was zeroing in on it with binoculars. Just at that moment Dubois came out of a companionway, and Rueda regarded the first officer darkly. Valaczek was staring at the approaching boat, too.

"Captain," the sailor with the binoculars announced, "that approaching vessel is heading right for us, on a collision course. It seems to be the American Coast Guard."

A second sailor came to the gunwale. "They swarm in these waters since the rise in drug trafficking."

Parrish and McGill were watching the boat approach. They could see men aboard now, in white uniforms. One of them was signalling with semaphore flags.

Valaczek came down from the bridge. "What the hell!" he said gruffly. "They're telling us to heave to! They want us to stop, for Christ's sake!"

Rueda and the third sailor came over to look now, too. The white boat with the Coast Guard stripe on its bow was making a wide sweep to come in alongside the *Maria Isabel*.

"Dubois, get up on the bridge!" Valaczek ordered.

Dubois nodded. "Aye, Captain." He scrambled up to the wheelhouse where he took the helm.

Valaczek now had a pair of glasses focused on the

boat. "Yep. They ask us to stop for a search. Goddamn it! They've never had any trouble with this ship or this line!"

"Maybe they got a false tip, Captain," the nearest sailor offered.

"That's unusual, isn't it?" McGill asked Parrish. "For the Coast Guard to stop a freighter out on the Stream?"

"They probably think we might be a mother ship for cocaine or heroin," Parrish guessed. But there was uncertainty in his voice. As he watched the boat swing in on them, he thought something about it did not look right, but he did not know what it was.

"All right, Dubois!" Valaczek shouted to the bridge. "Let's not forereach them. Cut the engines. Let's see what's going on here."

The ship slowed, the white wake gradually disappearing alongside it, and the throbbing of the engines was suddenly more noticeable. The white boat was coming up close now, and Parrish could see the men aboard fairly well. One had a black mustache, and it occurred to him that they did not look American. The freighter had come to a stop.

"*Maria Isabel!* Lower your gangway and prepare for boarding!" a white-suited man aboard the cutter spoke to them through a megaphone.

Parrish noted that the man who spoke had an accent.

"Jesus Christ!" Valaczek muttered. Then, shouting to the bobbing boat: "What's the trouble, Coast Guard?"

"Just a routine inspection, *Maria Isabel,*" came the reply.

"All right, boys, bear a hand there," Valaczek ordered. "Get that gangway down, and let's get this over with. I've got to make some time."

The sun had just touched the horizon between two green keys in the distance, but there was plenty of light in the sky. Two of the three sailors on deck unfastened an apparatus beside a winch, and began lowering the long, narrow ladder-stairway that was attached to the hull of the ship. It was lowered to sea level, and the Coast Guard cutter tied up to it. Parrish noticed that there was no big gun mounted on the cutter. Also, there was an American flag, but no Coast Guard colors. The four men below were preparing to board.

"Hey, Jake, that's odd," McGill said to Parrish, still standing beside him. "The stripe and insignia aren't painted on the cutter. I can't see very well in this light, but it looks like a canvas is stretched over the bow of the hull, and the insignia is painted on that. Isn't that odd?"

Rueda, not far away, was eyeing the boat suspiciously, too. Because the ship had stopped, Tony and Nita had appeared on deck now, and Tony came over to McGill and Parrish. Ana came out on deck behind Nita and stared toward the captain, looking curious. Finally, in a forward companionway, the fourth sailor appeared, frowning toward Dubois and Valaczek.

Valaczek himself was now eyeing the cutter more closely, and suddenly Dubois came up to him, hurrying from the bridge. "She's all down, Captain," he reported, staring at the cutter over the gunwale.

"Drop sea anchor!" Valaczek yelled to the sailor at the bow. "We don't want to lose way!"

"Aye, Captain!"

The voices of the men below came up to them now, as they gathered for boarding.

"Hey. Are those automatic weapons they've got down there?" Valaczek asked Dubois.

Dubois nodded slowly, as the first man came onto the gangway. McGill heard the remarks, and now saw the weapons himself. His heart was suddenly pummeling his chest. Two men were on the gangway.

"I think, also, Captain," Dubois said more quietly, "that they are speaking Spanish among themselves."

Parrish and McGill had just noticed the same thing. They exchanged looks now. Parrish turned and walked quickly to Valaczek, only twenty feet away. "Captain, you'd better deny them access until we have a better look at them."

Tony had come up to McGill now. "What is it?" he asked casually.

"Is something wrong, Jake?" Nita called from beside her mother.

Valaczek turned to Parrish. "It's too late for that now, Mr. Parrish." He gestured with his head, and Parrish saw that three men were on the gangway, and the last was stepping onto it. Two carried automatic rifles, and the other two had hand guns at ready.

Valaczek turned soberly to Dubois. "Break out our artillery, Dubois. Quickly."

"Aye, Captain!" Dubois nodded, and hurried to a compartment not far away.

Down at the bottom of the gangway, Cuesta turned to Pardal. Behind Pardal were Torreon and Morales, waiting in their surplus white suits to board the freighter. Cuesta carried a black market M-16 A-1 5.56mm automatic rifle, and Torreon carried a second one. Pardal and Morales held surplus Army .45's.

"They've had a good look at us now. Let's get up there fast. Where are the masks?"

Pardal stared hard at Cuesta. "I don't think we brought them aboard the yacht."

"Oh, Christ!" Morales muttered.

"We?" Cuesta hissed out. "*You* were to bring them, damn it!"

"What does it matter?" Torreon said tensely. "Let's go!"

Cuesta paused for only a moment. To go aboard

openly changed all his plans. "All right, let's get up there! Right now!"

They hurried up the gangway. When they reached the top, the gate in the bulwark barred their way. Cuesta raised it violently and came up on deck, followed quickly by his three men.

"Jesus," Jake Parrish muttered, feeling a coldness tighten him inside.

Dubois had just returned from the gun locker. He handed Valaczek a double-barreled shotgun and the burly sailor a .32 revolver. He still held two revolvers himself, not having had time to give the third one to a second sailor. The other three sailors stood about the deck, mouths ajar, staring at the intruders.

"Hey, what is this?" Nita wondered to herself.

"Oh, dear!" Ana murmured.

"Ah, you found weapons," Cuesta said harshly, a little breathless. Pardal, Morales and Torreon had fanned out at the entrance to the deck, guns at ready. "You will now drop them, please."

"You're not Coast Guard!" Valaczek said in a hard voice, only a short distance from Cuesta. "You're god-damn foreigners. What the hell is this!"

"Drop your weapons! Now!" Cuesta repeated loudly.

But Valaczek could not bring himself to give over his ship to intruders. In the next instant, knowing he was outgunned, he raised the shotgun's muzzle toward Cuesta.

Parrish, who along with McGill already knew who these men were, thought of the PPL in his back pocket, and realized he would never be able to bring it into play. "Don't!" he shouted at Valaczek.

But it was too late. Valaczek had squeezed down on the trigger of the big gun just as Cuesta dropped into a crouch and fired his M-16. The shotgun went off, missing Cuesta, but hitting Morales in the left arm.

190

Morales was slammed against the bulwark as Cuesta's gun exploded like a multiple echo of the shotgun's blast. Valaczek was hit in the stomach, the heart, and the face, and was thrown off his feet to the deck. Ana began screaming. Tony started for Dubois, hoping to get possession of the extra gun. Rueda, who had come up near McGill at the gunwale, reached for the gun under his shirt, and Parrish, seeing that, started running at Rueda.

Tony got only halfway to Dubois. Dubois fired one of his revolvers at the nearest gunman, Torreon, and missed. Torreon then cut loose with his M-16, the gun clattering loudly in their ears, smoke rising from it. Dubois was stitched across the chest with hot lead and slammed against a bulkhead not far from the women. Ana's screams became louder. Nita, scared breathless, grabbed her mother and held her tightly, huddled against her near the companionway. The armed sailor now aimed at Morales, but Pardal whirled and shot him three times in rapid succession, and the sailor was hit twice in the heart and once in the right lung. Rueda aimed his Belgian Centennial .44 at the back of Luther McGill's head, without any of the gunmen seeing him do so. But just as he was about to squeeze the trigger, Parrish hit him bodily from behind.

Rueda was knocked off his feet as the gun went off, barely missing McGill's head. Rueda and Parrish hit the gunwale together, Parrish losing his hold on Rueda. Rueda, the .44 still in his hand, aimed again at McGill. McGill's eyes widened in shock. But when the explosion came, it was not from Rueda's gun. It was from Morales' automatic. The shot hit Rueda in the back, rupturing his spine. He screamed, the gun dropping from his hand, his body thrashing on the deck. Pardal came over and shot him in the head. Rueda jumped, and was still. Pardal turned his automatic on Parrish. Tony was surprised that Parrish had made no attempt to draw

191

his gun. Pardal's finger whitened over the trigger.

"No, wait!" McGill cried out. He had just figured out that Parrish had prevented Rueda from killing him.

Pardal looked over at McGill. "Why?" he growled.

Cuesta grunted. "That is Parrish. Get rid of him, too."

Pardal nodded. "No, please!" Nita yelled, from across the deck. Ana had stopped screaming, and was staring blankly at the gunmen. Pardal aimed again at Parrish. Parrish held his breath, waiting for death.

Fifteen

"No, please!" McGill said loudly again. "He's one of us now. He married my daughter in Panama City."

Pardal glanced at McGill, the gun still aimed at Parrish's chest. Cuesta narrowed his eyes on McGill, and then on Parrish.

"It's true," McGill said. "Also, Jake knows all that I know about Victorio Salazar, and more."

Cuesta turned to Pardal. "Spare him for now. See if he is armed."

"If I kill him, I won't have to search him," Pardal argued, looking bulky in his too-small white shirt and pants.

"You heard me!" Cuesta said loudly.

Parrish got to his feet, and Pardal began searching him. The only sounds were the soft crying of the gulls and the muffled throbbing of the ship's engines. Valaczek lay in a pool of his own blood. Dubois, Rueda and the burly sailor also lay dead in various awkward positions about the deck. Blood ran from the deck through a scupper and off the ship in a slow trickle of sticky crimson.

Pardal held Parrish's pocket automatic up for Cuesta to see it in the fading sunlight. "Hey, look at this! A toy gun! But our bridegroom was afraid to use it against us or the Biaza pig that tried to put out the Ameco capitalist's lights!"

Torreon laughed. Across the deck near the fallen Valaczek, Tony swallowed back a rising anger; he had expected Parrish to use the PPL against the gunmen.

Cuesta came over to Parrish and looked him over. "Well. So this is the American gigolo, eh, who steals Ecuadorian wives from their husbands?" He stared hard into Parrish's face. Not far away, Parrish heard the guerrilla Morales groan slightly, holding his bloody arm, his face ashen with pain. He, Pardal and Torreon watched Cuesta as he walked away from Parrish over to Nita.

"Did you really marry this cabron wife-stealer in Panama?" he asked her nicely, looking her over with care. She had changed from the T-shirt and shorts into slacks and a rather loose shirt.

Nita glanced toward Parrish. "That's right," Nita said hollowly. "Jake is part of our family, now."

Cuesta turned and looked at the carnage at their feet, rubbing his chin thoughtfully. He turned to Pardal.

"All right, things are different now. Take everybody aboard the yacht. Bind their hands."

"Everybody?" Pardal said.

Cuesta scowled at him. "Everybody." He turned to the slim sailor standing at a nearby bulkhead. "Is this all of you? Is there anyone below? And tell the truth!"

The fellow shook his head. "No, no one below."

"Throw the dead overboard," Cuesta continued. Ana made a small choking sound in her throat. "Gather up all dropped weapons and confiscate them. Then wash this deck clean."

Torreon frowned at him. "Why?"

"Because I said so!" Cuesta said loudly. "I'll search the ship to make sure there's nobody else aboard. I don't want anybody else below, and I don't want anything aboard disturbed."

Now Pardal was studying Cuesta's face curiously.

"I don't want any evidence that we've been here. No

194

blood. No display of violence.''

A silence had fallen over the scene, except for the distant-throbbing engines. A smell of cooking food came to them from the galley. "We'll let them guess what happened here," Cuesta added with satisfaction. "Rather than telling them. It may give us more time after we're gone."

McGill was recovering slightly from the shock of the carnage and his narrow escape at Rueda's hands. "May we take anything with us?" he asked Cuesta. "Toilet articles, extra clothing?"

Cuesta came over to McGill, stared at him for a moment, and then hauled off and backhanded him. The sound of it carried across the deck. McGill fell backwards against the gunwale, holding his inflamed cheek. Tony was enraged. "Hey!" he yelled, starting toward Cuesta. But Pardal stopped him by stepping into his path with his big .45 pistol.

"What do you think this is, gringo, an Ameco picnic?" Cuesta growled at McGill.

McGill did not reply.

"Where is the trunk?" Cuesta growled at McGill.

"The trunk?" McGill said.

Cuesta hit McGill again, this time leaving blood at the corner of McGill's mouth.

"Leave him alone!" Nita yelled.

Cuesta ignored her. He held McGill's terrified gaze as his men bound Parrish, Tony and the first sailor. "Don't play any games with me, McGill," Cuesta said. "Fuentes sent a trunk with you. Where is it?"

McGill swallowed hard. "It's in. . .the baggage compartment. Down the deck there." He added, fearfully, "Either Valaczek or the first officer would probably have the keys on them."

Cuesta grinned behind his mustache. "Thank you."

"You shouldn't have told them!" Tony said angrily.

Cuesta gave him a look, then went and searched Valaczek's body. He found a ring of keys, and, in moments, had found the compartment and opened it. He forced McGill to identify the trunk, and then he and Pardal dragged it out onto the deck.

"All right, Torreon," Cuesta said. "Get all of them, except McGill, aboard the yacht. You, Pardal, get those corpses overboard, and the deck washed down. Also retrieve any stray slugs. Morales, we'll get that arm bandaged as soon as we're under way. For now, take a look at this trunk and see how we might open it." He had asked McGill about keys, and McGill had denied having any. Cuesta, knowing Fuentes, had believed him.

While Torreon was taking Tony, Parrish, and the three sailors down the gangway, with the women following down behind, Cuesta went below deck and checked to make sure nobody else was aboard. When he came back on deck, all prisoners were aboard the *Sea Witch*. Pardal had dumped the bodies of Valaczek, Dubois, Rueda and the burly sailor overboard, and was almost finished with washing the deck clean of their blood. Cuesta joined Morales who was attempting to open the trunk with a sophisticated lock-pick.

"These are good locks," Morales said. "Also, each one takes a different key. Fuentes did a good job of protecting what's inside."

McGill was standing near the trunk, his hands bound in back of him, his face slightly swollen from Cuesta's blows. "It had better not turn out that you have keys somewhere," Cuesta said easily to him.

McGill shook his head. "I don't, honest to God. Look, Mr. . ."

"Cuesta."

"Mr. Cuesta, surely Alvarez didn't send you to harass my wife and daughter. Leave them aboard the freighter, and Tony, too. They can't do you any good; they know nothing."

"But they can do me harm," Cuesta said. "They could identify me and my men, if we were picked up by the authorities before getting clear of these waters. No, I would rather have them with me, McGill."

Cuesta turned back to Morales. Morales withdrew a lock-pick from a second lock and shook his head. "It could take hours to open this trunk this way, and even then I could not guarantee results. Of course, I could do better with two hands."

Pardal was finished with the clean-up. He came over now, looking big and sweaty in the white uniform that McGill noticed for the first time, had no insignia sewn on it.

"Shoot it open," Pardal said.

Cuesta looked at him. "Not a bad idea." He stepped back and fired off a rattling, cacophonous blast at the nearest lock. He reached down and pulled the corner of the trunk lid. There was no release. The bullets had chewed up the lock without destroying it.

"Damn, that thing is difficult!" Morales said, holding his bloody arm where the flesh was torn below the elbow.

Cuesta turned to McGill, walking over to him. McGill watched him fearfully.

"What's inside this damnable trunk?" he said evenly.

"I don't know. Fuentes mentioned papers and documents. He didn't tell me any details. I don't think anybody knows, except Fuentes. And maybe Salazar."

Cuesta studied McGill's face closely. "Was it weighed when it came aboard?"

McGill tried to remember. "I don't know. It came aboard separate from us."

"You don't know much of anything, it seems."

"One of the sailors might know," McGill suggested. "Please, Cuesta. At least let the women go."

"Did Fuentes mention in what way these papers might be used by his swine of a cousin?"

197

McGill was in pain; the ropes on his wrists cut into his flesh, and his hands were swelling. "No, not to me."

Cuesta came up closer to him. "What is Salazar's address in Miami?"

McGill felt a little sick. He knew plenty about Salazar —but he instinctively knew that, once he had told Cuesta everything, his life and the lives of his family would have little value.

"Enrico Fuentes swore me to absolute secrecy on that," McGill said almost inaudibly.

"What?" Cuesta said angrily.

"I said, I can't tell you that without betraying the trust of Fuentes."

Cuesta stuck the muzzle of the M-16 into McGill's face. "You can betray his trust!" he said harshly.

McGill suddenly passed water in his trousers, not even aware of it for a moment. "I. . .can't," he croaked pitifully.

"Let me have him for a moment," Pardal spat out.

Cuesta sighed. "No. Not here. Let's get him and the trunk aboard the yacht, and get the hell out of here."

While Pardal and Cuesta wrestled with the trunk, and Morales held a gun on McGill, Torreon was enjoying himself with his prisoners. A sailor had asked where they were being taken, and Torreon had replied by swinging the butt of the automatic rifle into the fellow's face, cracking bone in his nose and cheek, almost knocking the man unconscious. Tony had protested, and Torreon then held the gun to Tony's chest, while Ana gasped in fear, and Parrish and Nita held their breaths.

Torreon now moved over to the women, huddling together on the gunwale of the yacht. Torreon looked Ana over first. She was almost as attractive as her daughter, and Torreon liked older women.

"What is your name?" he said to Ana.

Ana looked up at him, and Nita frowned. "Leave her alone, damn you!" she said loudly.

"Ana," her mother quickly replied. "My name is Ana."

"You are Ecuadorian?" Torreon said.

Ana hesitated. "Yes."

"And you married a Biaza pig?"

"Goddamn you!" Nita exploded.

"Take it easy, Nita," Parrish warned her.

Tony glared at Parrish. "Too many of us have been taking it easy," he said in a low voice.

Torreon ignored both Tony and Parrish. "You like it in bed with this McGill, hmmm?"

Nita glared at him, breathing hard.

"I'll bet you would like a younger, more robust lover, eh? I could make you yell with pleasure. Would you like that?"

Tony, with a growling sound in his throat, rose to attack Torreon, but he could do nothing with his hands tied behind him. He came over to Torreon and shouted into his face, "You dirty animal! I'll kill you!"

Torreon punched the butt of the rifle into Tony's stomach, and Tony went sprawling to the deck at Parrish's feet, unable to breathe, gasping like a fish out of water. Parrish felt helpless.

Torreon was grinning. He was enjoying this very much. Now he turned to Nita who was scowling darkly toward him, trembling all over.

"And you, offspring of a capitalist. I'll bet you can give a man a fever, hmmm? What are you hiding under those men's clothes? Shall we find out, eh?"

"Go to hell," Nita said shakily.

"I'll bet you like to be kissed down there. Between your legs. Does this cobarde gringo kiss it for you?"

Nita lowered her head, blushing angrily.

"Why don't you lay off it, Torreon?" Parrish growled. He had heard Cuesta mention their names, up on deck.

Torreon turned at last to Parrish. "Ah, the coward has a tongue after all! You want to make trouble, too, cabron?"

"Lay off the women," Parrish said quietly, avoiding Torreon's hard look. "That's all." He was scared, like everybody else. In the old days, he had ignored fear. Parrish remembered how he had felt, on the *Maria Isabel,* when the shooting had begun. He had calculated the odds and decided it would be suicidal to go against the gunmen. But, was it, perhaps, simply a question of cowardice. Maybe Tony was right in the way he looked at Parrish, as if he were a new species of insect.

"Now the prisoner gives orders to his captors?" Torreon said happily. "What an illogical circumstance! Could it be that he needs a small lesson in discipline, perhaps? A fractured knee-cap, a. . ."

"Torreon!" Cuesta's voice came. "Give us a hand here!" Cuesta ordered Torreon.

Torreon turned from Parrish reluctantly. Cuesta was too businesslike for his taste. On the yacht, when they had hi-jacked it and killed Wade Sumner, Cuesta had hurried Torreon with the girl when he was taking his second turn on her. That had angered Torreon.

Torreon moved to the gunwale and helped Cuesta and Pardal get the trunk aboard. It landed on the yacht's deck with a loud thump. Nobody had noticed McGill's arrival on the *Sea Witch.* But, he immediately had seen Tony lying on the deck, his face white with pain.

"Are you all right, Tony?" McGill asked.

Tony muttered an affirmative reply.

"Oh, Luther!" Ana gasped out. She rose, ran to McGill and embraced him. "Everything is going to be all right," he said soothingly.

Cuesta turned to Pardal, "All right, let's get going!"

Pardal went to the small bridge and started the engines. Torreon cast off a line, and the yacht slowly pulled away from the side of the freighter. In just moments they had moved off some distance from the *Maria Isabel,* heading in a southerly direction along the keys.

The prisoners stared back at the freighter. It sat with its anchor down, its engines running smoothly. Its decks washed clean, the compartment doors secured, and no sign of human life. In the galley, the food was cooking for the dinner meal, and places had been set on the long wooden table in the mess cabin.

That was the way the *Maria Isabel* would be found, later.

It would be a mystery that would haunt the area for some time to come.

Aboard the yacht, Cuesta ordered the McGills and Parrish below deck, locking them into the forward cabin where Wade Sumner had been interrupted at a crucial point in his love-making. The three sailors were left out on deck, and Parrish thought he knew why.

Darkness fell quickly. Interior and running lights were turned on. The gunmen got out of the white uniforms and back into their street clothes. Pardal clambered over the forward deck to untie the canvas covers with the red stripes and insignia painted on them. The canvases dropped into the sea where they quickly sank out of sight. The American flag and the Coast Guard paraphernalia were quickly discarded. The *Sea Witch* was herself again, her name displayed proudly on her uncovered bow.

Cuesta's wild plan had worked to perfection. Nobody was left aboard the *Maria Isabel* to tell any stories.

After they had been under way for about a half-hour, Cuesta ordered the three sailors to kneel at the gunwale, facing the water. Then Pardal walked behind them and shot each of them once in the back of the head.

The shots reverberated through the yacht, and made Ana jump, in the locked cabin.

"My God! What are they doing?" she whimpered.

Parrish peered out through a port hole and saw something hit the water with a splash. "It's the sailors," he said heavily. There were two more splashes.

"Jesus Christ!" Tony said, swallowing hard.

"They shot them," McGill said hollowly. "They shot them in cold blood."

"Oh, Jesus," Nita said.

"Oh, my God!" Ana muttered. "They'll kill us all! Luther, they're going to kill us all!"

"I think they're taking us somewhere," Parrish said, "to interrogate Luther and me, and to find out what's in the Fuentes trunk."

"But Nita and I know nothing!" Ana said hysterically. "They may kill us before we get there! And Tony!"

Parrish avoided her gaze. "I doubt they'll want to get rid of you or Nita," he said quietly.

Nita said nothing.

Tony, sitting on a bunk with his hands bound tightly behind him, like the others, asked Parrish with anger in his voice, "What happened, Jake? Up there on the freighter? You had a gun."

Nita turned quickly to Tony. "Tony, for God's sake! Don't we have enough trouble? What did you expect Jake to do? Commit suicide by pulling out that pocket automatic?"

"It might have helped," Tony grumbled. "It could have made a difference. That's why he was carrying the damned thing. To use it in case of trouble." He glanced toward Parrish. "You're not my friend anymore, Jake."

"Tony!" McGill objected. "If I had had that PPL, I wouldn't have drawn it, either! Valaczek was wrong to try shooting it out with automatic weapons against him. All it got him was death. Do you want that for Jake, for Christ's sake?"

202

"I want a friend to act like a friend!" Tony said loudly. "You're not good with a gun. Jake is. He should have used it."

"Don't make excuses for me, Luther," Parrish said heavily. "Tony's right. But I warned you, both of you. I told you not to expect anything, not to depend on me."

"Don't talk that way, Jake!" Nita said. "You did nothing wrong. You saved Papa's life, and nobody has bothered to say, thank you. Well, I'm saying it, Jake. Thanks for being there when Rueda tried to kill my father!"

McGill nodded. "Yes, I sure appreciate that, Jake. And Tony does, too, whether he shows it or not."

Tony mumbled something and looked away.

"Please, let's not let them divide us!" Ana pleaded. "Let's just hope they leave us alone until they get wherever they're going, and then. . ."

There was a sound at the cabin door. In the next moment it was pushed open, and Pardal and Torreon stood there, both of them grinning.

"What is it?" McGill asked quietly.

"You, and Parrish, and the boy. Up on deck," Pardal ordered. The scar through his right eye glowed pink in the soft light.

"And the women?" McGill asked breathlessly.

"They stay here," Pardal replied, "where Torreon and myself will look after them."

Ana rose hysterically from the bunk where she had been sitting, her dark hair mussed, her face pale with fear. "Oh, no!" she cried out desperately. "Oh, God, no!"

Sixteen

McGill fought the raw fear which grabbed at his insides with a clammy hand. "Does Cuesta want to interrogate us? Why not take us one at a time?"

Torreon laughed in his throat. "Because we would like a little privacy with your women. All right?"

Ana made a little whimpering sound. Nita came over to her, and embraced her.

"It's *not* all right, you bastards!" Tony said loudly. "You leave my mother and sister alone, goddamn it, do you hear me?"

Pardal looked at Tony. "I think I'll shoot this one; he's no good to us, anyway."

"Oh, Jesus and Mary, please!" Ana cried out. "Don't hurt him!"

But Pardal had only been bluffing. Cuesta did not want any of them killed, just yet. "Then tell him to stop making a fuss, lady."

Parrish, knowing what could happen to Nita and her mother, felt the anger crawling around his gut from some dark place deep inside him, an anger he had not felt on the freighter, an anger that surprised him with its intensity. Trying to keep it out of his voice, he said, "You can't question us all at once. Luther's right. Take us one at a time, or we won't go."

Pardal regarded Parrish with a wry, hard grin. "Won't go?" Pardal said, as if he did not understand.

Parrish looked to McGill for support, and McGill nodded. "That's right. You'll have to kill us to take us all."

Tony looked quickly toward Parrish, so did Nita.

"That can be arranged," Torreon said, aiming a pistol at Parrish's chest.

But Pardal, knowing Cuesta would not want any more shooting until he gave his okay, came between Torreon and Parrish, hauling off and kicking Parrish in the shin. Parrish yelled, and went down, hissing in sudden pain.

"No!" Nita yelled.

Pardal kicked Parrish again, in the side, and Parrish grunted in further pain. "You think I have to kill you to take you on deck, you cabron? I can drag you up there by your goddam hair!" Pardal grated out, his face dark with irritation.

Nita came over to Parrish and knelt beside him. "You bastard!" she cied out at Pardal.

Pardal took a length of rope from a pocket and bound Parrish's ankles quickly and tightly. Then he looked Nita over closely, and grinned. "On second thought, I'll leave the cabron in here with me and the girl," he said thickly. "Torreon, take McGill and the kid up to Cuesta. And take the woman with you." With his eyes he gestured toward the next cabin.

Torreon understood. "Yes, all right. Come on, the three of you."

McGill looked toward Parrish for approval of this move, and Parrish, realizing there was no choice, nodded. Tony saw the exchange.

"I'll stay here with Nita," he said.

Torreon grabbed Tony by the shirt and threw him bodily through the doorway into the next cabin. He hit the floor hard. Ana let out a yell and ran to him; they did not try to stop her. McGill, prodded by Torreon, stepped into the next cabin after his wife.

Pardal then closed the door between the two small rooms, and stood grinning at Parrish. Parrish heard, through the door, Torreon telling Ana to stay in the cabin, below. Then there was the sound of the three men going up on deck.

Pardal looked down at Parrish. Pain rocketed up and down Parrish's lower leg and through his side.

"Now," Pardal said to them. "We are all going to have a great time down here, yes?"

Parrish, lying on his side on the deck of the cabin, squinting in pain, exchanged a glance with Nita who was standing close to Parrish.

"So you say you married this gringo in Panama," Pardal went on, grinning at Nita. "If you are married, where are your rings?"

Nita glanced at her bare third finger on her left hand.

"We didn't have time for rings," Parrish spoke up.

Pardal scowled at Parrish and kicked him viciously in the thigh. Parrish sucked in his breath, then lay gasping. "I was speaking to the girl," Pardal said nicely.

"Goddamn you, leave him alone!" Nita yelled, trembling with emotion.

Pardal came over to Nita, turned her around roughly, and untied the ropes at her wrists. When they were free, she turned and hit out at Pardal wildly. He laughed, blocking her two blows easily. "Heh, heh! A spunky one, hah! It is your Ecuadorian blood, little pigeon!"

Nita pulled her arm loose from his grasp, and stumbled backwards across the small cabin. "You. . . ape!" she breathed.

"Hidden fire," Pardal said, looking her over. "And other hidden things, too, eh? Under those clothes?"

"Don't touch her, damn you!" Parrish breathed.

Pardal glanced at Parrish, but made no further move toward him. He fixed his brittle gaze on Nita. "You have shown him what you have under there, married or not," he said to her. "Why not show both of us now?

You would enjoy that, wouldn't you, gringo?"

"Goddamn you," Parrish muttered.

"I'd burn in hell, first," Nita said, breathing rapidly.

Pardal grinned, and drew the big automatic from his waistband. He casually pointed the heavy gun at Parrish. "I argued that this one should have been sent overboard with the sailors. I don't think Cuesta would make much of a fuss if I shot up both of your legs. Do you?"

Nita looked at the gun, then at Parrish, and made a moaning sound in her throat.

"Don't pay any attention to him," Parrish told her.

Pardal's bald head gleamed in the light, and the scar through his eye looked hideous to Nita. He aimed the automatic pistol at Parrish's right leg, and tightened his finger on the trigger.

"I think I'll start with this one," Pardal said evenly. He was not bluffing now. He would merely tell Cuesta that Parrish had given him trouble.

"No, wait!" Nita cried out.

Pardal turned to her, straight-faced. "Either you start, or I do," he said. "I would suggest the blouse first."

"Don't do it," Parrish gritted out.

But Nita was already unbuttoning her shirt. Pardal watched closely. She pulled it down, and his eyes widened slightly. She took the shirt off.

"Mother of God!" Pardal whispered.

"Shit!" Parrish growled, straining at his bonds.

Pardal ignored him. He had never seen such perfect breasts on a female. Nita was breathing hard, making them move more dramatically, and Pardal could not take his eyes off them. He could think of nothing but Nita's breasts. He came over and touched the muzzle of the gun against her cleavage, tentatively, and then moved it along the contour of her right breast. The metal was cool to her skin, and she flinched. "Extra-

207

ordinary," he murmured.

"Don't let him, Nita!" Parrish said hoarsely. For the first time in three years, he cared desperately about something. "Fight him, it doesn't matter about me!"

Pardal looked into her beautiful eyes and grinned. He saw the surrender there.

"Now," he said, "the trousers."

Nita licked her dry lips. She began unbuttoning the slacks.

But just at that moment, the door opened and Jesus Cuesta stood there. They all looked toward him, and he stared hard at Nita's nakedness. She stopped unbuttoning the slacks.

"What the hell is going on here?"

Pardal shrugged. "Entertainment. It is all night to the Yucatan, yes? Why not spend it pleasantly?"

Cuesta was in a black mood from lack of success in questioning McGill. "Because we need you to run this boat!"

Pardal made no response.

"Now get on deck and relieve Morales at the wheel," Cuesta said harshly.

Nita had fastened her slacks, and was now slipping the shirt back on. Pardal glanced toward her for a last look, then stormed past Cuesta angrily, his small eyes flashing fire. Cuesta turned to her.

"You women cause trouble! I should have dumped you into the sea!"

The charge was so outrageously absurd that Nita did not reply to it. Through the open doorway Ana's voice now came to her.

"Nita! Are you all right?"

Nita turned and saw Ana in the doorway, looking very distraught. "I'm okay, Mother." Ana came back into the cabin, and embraced Nita tightly. Behind her, Torreon pushed McGill toward them. When McGill came into the cabin, Parrish saw that he had several cuts and bruises on his face. Tony came along behind, limping, and his left eye was swollen shut.

"Oh, Luther!" Ana exclaimed. "Tony, my baby!"

"Oh, God!" Nita murmured, her lower lip trembling as she looked at her father and brother.

Cuesta picked up the rope that had bound Nita's wrists and rebound them, her hands behind her back. Then he turned to Torreon. "Leave the women to themselves. At least until we get where we're going."

Torreon nodded grudgingly, and they both left the cabin. Cuesta closed and locked the door behind them.

McGill had slumped onto a bunk. Tony went and sat on the floor near Parrish. Ana and Nita sat together across the aisle from the men, Ana wishing she had her hands free to tend to McGill's wounds.

"What did they do to you?" McGill asked Parrish.

"It's nothing," Parrish said. He elected not to say anything about Nita. If she wanted to tell them, that was her business. "I see Cuesta's goons worked on you up there, you and Tony."

Tony was looking Parrish over. "That bastard punched him," he said. "Over and over again. That Torreon."

"What did they want?" Parrish asked.

"Everything about Salazar," McGill said. "I decided to hold out. I didn't think Cuesta would go too far, here on the boat. Once Cuesta gets everything we know, there's no telling what he'll do."

Parrish nodded. There was only a small overhead light in the cabin, and he could not see McGill's injuries clearly. "That's smart, Luther."

"They think you and Tony know about Salazar, too. I was afraid to let Cuesta think you knew nothing."

"That big one hurt Jake," Nita said quietly. "He kept kicking him. Are you all right, Jake?"

"Hell, yes, Nita."

"Jake gave the big one hell because he bothered me.

That's why he was kicked again." Nita glanced toward Tony, and Tony held her gaze for a long moment.

"Is anything broken, Jake?" McGill asked.

"I don't think so. Tony, can you see out of that eye?"

Tony turned to Parrish, and for the first time since the shipboard shoot-out, he did not scowl at him. "Not much, Jake. But it's okay."

Parrish turned to McGill. "Have they made any further attempts to open the trunk?"

"No, I think they're waiting until they get to Mexico," McGill said. "I heard them mention that they're heading to some isolated spot on the coast. I gather that Cuesta knows an Indian who lives alone there somewhere."

"They probably want us around until they've had a look at the contents of that trunk," Parrish said. He looked toward Ana and Nita. "But I'm going to be honest with you. After Cuesta thinks he's gotten all the information he can get from us. . .I suspect he intends to kill us."

Ana shook her head sidewise. "Holy Mother! No!"

"Alvarez sees us as enemies of the rebellion," Parrish added. "Traitors to a cause. I'm sure Cuesta has his orders."

"Cuesta mentioned how they found out about us," McGill said. His nose was swollen, and his lip was bloody. There were cuts over his eye and on his left cheek. "They grabbed Esquinaldo in Guayaquil as soon as he left us at the ship. They must have made him tell them everything."

Parrish met McGill's gaze. "They can make anybody talk, Luther."

A silence fell among them.

"I know that," McGill said.

Tony turned to Parrish. "So what are we going to do? Just wait for them to kill us?"

210

McGill smiled tiredly. "Tony, even if we got loose from these ropes, there's nothing we could do. They're all up there together, with guns. Deadly guns. There's just no way to separate them or surprise them."

"I'd agree with that," Parrish said.

"Then there's nothing to do?" Tony said darkly.

"Yes, we can't wait," Parrish said. "Wait for opportunity. Maybe when we get off this yacht."

McGill looked around him. "This is Wade Sumner's boat. He's described it to me. And. . .there are blood stains on this bunk. . .My God, Jake! What have we all gotten into?"

By dawn they were approaching the Yucatan coast. McGill could see the green hills on the horizon. Cuesta had loaded drums of gasoline aboard so that he would not have to re-fuel anywhere. In early morning they sailed down the Yucatan coast and, before mid-morning, they put into a small cove.

Soon the engines were stilled. They heard an anchor thrown over. The white boat bounced on a light surf. There was some moving about on deck, and then Cuesta came for them.

"Everybody's up!" he said in a hard voice. "We're going ashore!"

He leaned down, cut the bonds on Parrish's ankles, and yanked Parrish to his feet. Parrish hissed in pain.

"Let's go!" Cuesta ordered them.

Nita looked at Parrish doubtfully, and Parrish smiled at her. "Can you walk?" she asked him.

Parrish nodded. "I'll make it, honey."

They filed up onto deck, the five of them, with Cuesta behind them, holding one of the M-16's. Torreon and Pardal stood there on deck, looking grumpy. Morales had his arm bandaged and was putting a ladder over the side of the yacht.

It was a sunny pristine morning. The sea sparkled

turquoise, and the line of shore was all greenery and sand. The shrieking of birds could be heard. A clearing had been made directly in front of them, and there were several thatch huts sitting in it. A lone Indian stood on a narrow beach, staring toward the yacht.

"That's him," McGill said quietly to Parrish. "That's Cuesta's contact."

"Be quiet!" Pardal said to McGill.

Cuesta stood by the gunwale, gesturing to Ana and Nita. "All right, women first. We're going ashore."

Ana cast a doubtful look at McGill, but his eyes reassured her. She let Cuesta untie her bonds, and then she went over the side, down the ladder. Torreon was waiting in a dinghy, and as Ana came down to him, he enjoyed peering under her dress to where her long thighs met. He grabbed those thighs as she came down, and she gasped, but made no comment to him. Torreon had missed having her the night before, but now there would be much time.

Nita came next, and she pulled away from Torreon as he tried to handle her. He grinned insanely. McGill was untied and he joined the women. Then Torreon took them to shore.

A few moments later, Torreon came back for Parrish and Tony. Morales also went with them. Then, while Morales went back for Cuesta and Pardal, Parrish, Tony and Torreon waded ashore. The Indian was talking to Torreon as they came onto the sand, making some coarse comments about the women in accented Spanish. He was not big, but he looked as hard as sacked salt, and he carried a long machete that could decapitate a man in one stroke.

The prisoners had to stand there on the beach while the other Alvaristas came ashore. Parrish and McGill looked around them. It all looked very primitive and wild. There was no road visible from the beach, but Parrish spotted a jeep-type vehicle sitting in the shade of a coconut palm near one of the stucco-and-thatch huts.

Tony looked down the open stretch of beach. Their hands were still unbound, and he figured they had an excellent opportunity for escape. He caught Parrish's eye, and nodded toward the expanse of beach. Parrish glanced at Torreon who was speaking with the Indian, and the long machete of the Indian, and at Nita and Ana. It was too long a shot, with his hurt leg and the women. He shook his head negatively to Tony. Tony's face showed disappointment.

"How long is it you are here?" the Indian, named Nardo, asked Torreon.

"We don't know yet," Torreon replied. "It will not be long, though. When this is finished, we will take the boat on down to Colombia."

McGill and Parrish exchanged looks. They both knew that none of them would be aboard the yacht when it left.

Cuesta, Pardal and Morales were coming ashore now. The trunk was in the dinghy. Cuesta called out to Parrish, McGill and Tony to come and help get the trunk ashore. The men followed orders, while only Pardal helped them move it. They brought it ashore fairly dry, and Cuesta ordered them to carry it up onto high ground, into the compound between the huts. The women and the gunmen went along. The Indian named Nardo and Cuesto spoke together in confidential tones, and then the prisoners' hands were once again bound, and they were led to a thatched hut. The small settlement was deserted—Nardo its only inhabitant.

"Inside! All of you!" Pardal commanded them.

A dusty iguana scurried out of their way as they filed through the low doorway, one at a time. The women entered first, then Tony and McGill, and finally Parrish. Inside, it smelled musty. The floor was dirt, and there was thatch above their heads. A spider hung from a web in the apex of the ceiling. Ana saw it and gasped. In a corner there were rat droppings and the burrow of some animal.

"Oh, Jesus," Nita said.

Pardal still stood in the doorway behind them. "We'll arrange more. . .convenient accommodations later," he said, grinning at Nita. Then he slammed a heavy wood door on them, shutting out most of the morning sunlight. One small window at the side, boarded over partially, allowed them dull light. They all heard Pardal slide a bar across the door on the outside. Ana, huddled beside McGill, looked around at the mud walls and shook her head slowly.

"We're all going to die here," she said without even knowing she was voicing the thought aloud. "I can feel it, none of us will ever leave here alive."

Seventeen

McGill turned to Ana and saw her blank staring eyes, and the pale drawn look on her face. She had had a sheltered life, his Ana. Things like this just did not occur in her world of high Ecuadorian society. She had been brave, had held up well through all of it so far. But, deep down inside of her she had suddenly given up and was withdrawing from reality.

McGill put his lips to Ana's cheek. He could not hold her because of his bound hands. She turned and stared at him as if she had never laid eyes on him before.

"It will be all right," McGill said softly to her. "Believe me, Ana. It will be all right."

"Those bastards!" Tony said bitterly. "Those dirty bastards!" His voice was uneven.

Parrish limped over to the small window. He peered through the spaces between the two boards, and examined the boards themselves. It all looked very solid. To break through would be difficult and noisy, even if they had the use of their hands. Besides, the window was barely large enough to climb through.

McGill came over to him. "What does it look like to you, Jake? What will they do next?"

"I suspect that trunk will occupy their attention until they get it open," Parrish told him. "The longer it takes them with that, the more time we'll have, probably."

Nita took her mother over to a wall, and Ana sat down on the dirt floor, leaning against the wall, Nita joining her there. Ana's dress was soiled and wet at the hemline; she looked very bedraggled. Tony examined the heavy door, while McGill and Parrish stared through the cracks in the window.

"Can one of us untie another's hands?" McGill wondered. "I saw someone do that in a movie once. They stood back to back."

"Those things generally work out better in John Wayne films than in real life," Parrish offered. "My hands are almost numb because they tied the ropes so tight. How are yours?"

"Not so good," McGill admitted.

"Mine feel pretty good," Tony said, coming over to them. "Maybe I could untie yours, Jake. Or Dad's."

Parrish met his hopeful gaze. "Remember, any attempt to escape is a risk. If they come in here while we're trying to untie our bonds, they might kill one of us, to teach the others a lesson."

"Wouldn't it be worth the risk?" Nita asked.

Parrish turned to her. "It depends. For instance, what would we do if we were all free to use our hands right now?"

The question was answered by silence.

"This window is well-boarded," Parrish continued. "If we tried to knock those boards off, we'd raise the dead. The door is solid and apparently heavily barred from outside."

Tony looked upward. "What about the thatched roof?" he wondered. "There might be a weak place in that."

"We can't even reach it, except at the eaves," Parrish said.

"Well, we have to do something!" Tony said emotionally.

Parrish nodded. "I agree. The question is, what? And when? When will the best opportunity arise?"

"If we wait for the best one, we may never leave

216

here," Tony insisted.

"Again, I agree," Parrish told him.

"Why don't I work on your wrists?" Tony said. "Just for something to do?"

Parrish sighed. "If you have to do something now, try Luther's. They may be less tightly tied than mine."

Tony went over and stood behind his father, back to back, and his fingers reaching for McGill's bonds.

"The knot is down lower," Parrish guided him. "There."

"I feel it now," Tony said.

Tony fumbled with the knot. Parrish watched bleakly for a moment, then went over and sat down near Nita. "I'm sorry you and your mother have become involved in this," he said softly to her.

"I'm so scared, Jake," Nita admitted to him.

Ana stared across the hut, not listening to any of them.

"I know," Parrish told Nita. "So am I."

"The one that was in the cabin with us. He's going to. . ."

"Listen to me," Parrish said. "Don't think about what might happen. Cuesta is in charge, not those other two apes. And Cuesta is all business. He has to answer to Alvarez when he gets back to Guayaquil."

"If you had told me a couple of weeks ago that any of this could happen to us, I'd have laughed," Nita said. "Now I may never laugh again." Her lower lip trembled.

Ana turned and looked at Nita without speaking.

"It's all my fault," Luther McGill said. "Every damned bit of it."

"Hell, don't say that, Dad," Tony said.

McGill looked at him. "It's true. I saw the trouble coming. Other Americans took their families and left. But old-timer Luther had to stick it out, like a dyed-in-the-wool colonial from the nineteenth century. I knew there was danger. I played with your lives, and I lost.''

"Luther. . ." Parrish protested.

"I wish to God I could give my life to save all of yours," McGill said with great emotion in his voice.

"Hell, don't talk like that," Tony said, tugging at McGill's bonds.

McGill did not hear him. "They offered me a job in Brazil a year ago," he went on. "There would have been a little more money, too. We'd have lived in Manaus, in luxury. But I thought the Guayaquil job was a tougher one, and that nobody could do it but me. I wasn't thinking of anyone but myself, even then."

"Jesus, cut it out!" Tony said angrily. "Just cut it out, will you?"

McGill and Ana turned to Tony. "You're just like your father, Tony," Ana said with a bland smile. "You've always been a good boy."

Everybody looked toward Ana. McGill swallowed hard.

Outside in the compound, Parrish could hear the sound of Cuesta's voice, and the screeching of metal against metal. They were trying to open the trunk. The musty odor of the hut smelled like death to him, and he hated it. He sat there, hoping Cuesta could not get the trunk open. He fantasized that Pardal came into the hut, and that they overpowered him and took the automatic rifle from him, bursting out of their imprisonment to kill all of the gunmen. But he was sure that now was not the time to make any move. Not with all the gunmen and the Indian out there in the compound. Parrish knew that he and the other captives had to hope that the gunmen became physically separated somehow, so that there was not such a concentration of guns.

"Christ!" Tony said suddenly, pulling away from his father's back. "I can't do it! I can't get hold of the damned knot!" He give it up, coming across the room and leaning on the heavy door to the outside.

218

"It's okay, Tony," McGill said. "We'll give it a try later, when we're all rested some. Maybe the ropes on Ana or Nita will be easier to get at."

Nobody responded to McGill.

They all thought that it sounded a little silly to talk about escape.

That possibility seemed, at that moment, extremely remote.

Out on the sand of the compound, sweating in the morning sun, Torreon turned and threw down a short crowbar he had been using on the Fuentes trunk. "Sonofabitch!" he muttered. "That damned thing is impregnable!"

Pardal sat on a dead log nearby, staring glumly at the trunk. Cuesta, Morales and the Indian stood in a loose semi-circle, looking at Torreon. Cuesta hated men who lost control of themselves. He glared at Torreon and then knelt beside the trunk. Where Torreon had jimmied it, the lid and top of the trunk were bent, but the metal was tough and the locks had held.

"Well," Cuesta said. "It's obvious we need some tools. Maybe a metal saw that will cut through these locks."

Nardo turned to him. "I know where there is some plastic explosive." Cuesta had used this place and this Indian on previous occasions when Cuesta used to hijack boats for gun running, years before.

"Explosives?" Cuesta said. "Where?"

"It is at a nearby village. Not much more than an hour through the jungle. I could take the jeep and be back this afternoon."

Cuesta looked at the trunk, then at Torreon who had handled explosives many times in the past. "Could you blow this with plastics? Without damaging what's inside?"

Torreon was suddenly in a better mood. "I can lift

219

that top off without bending the hinges,'' he said.

Cuesta turned back to Nardo. "All right. You go with Torreon. But don't let anybody know our identity, and don't mention this camp. Torreon will inspect the explosives to see if we can use them.''

Nardo nodded. "We can leave immediately.''

The two left shortly thereafter, in the small jeep parked in the compound. A tiny road led into the jungle, and the road wound its way out to a larger one that snaked through the wilderness to civilization.

When they were gone, Pardal went and peered through the window of the prisoners' hut. When he returned, Morales had opened a can of fruit and was eating some peach halves. His shot arm was still aching badly, despite the fact that he had removed most of the buckshot from it. Cuesta was sucking on a thin cigar, sitting on the same dead log as Morales, staring toward the trunk which was battered and bent now, around the lid.

"They're making no trouble,'' Pardal reported. He had taken his shirt off, revealing a tanned, hairy chest and pot belly. He looked like a 1700's pirate, standing there with the big pistol in his waistband. "When do we resume our interrogation?'' He enjoyed hurting people, and was looking forward to another session with McGill, or one with Parrish.

"I'm more interested in the trunk than in trying to learn more about Victorio Salazar,'' Cuesta said. "What danger can Salazar be to Alvarez, anyway, without this trunk and what's in it?''

"Alvarez seemed to think Salazar is important,'' Morales reminded Cuesta. He wished that he had not come on this mission. He had asked Cuesta to stop Pardal and Torreon from raping the mistress of Wade Sumner, but Cuesta did not want trouble. Now both of them were behaving badly with these women, too. His peasant's brain honored the sanctity of womanhood.

220

Morales did not like killing, but if he had to kill, he liked to kill cleanly. To maul a woman first was a violation of his personal code of honor.

"Yes, Alvarez has many ideas that may or may not be sound," Cuesta told Morales. Morales eyed him narrowly. "We must decide on our own, out here in the field, what is important and what is not. Only we can judge the situation here, and what is most important at the moment."

"Nevertheless, we have nothing else to do until Torreon returns," Pardal said. "I don't like them all in the same hut. We might go ahead and split them up. For instance, the women in one hut, the three men in another?"

Cuesta eyed him sourly. "Do you think of nothing but the women, Pardal? You are getting as bad as Torreon."

Pardal shrugged. "Does it hurt the revolution to devise a diversion occasionally? Will the great reform fail if we pause once in a while for a random pleasure?"

"Leave the women alone, for God's sake!" Morales said harshly. "Haven't we made it bad enough for them? Isn't it enough that they will forfeit their lives? Must you mistreat them gratuitously, also?"

Pardal scowled deeply at Morales. "Now you, peon, tell me when to think of women and when not?"

Cuesta sighed. "Never mind, Pardal. Maybe we do have time to conduct some interrogation, though. Why not bring that cabron Parrish? We have not spoken to him yet. Maybe he knows more than we think."

Pardal grinned. "Good. The sooner we take care of this business, the better. And the women?"

Cuesta waved a hand impatiently. "Put them where it pleases you, I don't care!"

Pardal grinned again, and gave Morales a triumphant look. "I will be back shortly," he said.

All of the captives knew that the development was a

bad one when Pardal came into their hut and said he was taking the women away and separating them.

"No!" Ana said rigidly. "I won't go! I won't leave my husband!"

"You will have your daughter with you," Pardal said genially. "Of course, if you wish to resist, I can carry you to the other hut. That will be perfectly all right with me."

Ana eyed Pardal fearfully, and Nita rose to her feet. "We'll go peacefully," she said in a hoarse voice.

"No, don't go!" Tony objected. "Don't you see what he has planned? We won't know what's happening to you, if you're off in some other hut! Don't go!"

Nita turned to him with a gentle look. "I don't think we have any choice, Tony," she said quietly.

Ana got to her feet. "Maybe Luther could come. Would you come along, too, Luther?"

McGill studied Ana's tight-lined face. She was like a cracked mirror that has not yet fallen to pieces.

"I think they want me to stay here, my dear," he said thickly. "Don't worry, we'll be right here, not far away."

"Don't you hurt them, damn you," Parrish growled tautly. He knew that they all might still die there, but it tore him apart inside to think that the women might be mistreated in the meantime.

"Oh. You are to come, too," Pardal said with a grin that was more like a sneer. "For questioning."

Parrish exchanged looks with McGill. He knew absolutely nothing of value to these men, but if they suspected that, he would be disposed of immediately.

"Let's go," Pardal ordered them.

The women were taken by Pardal to a hut on the other side of the compound. There was no window; when the door was shut and barred, the darkness was overwhelmingly thick. Ana and Nita looked at each other, trying not to panic.

222

Outside, Cuesta had brought a straight chair into the middle of the compound, and set it facing the beach. He shoved Parrish onto the chair and bound him with strong rope.

"The woman-stealer," Cuesta said from behind his thick black mustache.

"I doubt he is married to the girl," Pardal said, "but he has a thing for her. Hey, cabron?"

"Whatever you say," Parrish grunted.

Pardal laughed gratingly. "I am going to rape her later. What do you think of that, cabron?"

Parrish glared at him.

"I suppose she is a juicy morsel," Pardal said. "What is it like between her legs? Hot as a furnace, eh?"

"Go jerk yourself off," Parrish said.

"I'll show her what screwing really is," Pardal added.

Cuesta broke in, casually. "I think this cobarde knows something about that, himself. You taught the minister's wife, in Guayaquil. Didn't you, Parrish?"

"Is this what you brought me out here for?" Parrish said.

Pardal swung his fist into Parrish's face, connecting solidly with Parrish's right cheek. Parrish grunted in shock and fell to the sand, taking the chair with him. He lay there then, sand on his face, dazed and hurting. Rough hands grabbed him and pulled him and the chair erect again. He was breathing hard now.

"We don't like smart answers to our questions," Cuesta told him. "I thought you understood that by now."

"I think he is learning," Pardal grinned, rubbing his knuckles.

"Why would McGill tell us voluntarily that you know about Victorio Salazar?" Cuesta said, after a moment, "except to spare your life aboard the freighter?"

223

Parrish had expected that question. In his anxiety to save Parrish, McGill had overplayed his hand. Parrish thought of an answer that might keep him alive.

"That was the reason," he said. "I know nothing of Salazar, I'm just a hired hand. Actually, Luther probably knows little, himself. But he wants you to think he does, just to keep alive. I can't blame him."

Cuesta narrowed his dark eyes on Parrish. "And you? You don't want to keep alive? Is that why you are so honest about this?"

Parrish looked up at him. "You intend to kill us all. What difference does a few hours make?"

Cuesta and Pardal exchanged looks. Cuesta came closer to Parrish, squinting in the glaring sun. "How long did you work for McGill?"

Parrish shrugged, wondering if his ploy had worked. He half-expected Pardal to draw the heavy pistol and shoot him dead at any moment. The sun was like a flat-iron on the back of his neck. A black fly buzzed around him for a moment, then flew off.

"A couple of years, I guess."

"You were invited to his house on occasion, I suppose?"

Parrish met Cuesta's hard gaze. "Yes, of course."

"You knew the family well?"

Parrish raised dark eyebrows. "Yes, fairly well."

"Well enough," Cuesta said evenly, "so that when Luther McGill felt the need of someone he could trust with his life and the lives of his family, he scoured Ecuador to locate you. Isn't that true, cabron?"

"You have good sources," Parrish said quietly.

"That's right. And yet, you expect us to believe that McGill, going to all this trouble to involve you in this rabbit run from Ecuador, would not confide in you?"

Parrish met Cuesta's look with a mask of resignation. "You tell me," he said.

Cuesta's face was smug with triumph. "We are not

224

fools, Parrish. Don't treat us as such."

"Luther only mentioned Salazar," Parrish said truthfully, hanging his head, making it sound like a lie. "I know nothing about him, except that he was to receive the trunk Fuentes sent with Luther." He glanced toward the trunk where it sat out in the middle of the compound on trampled-up sand.

"He's lying," Pardal said with certainty. "I will go to work on him."

Cuesta grinned. "You see how eager Pardal is to get at the real truth? Isn't it a pleasure to witness such loyalty, such willingness to go beyond the call of duty?"

Parrish glanced at the big bulking Pardal, and sweated more profusely. He was surprised at himself. He did not feel fear. It was there, all right, but it had not taken hold of him. He wondered if the difference were Nita and her open affection for him, her belief in him. Maybe he was worthy of her love. But all that was academic, now—neither of them would ever leave this place alive.

"He's a goddamn gem of a man," Parrish responded to Cuesta.

"Let me have him," Pardal said. "I'll get my things."

"You see? The man absolutely loves his work! He suggests getting his tools, Parrish, the tools of his trade, so to speak. A hammer. A pliers. He's very good with the pliers. He almost got to use them on Esquinaldo, too, but Esquinaldo spoiled it for him. He spilled his guts, told us everything. It was a shame, really, for Pardal. He so likes to use his tools!"

Parrish eyed Cuesta. "I'm not telling you anything," he said quietly, implying that he knew everything.

Cuesta stared at him for a moment, then nodded to Pardal. Pardal grinned and walked away. Cuesta came and bent over Parrish. "We have much time, much patience. For you, it can only get worse."

Parrish believed him.

"When I return, we will see how well you appreciate Pardal's methods."

But a series of delays prevented the twosome from coming back to him. Pardal, who had left his *tools* on the yacht, felt too lazy to make the trip in the dinghy. Instead, he and Cuesta got into a discussion about the trunk, forgetting all about Parrish.

"I wonder what Alvarez thinks is in it?" Pardal said, as he and Cuesta stood in the shade of a hut at the edge of the compound. Cuesta had opened a bottle of rum, and they were taking swigs from it.

Cuesta shrugged. "Whatever it is, that pig Salazar will never lay his fat hands on it."

Pardal swigged the rum and handed it to Cuesta. "Wouldn't it be something if there were money in it? Sucres that Fuentes was stealing from his country?"

Cuesta glanced at him. "I would not be at all surprised. Fuentes is a notorious thief!"

"It would make an interesting situation if there were a lot of money, say, thousands of sucres."

Cuesta cast a look at him."

"I mean, as soon as Alvarez solidifies the Guayaquil government, the international banks will be trading in sucres again."

Cuesta was surprised at Pardal. He had not thought that the big man had enough brains to know about international banks. "So when did you become a financial expert?" he said.

Pardal shrugged his thick shoulders. "It would be an interesting situation, that is all. I mean. . .all that money. . .thousands of miles from Ecuador." He looked over his shoulder to make sure Morales was nowhere near them. Morales had gone to a hut to rest until Torreon and Nardo returned. "All that money for just the two of us."

Cuesta regarded Pardal impassively. "The two of

us?" he said.

Pardal made a face. "I'm only counting you and me."

A grunting sound came from Cuesta's throat. "In the first place, Pardal, it is unlikely that there is anything in the trunk but papers important to the Biaza government. In the second place, if any of us were to steal from Alvarez, he would send people after us."

"If he did not know where to look?" Pardal wondered. "He does not know we are in Mexico. Nobody does, outside this small group, if you follow me."

Cuesta nodded. "I follow you very well. But, believe me, Alvarez would be very patient about hunting us down. Very patient."

"Well. It was just an idea, of course." Pardal watched Cuesta's face closely. "Nothing serious."

He and Pardal broke open some supplies they had brought ashore from the yacht, and went under a coconut palm and ate some canned beans and tuna.

Meanwhile, Parrish sweated in the heat, wishing they would come back and get it over with. His ribs and lower leg still hurt, and now his face was swollen and throbbing. He was tensed and prepared for further pain. Flies buzzed around him, and he felt slightly faint, sitting there on the hard chair.

In early afternoon, Cuesta and Pardal finally returned to him. Pardal was carrying a length of pipe he had found in a hut on the edge of the camp, a galvanized iron weapon just over a foot long and about two inches in diameter. Seeing Pardal approach with it, Parrish calculated that he would last about five minutes under interrogation with that kind of *persuasion*. His only hope was that Cuesta would stop Pardal from killing him, hoping Parrish would talk later.

Pardal and Cuesta had just come up to Parrish, when the distant sound of a car engine was heard. Cuesta and Pardal immediately forgot Parrish again, watching the road opening into the forest. In just moments the small vehicle of Nardo came coughing into the compound, raising a small cloud of dust behind it.

"Get Parrish back into the men's hut. We'll tend to him later," Cuesta ordered.

Pardal evidenced no disappointment. He was as interested in the trunk, now, as he was in Parrish. He untied Parrish from the chair, and then shoved him roughly along. At the hut, Parrish was thrown inside, and the door re-barred.

Nardo and Torreon were unloading small packages of plastic explosives from the jeep. "We got it," Torreon told Cuesta, holding one package up. "And it's good stuff."

"Great," Cuesta said.

"There was no difficulty," Nardo told Cuesta. "No questions asked. But we learned some information that may be of interest to you."

Cuesta looked from the Indian to Torreon. Morales, who had gotten up when the vehicle arrived, now came over to the car, massaging his hurt arm.

"Guayaquil has fallen," Torreon said. But he was not smiling, Cuesta noted. "Our Alvaristas are in complete control of the country and the government."

Cuesta nodded. "I thought as much."

"Why, that is excellent news!" Morales said. "Now we can go home as heroes!"

Cuesta glanced at him without expression, then turned back to Torreon. "There is more, isn't there?"

"Yes," Torreon said. "Both Fuentes and Alvarez are dead."

Cuesta was not prepared for that. His mouth fell slightly open, and he just stared at Torreon. "Dead? Alvarez dead?"

"Holy Jesus!" Morales breathed.

Pardal stared past Torreon, trying to comprehend it.

"There are only rumors as to what happened. But he

228

died of a gunshot wound. Perez and Linares have taken control of the Alvaristas and the new government. The news people are calling it a military junta. The generals allege that Alvarez was murdered by some Biaza fanatics who got past the guards."

"They killed him," Cuesta said. "Perez and Linares."

"That was my conclusion," Torreon told him.

"He never trusted them," Cuesta added. He wondered if Perez would have approached him to join the conspiracy against Alvarez. There was no doubt in his mind what his decision would have been. Cuesta had no loyalty to anybody, no god but the god of power. If a man lived by more idealistic rules, he was a fool.

"Now what?" Pardal wondered. "Where does this leave us?"

Torreon made a grating sound in his throat. "We are on our own. If we return to Guayaquil, we have no idea how we will be received."

"Then let us not return to Ecuador," Pardal said.

Morales was frowning at him. "Not return? But what about the reform movement? If Alvarez has been betrayed by Perez and Linares, is there not good reason for us to return immediately? To help unseat these traitors to the cause?"

The other Alvaristas all looked at Morales, but said nothing.

"I have contacts in Mexico City," Nardo said. "I can get you papers that would keep you in this country as long as you wish."

Cuesta turned and looked at the battered trunk. "I think we must first open the trunk, as Alvarez instructed us. Then we will decide what our course of action ought to be."

Pardal nodded. "Agreed," he said more boldly than usual, realizing, suddenly, that Cuesta had no more authority there than any of them.

Torreon proved to be quite an expert with explosives. He worked slowly but efficiently. Minutes later, he had affixed the small blobs of explosives to the four locks and set the fuses. He turned to Cuesta. "It is ready."

Cuesta nodded. "All right, let's do it."

Torreon took the four fuses and twisted the ends of them together. "Get back!"

Cuesta, Morales and Pardal moved away from the trunk. Nardo was already standing at a distance from it. Torreon took a cigarette lighter from his pocket and touched the flame to the twisted fuses.

There was a sparkling of fire. Torreon ran back to join Cuesta and the others. They crouched low to the ground.

A yellow explosion detonated the tranquil scene, and smoke billowed around the trunk, obscuring it from view. When the smoke had cleared, the trunk's lid sat crookedly on its hinges. Every lock had been blown off. Torreon lifted the lid.

The five of them stared inside. There were stacks of files, documents and letters tied in bundles. Cuesta reached in and picked up a pile of letters, bundled neatly by some unknown ministry employee.

"It appears to be just as Fuentes said," Cuesta commented. There was as much disappointment in his voice as in Pardal's face.

"There is no money?" Pardal inquired over Cuesta's shoulder.

Torreon glanced at Pardal, and then looked back into the trunk more closely.

"No, apparently not," Cuesta said, digging through the papers.

"Why should there be money?" Morales said. "Nobody ever said there would be money."

Cuesta had stopped digging. "Hey, wait. Look at this."

Cuesta cleared a place with his hands. "There's a

false bottom, just six inches down, maybe eight."

"What?" Pardal said excitedly. He excitedly began removing papers and files from the trunk. Torreon and Cuesta joined him. A few moments later they had the false bottom cleared.

"Most of the trunk lies below this level," Cuesta said a little breathlessly. The surf washed up rhythmically behind him, and a gull shrieked out over the water. "Here. I think we can pry this corner upward."

Pardal helped with a wide-bladed knife. They pried and pulled, and suddenly the moveable wood divider came up. Cuesta pulled it away.

Their faces all changed.

"Jesus in heaven!" Morales said.

"I don't believe it!" Cuesta whispered.

"God*damn!*" Pardal exclaimed.

There were ancient Inca burial artifacts made of hammered gold. There was pre-Inca gold—jewelry, small statues, chains, ritual pieces. There were bags of precious gems, some old, some new—diamonds, rubies, emeralds from Colombia. There were rolled-up canvases painted by classic South American artists, as well as small works by Titian, Tintoretto, Goya, El Greco, Rivera. There was a leather-bound book of stamps, all valuable collectors' items. In one corner were two boxes of Spanish coins—doubloons and royals, worth thousands of dollars apiece.

"That bastard!" Cuesta said hollowly. "That greedy, soulless sonofabitch!"

But Pardal and Torreon were too excited by the riches before them to concern themselves about a dead enemy.

"It's. . .incredible!" Torreon said in a hushed voice.

"How much is it?" Nardo asked.

All four men turned toward him soberly. Pardal drew the .45 automatic he carried at his waist, aimed it at Nardo's chest, and fired off a blasting round. Nardo jumped backwards with the shot, a look of abject surprise on his face. Then he was on the sand, staring at Pardal as if he must be insane. He dug his right hand into the sand for a moment, and his eyes glazed over.

Pardal turned to Cuesta. "How much is it?" he asked, like a child full of wonder.

Eighteen

Pardal received no criticism for his shooting of their Mexican ally. None of the other three even mentioned the incident. They all turned back to the trunk, and Cuesta addressed himself to Pardal's question.

"It would require an expert to tell us with certainty," he said quietly. "But there are millions here, even measured by the holy American dollar. Millions upon millions."

Pardal licked heavy lips unconsciously.

"We cannot return it to Alvarez," Torreon said, watching Cuesta's face.

"And we sure as hell don't want to turn it over to Perez and Linares," Pardal put in.

"No," Cuesta said. "We don't want to do that."

Morales came up to Cuesta and looked into his face. "But Alvarez is not the movement! And this is stolen wealth, is it not? It surely belongs to the Ecuadorian people! It seems to me that we have an obligation to return to Ecuador, seek out the true followers of Alvarez, like ourselves, and use this capital to carry on with Alvarez' great fight for freedom."

Pardal turned and gave Morales a contemptuous look. "Are you joking, Morales?" He looked at Cuesta. "Is he joking?"

Cuesta sighed slightly. "What Pardal is trying to say, Morales, is that what you propose is impractical. There

233

probably are no reform leaders left in Ecuador. If Alvarez was killed, so were any Council members who might oppose Perez. The movement is dead. We must accept that fact, and go on from there."

"Also," Torreon put in, "it would be suicidal for any of us to return to Ecuador now. We were close to Alvarez. That would be enough for Perez to have us shot, or at best, thrown into a stinking prison for the rest of our lives. Is that what you want, Morales?"

Morales shrugged. "No, of course not."

Cuesta picked up a pre-Columbian burial mask and turned the gold over in his hands. "I don't think it's appropriate to concern ourselves with returning this to the Ecuadorian people, Morales. If we tried, we would fail, and it would be lost to those in power. This cache can never get back to the Ecuadorian people. So it is ours to do with as we think best."

Pardal and Torreon exchanged satisfied looks. Morales looked pensive. "Well," he said. "Maybe you're right, Jesus."

"Of course I am," Cuesta said smoothly. He put the mask down. "As leader of this expedition, I formally take possession of this cache, and I recommend that we divide it up among ourselves, to use as we see fit."

"I agree!" Pardal said vehemently.

"Of course, that does not imply equal shares," Cuesta hastily added. Pardal's and Torreon's grins washed away. "As a Council member, naturally I will take a larger amount for myself as payment for past services to the movement."

"There is no Council now, Jesus," Torreon said darkly.

Cuesta held his look. "I will be fair with you, don't worry. Each of you will be a rich man. I promise you."

Cuesta returned several items to the trunk, and then put the false bottom back in. "For now, let's replace these documents, and take the trunk to that larger hut."

234

Torreon did not move. "I can't speak for the others, but I want a full quarter share of the proceeds from the trunk."

Cuesta turned to him. "You are very bold, Torreon."

"Not so bold as you."

Cuesta cast a brittle look at Torreon. "I said we'll talk about it later," he growled, resting his hand on the butt of the pistol in his belt.

Torreon said nothing. Pardal went and somberly closed the lid of the trunk. Morales came over between Cuesta and Torreon, and regarded Cuesta with serious eyes.

"If we can manage to quit arguing about the riches in the trunk," he said sourly, "maybe we might talk about our prisoners. What are we to do with them now?"

Cuesta looked from Torreon to Morales. "What would you suggest we do with them, Morales?"

Morales shrugged. "Alvarez is dead. What purpose is there in killing them, now? We have prevented Salazar from getting his hands on Fuentes' trunk. And, as you pointed out, there is no movement to protect. Is there any need to commit further murders?"

Pardal frowned at Morales. "Damn, how you parade your stupidity!" he said harshly.

Morales scowled at Pardal.

"These are not murders we have committed," Cuesta said levelly to Morales. "I thought you understood that, Morales. They are political executions under the authority of the movement."

Morales shrugged. "Murder. . .execution. It is all killing. Maybe there has been enough, now that the movement has failed."

Pardal shook his head. "Jesus!"

But Cuesta had an answer that Morales would accept. "Are these people any less traitors to the cause, just because Alvarez is dead?" he suggested to Morales.

Morales' simple face looked perplexed. "I suppose

not," he replied uncertainly.

"Alvarez told us to kill them, not because he held any animosity toward them on a personal level, but because they are an affront to everything we fought for. Alvarez rightly said that an example must be made of them. The world must take notice. We cannot fail him now."

"I guess you are right, Jesus," he said, trying to absorb Cuesta's seductive argument.

"When will we do it?" Pardal wondered.

Cuesta looked over at him. "We'll be here another night or two, until we've made our plans. There is no hurry."

"Then I'll have my pleasure with the women," Torreon said.

"The same with me," Pardal quickly put in.

Cuesta raised his dark eyebrows. "Do what you will with the women. Later, this evening, we'll discuss the division of the cache, and what we'll do from this point on." He eyed Torreon. "Any questions?"

"I suppose there is no further point in questioning the prisoners?" Pardal said with disappointment.

"I see none," Cuesta said. "Let Salazar live out his exile in Florida. Who cares, now that the movement has failed?"

Morales shook his head slowly, but said nothing.

"Then let us get rid of Parrish and the boy, at least," Pardal said.

Cuesta pursed his lips. "No, there is time. They are no danger to us—a coward, a boy, and a middle-aged businessman. The contents of the trunk are our first consideration now. Should we convert it all to cash through a fence, or divide it up now? Where should we go, so that we may reap the greatest benefit from this windfall? The least dangerous thing would be to stay right here in Mexico. Many questions we must discuss later. McGill may be valuable to us in such a discussion. We will promise him his life, of course, and the lives of his family."

Inside the men's hut, Parrish stood at the one window and peered through the boards toward the compound, squinting to see better. "Yes, they shot the Indian, all right." He had reported to McGill and Tony that there had been rich-looking objects taken from the trunk. "The poor bastard must have asked for a share of the wealth."

McGill was sweating. The death of Nardo had reminded them all just how callous Cuesta and his men were. "What are they doing now?" McGill asked.

"Dragging the trunk away," Parrish said. "I can't see them now."

Parrish turned from the window and sat down next to McGill. Tony was leaning against a wall, looking scared and frustrated.

"So what was in that damned trunk?" Tony asked Parrish.

"I couldn't see well, but it looked like gold artifacts . . .maybe paintings. Probably stuff from museums. It seems that Fuentes was using you, Luther, to steal his government blind."

"Are you sure they said Fuentes is dead?" McGill said.

Parrish nodded. "And Alvarez. This is a bad situation for us. Even if Cuesta had had ideas of letting us go, he can't now, not if he keeps that trunkful of stuff."

"I don't think he ever intended to let us go," McGill said heavily.

"He won't care about Salazar now," Tony offered. "He won't give a damn about what we can tell him about Salazar, or anything else."

"That's probably true, Tony," Parrish said, watching Tony's tense face.

"So our lives are forfeit as of this moment," Tony

added.

"At least they've been diverted from Ana and Nita," Parrish reminded them, trying to think of something positive to say.

"I'd say we're out of time," McGill said.

Parrish nodded. "Yes. I don't know how, but we're going to have to try to make a move against them. And soon."

"I tried to untie Dad's ropes," Tony said. "It didn't work. And we can't do anything with our hands tied behind us."

Parrish looked around the hut. There was no furniture, no debris lying about. He got to his feet awkwardly, and moved about the hut. The interior walls were stuccoed mud bricks with white-wash. He saw nothing protruding from the walls, no sharp edges that would cut. Going to the window, he saw that a nail came through one of the boards, and it had a sharp point. But, there was no way for him or the others to get their bonds up high enough to the window. He turned toward the door, scanning its surface meticulously. He saw nothing at first. Then he spotted it—a primitive nail had come through the wood, one of the square-shaft kind, and had been bent over on the inside of the door, along a bracing beam. An exposed edge of its shank was close to razor sharp.

"Hey. Maybe I have something here," he said.

"What is it?" McGill said. He and Tony walked over to the door.

"This bent nail. . .it has an exposed edge. And it's at a good level." He felt the rope dig into his wrists when he moved them slightly. "My wrists are all swollen. I'd never get the cutting edge down to the rope. Let me see what your rope looks like, Tony."

Tony turned his back to Parrish, and Parrish examined the bonds. "Yeah. Yours are the best. Turn around to that door and let me guide you to the nail."

238

"God, do you think it will work?" McGill wondered.

"Hell, I don't know," Parrish said. "Even if we got our hands free, we'd have to get out of here without attracting attention. Then we'd have to somehow surprise our captors, unarmed, and survive a confrontation with them. But frankly, I don't know what else to do. It's better than just sitting here and waiting for death."

"Am I close?" Tony asked.

Parrish knelt beside Tony. Tony's hands were six inches above the bent nail. "You're going to have to lower yourself, Tony. Bend your knees some."

Tony followed Parrish's instructions. His rope touched the bent nail. "Okay?"

"Right on it," Parrish told him. "Now, push against it. That's it. Now, move your hands back and forth, gently. Get on the window, Luther. Tell us if you see or hear anything."

"Right," McGill acknowledged.

Tony moved his hands back and forth over the nail, slowly and forcefully. "I can feel the nail," he said.

"Yes, you're against it," Parrish told him. "The rope is fraying. Keep working at that same level. . .Yes, that's good."

Tony's arms and legs were trembling from the effort. "I have to rest," he said.

"That's okay," Parrish said. He bent and looked at the rope. "Yes, you've got a start on it. Several strands are frayed. We'll go back to it just as soon as you get your strength back."

"God," Tony said, leaning against the door. "I wish I could believe all of this is going to get us somewhere."

Outside a large dilapidated hut, where the trunk had been stashed, Morales was fixing a midday meal. He crouched in front of an open fire, while Torreon served as chef, barking out culinary orders. Inside the hut,

Cuesta and Pardal were discussing the advantages of settling for a while in Mexico City or Cuernavaca.

Torreon, impatient with Morales' progress with the torta batter, announced that he was going to get one of the women to assist Morales. Cuesta made no objection, so Torreon went to the women's hut alone. He had lost his interest in tortas, and was intent upon another kind of gratification.

When he entered the hut, his eyes fixed on Ana. She was sitting on the floor with her knees up, her thighs exposed.

"You," he said gruffly to Nita. "Can you cook tortas?"

Nita hesitated. "Yes," she said.

"Come with me," he told her. "You can help Morales. Don't worry, I'll bring you back here when you're finished there. Maybe we'll give you something to eat, eh?"

"All right," Nita said heavily. "But bring me right back to her."

"Of course," Torreon said easily.

He pulled Nita to her feet, led her outside into the sun, and crossed the compound.

"I've brought you an experienced cook," Torreon told Morales. "I'll eat later." He laughed and walked away.

When Torreon appeared inside the women's hut again, Ana merely looked up at him blankly. "Where is Nita?" she asked dully.

Torreon stared at her thighs and then knelt down beside her. He put a hand on her knee, and then moved it along under the side of her thigh. Ana jumped, and tried to draw away.

"Where is Nita?" she said again.

Torreon stroked the soft smooth flesh. "She is cooking. If you give me trouble, I'll give her to the other men."

"Oh, no," Ana murmured.

Torreon moved his hand up Ana's inner thigh. "If you're nice to me, Nita will be all right. Do you understand?"

Ana stared into his dark eyes and said nothing. She was trembling slightly. Torreon pushed her dress up above her hips. She flinched, but did nothing to stop him.

"You're a fine-looking woman," he said excitedly.

Ana cowered away from him.

Torreon moved behind her and began untying the bonds at her wrists. "I think this will be nicer for both of us. You see, we are not such bad fellows."

Ana's hands were untied. She brought them forward and rubbed at her swollen wrists. But she stopped abruptly when Torreon's hand pushed between her legs, caressing her. She quickly put her own hand over his, her eyes widening.

"Please! I am Luther's wife. He would not like this." Breathlessly, with great tension.

"But you will like it," Torreon grinned.

His hand moved more insistently on her. Ana, panicking, cringed away from him. "Don't! Don't touch me!"

Torreon moved over to her quickly, grabbed at the cloth on her hips and ripped it downward. It tore, and came off her. Torreon threw the cloth to one side, and then stared at her new nudity.

"No!" Ana yelled breathlessly. *"God, no!"*

Torreon unfastened his trousers, and reached for himself. Ana's eyes widened. *"Luther, help me!"*

Torreon struck her across the face with the flat of his hand. The slap resounded loudly in the hut. "If you keep that up, I'll take that daughter of yours next!" he told her harshly.

But Ana was beyond listening to reason. "Please! Please!"

Torreon forced her thighs further apart. Ana resisted,

241

but he was very strong. He grabbed at her legs and pulled her knees upward.

"Oh, God, don't do this!" Her voice was thick with hysteria.

"Shut up, you damned bitch!"

Ana was in the midst of a long, heart-breaking wail when Torreon mounted her, savagely thrusting into her. "There!" he growled. "Isn't that much better than your soft husband can give you?"

Tears streamed down her cheeks, and she had squeezed her eyes tightly shut. Torreon was moving, thrusting and mauling. The pain was bad for a couple of moments, then she did not feel it anymore. Finally he collapsed onto her, breathing heavily and sweating.

Ana lay there under him, but she was in Guayaquil, in her beautiful home, making lunch for McGill. There was a smell of jasmine coming through the kitchen windows.

"What's the matter, are you speechless with pleasure?" He frowned slightly, and separated them. Torreon rose and stood over her, adjusting his trousers. "You didn't do much to help," he said.

Ana's eyes, behind her closed lids, saw the sun-bathed patio and the delicate green vines resting against the garden wall.

"If you want to know the truth, it wasn't much."
Silence.

"I think you have forgotten how, with that milkweed husband of yours. Is that it?"
Silence.

Torreon did not like it that he was getting no answers. "Maybe your daughter will be better," he said.

Ana slowly opened her eyes.

"Did you hear me? I think we will try your daughter, now."

When Ana finally opened her mouth, a long, blood-curdling scream filled the hut, until Torreon's fist struck her hard across the face. She grunted under the impact, and fell silent again. Blood wormed out of the corner of her mouth.

"You stupid. . .woman!" Torreon hissed out.

Across the compound, Pardal had come out of the big hut at the sound of the screaming, arriving just in time to prevent Nita from running back to her mother. Nita fought and kicked and screamed as Pardal tied her to a support post on the side of the hut.

Inside the men's hut, McGill was rabid with fury and fear. He paced the hut in a frenzy now, swearing and shouting, "You bastards!" he shouted out the barred window. "You dirty, cowardly bastards! You sewer filth!"

"They did it," Tony said in a broken voice. "They couldn't leave them alone!"

"Come away from the window, Luther," Parrish said heavily. "You can't help Ana that way."

"If I could, I'd kill every one of these animals without mercy! I want to do terrible things to them, Jake! I want to tear them limb from limb!"

"I know, Luther," Parrish said quietly.

"Jesus Christ," Tony muttered, drying his eyes. "This is awful. This is bloody awful!"

Parrish looked from McGill to Tony. They were both in bad shape. They had to be careful, or they would lose the will to survive. "We can't give up, Luther," he said.

"Oh, my God," McGill moaned. "Oh, holy God."

Parrish went over to Tony. "Let's go back to the rope," he said.

Tony looked at him quizzically. "The rope? How the hell can I think about a goddamn rope now? I don't give a damn about that, Jake! To hell with it!"

Parrish stood there, not knowing what to say. It was Tony's mother who had been assaulted, and McGill's wife. Parrish felt like an outsider who had no entitlement to intervene in their anguish. But time was important.

"We have to think about escape," Parrish said gently. "To keep Ana out of further danger."

"Further danger!" Tony said loudly. "What further danger, for God's sake?"

McGill turned toward his son. His face sagged with pain. "Listen to Jake, son. We don't have time to feel sorry for ourselves. I just want a chance at them. Just one shot!"

Tony looked toward his father. "Shit!" he said bitterly. But he moved over to the door and turned his back to it.

Parrish knelt beside him. "Okay, Tony. Just a little lower. . .let's start again."

"You goddamn womanizer!" Cuesta spat out. Without any warning, he threw a hard fist into Torreon's face.

Torreon, caught off-guard, hit the ground on his back. He was gasping raggedly and holding his face, his eyes wild.

"What's the matter with you, are you crazy?"

"I told you!" Cuesta shouted down at him, looking stocky and dangerous standing over Torreon. "No trouble before I've spoken with McGill! I made it very plain!"

Torreon awkwardly got to his feet, eyeing Cuesta. "So, do you call this trouble? A couple of yelling women?"

"McGill will be furious, you cretin! Do you think he will want to discuss banks and art collectors now?"

"Don't ever hit me again, Jesus," Torreon growled at him. "Don't ever lay a hand on me again."

"He's right, you should have waited," Pardal said, siding with Cuesta. Torreon wondered if they had made some deal between them.

Over at the side of the hut, Nita stood tied to the post, glaring fiercely at them. Morales was near her, resuming his frying of tortas. "I don't like this," he said so Cuesta could hear him. "I don't like any of it."

"Let me go to my mother!" Nita said in a shaking voice. "Damn you, let me go to my mother!"

They ignored her.

"Now listen to me, both of you," Cuesta said. He glanced at Pardal, even though Pardal had stated his agreement. "There will be no further assaults on the prisoners—any of them—until I say so."

Morales made an acid sound in his throat.

"I mean it," Cuesta said to Torreon. "We have a changed situation here. We have riches within our grasp, but we have to begin acting like mature men. How to protect what has just become ours is the most important thing that we've ever had to consider. We need to know how to convert it to money without losing it to the authorities or thieves. We need to protect it and make it serve our futures. There will be all the women we want, when we have solved these problems. Surely we can restrain ourselves until then."

Torreon had made no attempt to interrupt the speech. Now he met Cuesta's gaze. "I'll find a way to make my share work for me," he said gruffly. "Once we've divided it up."

Cuesta narrowed his dark eyes on Torreon. "I should give you a share of the cache now, and set you loose in the jungle with it," he said quietly.

There was a silence among them. Finally, Cuesta turned to Pardal. "Go get McGill. Maybe it's not too late to talk with him, if I show him his wife and daughter are all right." He cast a hard look at the subdued Torreon. "Is she presentable? His wife?"

Torreon shrugged. "I suppose so. Although she was pretty crazy-acting when I left her."

"I wonder why," Cuesta said harshly. "Check her

out first, Pardal. But do not molest her!"

Pardal nodded casually. "Of course not," he said innocently.

In the men's hut, at that very moment, Parrish let out a low exclamation of surprise.

"That's it! It cut through!"

McGill came over and stared blankly at the cut rope on Tony's wrists, as Tony pulled and yanked it off him. McGill was so upset inside that he could not keep his mind on what Tony and Parrish had been doing.

Tony pulled his hands around in front of him, as the rope dropped to the floor. He was free. "I'll be damned," he said in disbelief. "I'll be damned."

"Luther, get over to the window," Parrish ordered McGill.

McGill dully followed orders. Tony was rubbing at his wrists, to get the circulation back. "Damn, it's like needles in them," Tony said.

"Are you all right?" Parrish asked. "Can you use your fingers?"

Tony nodded. "I think so."

"Good," Parrish said. "Here, untie me first. Then your father." He turned his back to Tony, so that Tony could get at the bonds on his wrists.

"God, your hands are all blue," Tony said to Parrish.

"Never mind. Just untie the rope. Quickly. Every second counts."

Tony knelt behind Parrish, fumbling with the bonds. They were tight, and he could not budge the knot. He grunted with the effort, working feverishly.

"I thought I heard something," McGill said quietly.

Parrish glanced toward him. "Is it somebody coming?"

"It might be."

"I've got the knot coming," Tony said. "The rope isn't cutting in as much, either."

246

"There's somebody out there," McGill said.

They could hear the sound of the bar sliding open. Tony and Parrish looked up quickly. "Hell!" Tony gritted out.

"Keep at it!" Parrish said urgently.

Suddenly, the door sprang open, and Pardal stood in the opening.

Tony had quickly turned away from Parrish, rising and putting his hands behind him. But Pardal had seen the movement. His eyes narrowed on Tony now. "What the hell is going on here?"

"Nothing," Tony said too quickly.

"You're free, aren't you?" Pardal growled, going for the gun at his waist.

Parrish saw the look of desperation in Tony's eyes. Then, Tony was hurling himself at Pardal. He slammed the big man against the door behind him, hitting out at Pardal with both fists. Parrish hurled himself at Pardal, smacking into him with his shoulder. Pardal, Parrish and Tony all went down at the doorway, a tangle of arms and legs. Parrish could do little after they hit the dirt floor, and Pardal was effectively blocking Tony's blows. He had managed to withdraw his gun and as Tony drew back to slug Pardal again, he swung the barrel against the side of Tony's head. Tony fell back, grunting in pain, dazed as he hit the floor.

Pardal got his feet under him and stood up, looking insane with fury, breathing hard. Parrish was still on the floor. Pardal kicked him savagely in the head, just as Parrish was trying to get up. Parrish hit the door and then fell to the ground, bleeding across the cheek, barely conscious. Tony, not far away, tried to get up off his back, but he was not seeing clearly.

Pardal stuck the muzzle of the Colt .45 into Tony's face. "I ought to kill both of you for this. If it were not for Cuesta, I would."

"Hey," McGill said. He seemed in a daze. He had

started for Pardal when they were all down, but had backed off when he saw the gun. "What are you doing? Leave my boy alone!"

Pardal looked up at him, very angry. He stuck the gun back into his waistband, then pulled a short length of rope from his pocket. He grabbed Tony and roughly pulled him over onto his stomach, tying his hands behind him more tightly this time. Tony grunted under the new pain.

"There, by God. Maybe that will hold you for a while longer." Pardal turned to Parrish. "I'll bet you freed him, didn't you, cabron? Eh?"

"You. . .figure it out," Parrish gasped out.

Pardal wanted to hurt Parrish, to beat him to death. But Cuesta would not approve. Not yet. He turned to McGill. "Cuesta wants to talk with you. Come with me."

"I want to see my wife!" McGill demanded, breathing as if he had just run a mile.

Pardal turned to Parrish. "You had better come, too. I think we ought to ask you some questions about what has been happening in here." He yanked Parrish to his feet. "Come on, let's go!"

McGill and Parrish were herded out through the doorway. Pardal locked Tony in, then prodded his two prisoners across the compound to the big hut.

As soon as McGill and Parrish got there, McGill saw Nita tied to the post. He broke from Pardal and went to her, his eyes moist. He had feared they had hurt her, too. "Oh, God, Nita!"

"Hi, Papa." She looked past him to Parrish, and saw the blood on Parrish's face. "Oh, Jake!"

"I'm okay," Parrish told her. "So is Tony."

Cuesta was sitting at a table, eating a canned meat tortilla. Torreon had finished eating and was staring at Parrish. Morales had gone off to tend to some chores.

"They had cut the boy loose," Pardal told Cuesta. "I

think it was this one." He jerked a thumb toward Parrish.

Cuesta, still chewing, rose from his chair, wiping his hands on his trousers. He was a millionaire, and no longer had to feel inferior to men like Luther McGill. He walked over to McGill, grinning. "Well. You had escape plans, eh?"

"I demand to see my wife!" McGill said, looking very pale and distraught.

Cuesta glanced at Parrish. "I didn't figure you as a man who had the guts to try an escape."

"Let me see my wife," McGill repeated, his face drawn and taut.

Cuesta turned to him again. "I promise you that you will be united with her, as soon as we have had a little talk."

"Talk?" McGill said. "I told you. I don't know anything about Salazar. No more than I've told you."

"No, no. I'm not speaking of Salazar. That is all finished, now. The fighting is over in Ecuador, and both Fuentes and Alvarez have perished in it. We need no longer be enemies."

"The Alvaristas have taken over Biaza's government?" McGill asked.

"The rebel generals have taken control," Cuesta told him. "Neither your friends nor mine, McGill. We have both lost, it seems."

Cuesta leaned against the hut wall. "As you probably have seen and heard from your hut, we have opened the Fuentes trunk, and found some interesting things inside it. It seems Fuentes was a thief, McGill." Cuesta grinned again. "But no mind. I'm presuming you knew nothing of the theft. And even if you had, it would make no difference now. Not to us, here."

"I was told I was taking government papers to Miami for Fuentes," McGill said blankly.

"Of course. You were duped by Fuentes just like all

249

of us were." Cuesta dropped his gaze to the ground. "My men and I are taking custody, for the time being, of the items inside the trunk," he went on. "And we are thinking of leaving them here in Mexico for safe-keeping. Also, we may have to convert certain of them to cash from time to time. We cannot return to Guayaquil, any more than you can."

"Should I take this one back to the hut?" Pardal asked Cuesta, disappointed in Cuesta's lack of interest in Parrish.

Cuesta turned to Parrish. "No, he can hear this. We have nothing to hide, now. What we want is your cooperation, in return for your lives."

McGill frowned at him.

"You're suggesting you'll set us free?" Parrish asked.

"Exactly," Cuesta said.

Parrish did not believe him, but he played along. "In exchange for what?" Parrish asked.

Cuesta glanced toward him impatiently. He turned back to McGill.

"You have spent some time in this nation's capital, is it not true?"

McGill nodded. "Yes."

"Then you probably know procedures necessary for procurement of safe deposit boxes?" Cuesta said.

McGill tried to concentrate on the questions. But all he could think of was Ana, and Tony with his bruised head. "Why, I suppose so," he replied.

"Is it necessary to be a citizen to obtain such a bank box?" Cuesta said.

McGill shook his head. "No. You fill out a form. If you're not a national, you show a visa or passport."

"Ah. Is it necessary to inventory what is in the box? For the bank?"

McGill tried to remember, tried to keep his mind on what Cuesta was saying. "I don't remember having to

250

do so."

Parrish spoke up again. "There are waiting lists, Cuesta. Some people have to wait years to get a box. And you'd have to have a lot of boxes, for what you've got in that trunk."

Cuesta turned to Parrish. It might be that he was talking to the wrong man. "In Ecuador, waiting lists can be circumvented, . .with small gifts," he grinned. "I would guess one might accomplish the same thing here."

"You might," Parrish admitted.

Cuesta turned back to McGill. "And what would the situation be in Mexico City, for disposing discreetly of gold artifacts and paintings?"

McGill glared at him. "I want to see my wife." He looked past Cuesta to Torreon, barely restraining himself from throwing himself at the man.

"Yes, yes," Cuesta said. "I told you, later."

"He wants to see her now," Parrish said evenly.

Cuesta gave Parrish a blistering look.

"Yes," McGill said firmly. "I want to see her now."

Cuesta turned from Parrish to McGill, then glanced at Torreon. Torreon shrugged. Cuesta spoke then to Pardal. "Go and bring Mrs. McGill," he said heavily.

Pardal stood there for a moment, questioning Cuesta's decision with his eyes. But then he turned and left.

"Now, about disposing of art and artifacts in the capital," Cuesta went on.

But McGill was unattentive. He stared after Pardal, trying to see if he had reached the women's hut. "Uh. . .Well, there are collectors in the city, of course." In a low monotone.

"There are a couple of well-known art collectors in the city," Parrish said.

Torreon was still at the table. "Cuesta is speaking to McGill. Why don't you shut your cabron mouth?"

Cuesta turned once again to Parrish. "What about artifacts? From the Incas and before?"

"There are probably collectors in the city. If it were me, I'd try a couple of museums first. If they weren't interested, the curators would probably be able to give you a list of collectors, if you went about it right. Most of them. . ."

He had noticed that McGill was staring across the compound, and so were Nita and Torreon. He turned and saw Pardal leading Ana by the arm.

"Oh!" Nita gasped out.

McGill's jaw had fallen open. "Ana," he said thickly.

Pardal led her up to them. Her dress was soiled, her dark hair hung wildly down about her shoulders, and her left eye was swollen, almost closed. She stared blankly past all of them, as if none of them were there.

McGill, his hands still tied, went over to her. "Ana! Oh, Jesus, Ana!"

Ana did not look at him. She stared out to the trees beyond the clearing, her dark eyes vacant of emotion or understanding.

"Cut his bonds, for God's sake!" Nita said, from the post. Her eyes were misty again.

Cuesta stared at her, and then looked toward McGill. He caught Pardal's eye and nodded. Pardal took a knife from a sheath on his hip, and cut McGill loose from the rope at his wrists. McGill moved quickly to Ana and put his hands on her shoulders.

"Ana. Look at me. Don't you know me?"

She glanced at his face as if she had never seen it before. McGill stood there for just a moment, while an animal sound began in his throat, and then he turned and threw himself across the table to get at Torreon. He hit Torreon hard, and they went down to the ground together, McGill going for Torreon's throat. Torreon, muttering obscenities, threw a hard punch into McGill's

252

head, and McGill fell back.

Torreon got to his feet. "Sonofabitch!" he growled out. He watched McGill warily as McGill also got awkwardly to his feet. But McGill did not attack him again. Instead, he suddenly reached for the .45 pistol on Pardal's belt.

Pardal had just started to turn away and was caught off-guard. Suddenly McGill had the .45 in hand. McGill was the only one armed now, except for Cuesta. Parrish was just about to warn him, when McGill turned to Torreon, holding the gun out in front of him.

"Luther, no. . ." Parrish shouted.

But it was too late. As McGill aimed the big gun awkwardly at Torreon's chest, Cuesta's pistol roared. McGill jumped sidewise, fell over the table, and hit the ground, the gun falling beside him.

"No!" Nita cried out. "No, no!"

Ana stared at her husband's inert body, her eyes empty of all expression. Parrish swallowed hard, watching the crimson flow of blood. "Good God," he muttered.

"What the hell did you have to do that for?" Cuesta said irritably.

Pardal knelt beside McGill and touched his throat. Then he turned his big face up to Cuesta and said, "He's dead."

Nineteen

Nita was inconsolable. Her sobs rent the hot air.

The two women were returned to their hut, their hands left free.

Parrish was led back to the men's hut. Very gently he told Tony about his father's death. Tony was so stunned that he could not speak. He slumped to the ground and just sat there, not responding to Parrish, not caring any more what happened to him.

Parrish was now responsible for their survival.

Out in the compound, Cuesta helped Torreon drag McGill's body beyond the huts and bury it in a shallow grave. Cuesta was in a bad mood, now. He blamed Pardal for letting McGill get hold of his gun, and he was also angry with himself—he wished that he had let McGill kill Torreon. Torreon was becoming a dangerous nuisance.

The four gunmen now sat around the table under the thatch canopy. "We can't stay here," Cuesta told them, his swarthy face damp with perspiration. "There may be people in that village who visit Nardo occasionally." Nardo, too, had been buried out beyond the huts. "The question is, where are we going? If we're going by land, we'll use the jeep and destroy the yacht. I say we should pack the artifacts and other things into bags, load them into the jeep, and drive to the capital. Nobody will

254

know we are here illegally. We have Ecuadorian passports. We can stash the stuff in several banks until we can find buyers. The proceeds, of course, will be 'clean' money, which we can deposit in our own new accounts."

"That sounds like a good plan, Jesus," Pardal agreed with him. "We could not get this stuff safely into the United States, anyway, without great risk. We don't know the Florida coast like Sumner did."

Morales was very quiet. McGill's death had disturbed him. "How far is it to the capital here?" he wondered.

Cuesta shrugged. "One day's drive, maybe two. Once there, we would be lost in the city, no one would ask any questions or give us a second look."

"Let's talk about the loot," Torreon said flatly. "And how you intend to divide it up."

Cuesta looked across at him. "I blamed Pardal for McGill's death," he said deliberately. "But it was really you who caused it, Torreon. By mauling the McGill woman. I should cut you out of the shares completely."

Torreon was still unarmed, so he went carefully. "Cut me out?" He said in a hard voice.

"I should, but I have no plans to do so," Cuesta told him. "I propose an equitable distribution, one that ignores the trouble you have caused us here." He paused significantly. "I will take forty percent of the proceeds for myself. I am, after all, an officer of the movement and a member of the Council. The rest of you will share the balance. Twenty percent of this cache should make you very wealthy men."

"You take twice as much as we get?" Torreon said glumly.

"It is only fair," Cuesta said, holding Torreon's hard gaze, "considering the responsibilities each of us has borne. Do you take issue with it?"

"I take issue with your logic," Torreon said. "We all shared the dangers during the fighting and on this

255

mission. McGill came close to killing me with this one's gun.'' Her jerked his head toward Pardal. "And Morales was wounded by that freighter captain's shotgun."

Morales turned to Torreon. "I don't want any of it," he said.

Torreon looked at him incredulously, as if Morales had gone crazy with the heat. "What?"

"That's right," Morales said, turning to Cuesta. "I want nothing. I will settle for the yacht so that I can leave by the sea. There is a little port I know in Cuba where I would be accepted without question. I have distant relatives who emigrated there from Ecuador in the fifties."

Cuesta raised his dark eyebrows in surprise. "Well. Of course, if you have no interest in the cache. You could have the yacht, yes. And I won't claim a bigger share, it can go to you, Torreon, and Pardal. That will give you thirty percent apiece, instead of twenty. Would that satisfy you?"

Torreon hesitated only a moment. "Yes," he said.

"That would be quite generous, Jesus," Pardal offered. He turned to Morales. "But are you certain?"

"I am certain," Morales told them. "I want to get all of this behind me. An unpleasant task awaits us, and I will help in that. The McGills and Parrish must be killed, I see that. Although I personally would spare the women. When that is finished, I'll leave in the yacht."

Cuesta nodded. "Very well." He looked up at the mid-afternoon sun. "It could be done yet today, if you wish. I doubt that I can get any more of value from Parrish, anyway."

"I'm for getting it over with," Pardal said. "The men, of course. There is no hurry with the women."

Morales gave him a narrow look.

"There are a couple of things I would like to get off the boat," Pardal said. "If you're sailing later today."

256

Morales nodded. "Yes, later today. Perhaps after an early evening meal here."

Cuesta turned to Pardal. "All right, you go get what you want off the yacht. Torreon, you go get the automatic rifles, and then let's have a little talk before you go get the men."

Torreon nodded. He headed toward the small hut where the guns were hidden under some palm fronds. Morales rose heavily and followed after him.

Pardal walked down to the water, Cuesta going along to help push him off in the white dinghy. The sun glinted off the water and into their eyes. The surf splashed dully onto the sand. Pardal threw the small anchor into the dinghy, and Cuesta helped him shove the boat down into the water. Pardal turned to him, then.

"The shares narrow in number," he said.

"Yes," Cuesta said. "I've never understood what is in that Morales' head. But, if he wants to give up his interests to us, it only makes the division of the loot a more comfortable one."

Pardal stood beside the dinghy, his bald head sweating slightly in the sun, his bare feet in the surf. "We could make it even more comfortable," he said.

Cuesta held his squint-eyed look. "Yes?"

"When Morales is gone. We could, if we wished, narrow the division of the shares even further. You and I."

"Torreon?" Cuesta said.

"Yes, Torreon. You said it yourself, he does not deserve a share. Also, the fewer of us involved, the better. I think you would agree with that."

"I didn't think you were so enterprising, Pardal."

"I would be satisfied with forty percent of the proceeds," Pardal told him. "That would give you sixty, Jesus."

Cuesta grinned slightly. "Then you think the life of a compatriot is worth a larger share to us?"

257

"If it is Torreon's, why not?" Pardal replied evenly.

Cuesta eyed him with new interest. "You wouldn't have your sights set on my sixty percent, too. Would you, Pardal?"

Pardal's face was expressionless. "The thought never occurred to me, Jesus."

Cuesta nodded. "Go get your stuff off the boat. I'll give your idea some thought."

Pardal grinned harshly, got into the dinghy, and pushed off. Cuesta watched him soberly for a couple of moments, as he rowed out toward the *Sea Witch*. Then he turned and headed up toward the big hut.

Torreon and Morales were already there, with the two M-16's. Cuesta came up to them and sat down on the edge of the table. There was still a low fire in the stone pit and the residual smell of their meal. They had not bothered offering the captives food or water.

"You will take care of the men now," Cuesta said. "And since we may be here for a couple of nights yet, I don't want the corpses piling up around us. These shallow graves do not hide much. Take Parrish and the boy out into the jungle. Nardo said there is a small Mayan ruin directly to the west several hundred yards, maybe a half-mile. That would be a good place. Try to hide them under some brush."

Torreon nodded. "No problem."

Cuesta rubbed his chin. "In fact, maybe you had better give them a quick burial, like Nardo and McGill. There are Indians in this jungle. We don't want any trouble before we get out of here."

"We could make them dig their own graves," Torreon said.

Cuesta nodded. "Not a bad idea. It's an old Mexican custom."

"There is an extra shovel," Morales said somberly. He wanted to get all this over with. "I'll get both of them."

Morales left for a moment, and Cuesta turned to Torreon. "Leave one of the automatic rifles here, just in case. I'll give Morales this pistol."

Torreon took a magazine of cartridges from his pocket and jammed it into the hefty-looking gun. Then he worked a cartridge into the chamber. He looked very deadly, with the gun. Cuesta, watching him, decided he looked too deadly. Torreon was trouble. Tonight, when Torreon was relaxed, perhaps sleeping, he and Pardal would put an end to Torreon's violence. Morales would not be there to raise moral issues; he would be on his way to Cuba.

In the women's hut, Nita huddled beside her mother and wept silently. Her father was dead, and her mother might never return from that dark place where she had retreated. Nita had already lost both her parents, and there was more to come. Much more. Tony and Parrish would be murdered next, and then she would be left alone with her blankly staring mother. The rebels would use them then, entertain themselves with them, before killing them. That was her future. She had no illusions.

"Mother, are you comfortable?"

Ana did not hear her.

"Papa always said that it is not the length of life that counts, but how it is spent. How we make the most of the time we have."

Ana turned to gaze dully at her.

"I think he would want us to remember that," Nita told her.

Ana turned away, looking across the dimness of the hut. "You aren't properly dressed yet, Nita. You mustn't be late for school. I've told you before, they won't tolerate tardiness."

Nita studied her mother's bruised face. At least she had spoken. But the sound of her voice choked Nita up inside.

259

"Can you hear me, Mother? Will you talk to me?"

Ana turned to her. "Where's Tony?"

Nita swallowed back her welling emotion. "He's with Jake."

"Well, I know he hasn't had any breakfast. He always tries to get out of the house without any breakfast. Will you tell him I have eggs for him here?"

Tears streamed down Nita's cheeks. "Yes, Mother. I'll tell him."

Ana had walled herself away. The past had become her reality. The past was safe and gentle. She licked her dry lips. "Tony has to learn that breakfast is an important meal. I wish you'd impress that on him, Nita."

Nita nodded, her lower lip trembling. "I'll have a talk with him, Mother. I promise."

Suddenly, she stopped breathing. There was the sound of men's voices and footsteps, but they were not coming to her hut. They were going to Tony and Parrish.

"Oh, God," she wailed under her breath. "Oh, God."

Just a short distance away in the men's hut, Parrish and Tony had heard the voices of Torreon and Morales, too. Parrish had been trying to cut his own bonds against the same nail that Tony had successfully used before, but had had little luck. Now he turned to Tony quickly.

"They're coming for us," he said, his mouth dry with fear. But it was not a paralyzing fear; it was the kind that made his adrenalin flow and galvanized him for defense.

Tony looked very scared. "We're still tied up. What can we do?"

"I don't know," Parrish admitted. "Hope for opportunity, I guess. If it comes, we have to be ready to take advantage of it. Okay?"

Tony nodded. "Okay." His voice was uneven and hoarse. "I'll try to. . ."

He stopped. The bar was being slid away from the door.

In a moment, the d;or swung open. Morales stood there, Torreon beside him. Torreon held the M-16 lightly in his grasp, and Morales had a pistol in his belt. He carried two shovels under his arm.

"All right. Out," Morales said gruffly.

Parrish went first, eyeing the automatic rifle.

Tony came out after him. "What are you going to do with us?" he asked fearfully.

"We are going for a little walk in the woods," Torreon said pleasantly. "To do some digging at a Mayan ruin."

Parrish knew exactly what they had in mind. This would be the end of it for them, if they could not think of something, if some good luck did not come their way. He glanced toward Cuesta, and Pardal who was now beaching the dinghy, and was glad that at least there would be only two of them.

"Let's go," Torreon ordered, prodding Parrish with the rifle.

The four of them started out, Parrish in front, then Tony, then Torreon, and finally Morales with the shovels.

Parrish moved into the trees at the back of the clearing, with the others close behind. There was a trail through small trees and underbrush, but then the path disappeared into the wild growth. It was late afternoon and very hot. Sweat ran down their faces, their shirts sticking to their backs and chests. Mosquitoes attacked them, and neither Parrish nor Tony could defend themselves from them. The insects whined in their ears, and bushes slapped at their faces. Morales took the lead position and guided them due west.

Finally, a stone structure appeared in a small clearing,

and Morales halted them there. The structure was cubic in shape, with a mound of dirt on its top, and crumbling ancient stones for walls. It had been a Mayan outpost of some kind. There were a few glyphs and serpent's heads cut into the stone.

"This is it," Morales said.

Torreon nodded and looked around at the ground. There was no underbrush underfoot, and the ground looked as if it might allow easy digging up against the rear wall of the structure.

"Okay, you two, over here!" Torreon commanded Tony and Parrish.

Morales dropped the shovels, and then quickly cut Tony's bonds, then Parrish's. "Now," Morales told them. "Take the shovels, and dig. You will need a hole three feet by six and three deep."

"Our graves," Tony said.

Morales did not respond.

"I want a separate grave," Tony said. "It's a last request, and it's a reasonable one."

"One hole," Torreon said in a low voice.

Tony glared at him for a moment, then picked up a shovel. Parrish did likewise. They began digging, starting at opposite ends, facing each other. Parrish ran into a root and cut through it with a few chops of the shovel blade. Morales stood only a few feet from the hole. He had drawn the .45 pistol and was holding it at his side. Torreon was leaning against the nearby wall of the ruin, a creeping vine at his back. He held the rifle cradled in both hands, his finger in its trigger assembly.

"Come on, hurry it up!" Torreon said impatiently. "We don't have all day for this!"

Morales glanced toward him soberly. Tony looked up, sweat running down onto his face. "You think this is easy? Why don't you try it yourself?"

Torreon grinned. "It is going to give me a certain amount of pleasure to kill you, offspring of McGill.

Almost as much as this cabron beside you.''

Parrish glanced at Tony and caught his eye, then stabbed his shovel into the rocky ground abruptly. ''The boy's right, this is tough. We can't dig here. There are too many roots. We'll have to dig on the other side of the ruin.''

''You will dig right there!'' Torreon said flatly.

''There's a root here as big as my thigh, goddamn it! Look!''

Tony understood that this was it. Parrish was going into an act to make a play against Torreon. Torreon hesitated a moment, and came over to the edge of the partially-dug hole. ''What root?'' he said gratingly.

''Stand away from them!'' Morales said loudly, seeing Torreon bend toward the hole.

But his warning came too late. Parrish swung the flat blade of the shovel savagely into Torreon's face. The shovel struck Torreon hard, catching him by surprise. His eyes widened as his nose fractured in three places and his jaw cracked under the impact. He went flying backwards, holding tightly onto the rifle, and hitting the ground with his legs in the air.

Morales made a growling sound in his throat. He aimed the pistol at Parrish's back. But Tony was already lunging toward Morales from the side, his hands going for Morales's neck. He hit Morales with all his weight, knocking the bigger man off-balance. The pistol went off, the hot slug digging into the ground.

Parrish leapt from the hole, the shovel still in hand. Bloodied Torreon was rising off the ground, trying to aim the rifle at Parrish, but he couldn't see clearly through the pain and his tearing eyes. Parrish swung at the rifle with the shovel, and the gun was knocked from Torreon's grasp. Torreon rolled onto his side and tried to scramble to his feet. Parrish got a good hold on the shovel and swung his weapon a last time, aiming at the side of Torreon's head. This time the thick steel hit

263

Torreon with tremendous force. There was a loud cracking sound as Torreon's skull caved in under the blow, and he collapsed onto the ground. Blood began seeping through his hair, his ear, his eyes.

Tony and Morales were wrestling for the gun. Morales broke loose from Tony's grip, struck Tony across the neck and shoulder with the barrel of the gun, and rolled away from Tony. Coming up onto one knee, he aimed the gun at Tony's face.

But Parrish had dived for the rifle, and now he swung it toward Morales and squeezed the trigger. The big gun clattered raucously in his ears. Five hot slugs were stitched across Morales' back. He arched against them, and then fell back, his eyes staring out into the jungle.

Tony could not believe it. "We did it!" he said hollowly. "We actually did it!"

Parrish rose, holding the M-16 loosely at his side. "You did great, kid," he said.

Tony got up and looked at Morales, then came over and stared hard at the bashed-in Torreon. "Jesus Christ. Jesus Christ!"

"Are you okay?"

Tony swallowed, and nodded. "Yeah."

"If they heard all that, I'm hoping they'll think it was Torreon and Morales letting us have it," Parrish said.

Tony was staring at him in a different way. "I've said some crazy things to you. . .some very crazy things. I should have had faith in you."

"You had no cause," Parrish said. He held the thick gun up at chest level. "You ever shot one of these things?"

Tony shook his head. "No," he said.

"Okay, get Morales' pistol and any ammo he has on him. "We can't delay now. Cuesta will be expecting Torreon and Morales back."

Tony retrieved Morales' pistol and an extra magazine of cartridges. "Okay. I'm ready," he said.

Parrish caught his gaze. "It's the lives of the women at stake now, Tony. There can't be any mistakes from here on in."

"I understand," Tony said breathlessly.

"Then let's get back there," Parrish told him.

Twenty

Ana jumped as the door of the hut swung open and big Pardal stood there. The sun seemed to armour his arms and legs with a white metal. Ana stared in awe of the sun-lighted figure.

Nita put a hand on her mother's arm. "What do you want?" she said in a hushed voice.

"Well. I see you have made yourselves comfortable. It feels better with the ropes off, heh?"

Nita just glared upward at him.

"Is that you, Luther?" Ana said.

Nita glanced toward her. "It's all right, Mother."

Pardal grinned down at them. "We tried to make you more comfortable while you wait, yes? Now you can repay us."

"Where are Tony and Jake Parrish?" Nita said, almost afraid to ask. "I thought I heard shooting."

"Shooting? Ah, that was probably Torreon. He is out hunting for deer. Your men are tied up in their hut. If you cooperate, they will live."

"Cooperate?" Nita said darkly.

"Yes, you come with me. We will have a few drinks, and who knows what nice things will happen."

Nita looked at him with fire in her eyes. "You talk of drinking, you ape, when you have just killed my father?"

Pardal frowned. He came over to Nita, grabbed her

arm, and yanked her roughly to her feet. He held her close, and put a big hand on one of her breasts. She jerked away, but he held her, and replaced the hand. He moved it slowly on her.

"We can do this easily," he growled, "or with difficulty. It is up to you."

Nita felt the hand on her breast, and the touch of him made her nauseous inside. "Get your hands off me, damn you!"

Ana, still sitting on the floor, looked upward at them. "I want you to help me get lunch ready, Nita. Your father always likes his lunch on time."

Nita glanced at her mother. Nita was alone, for all practical purposes, and it was a chilling thought.

"I could take her, instead," Pardal threatened Nita, with a harsh grin.

Nita met his hard look fearfully. He grinned, and pulled her to him, mauling her mouth with his. She squirmed and pushed to get away from him, and finally broke free, gasping for breath.

Pardal had enjoyed the struggling. "Or, if you give me too much trouble, I can go shoot your boy friend," he added.

"Don't. . .do that," she murmured.

"Then come with me. Quietly," Pardal advised her.

Nita hesitated, looking down at Ana. Then she turned and moved out through the open doorway. Pardal followed her, closing and locking the door behind him.

Impulsively, she turned toward the men's hut, and called out urgently, "Jake! Are you there? Tony?"

No reply answered her. Pardal grabbed her roughly by the arm and moved her along. "Never mind that! Come along!" Pardal warned her.

But with the silence from the men's hut, a sudden anger rose into Nita's chest, and she turned and began hitting out at Pardal. "You killed them, you murderers! You killed them!"

Pardal was having a time holding her. His hand grabbed at her shirt, and he savagely ripped at it. It opened up along the front, buttons flying, and tore away at the collar. Pardal grabbed at it again, from the back, and tore it off her.

"Damn you!" she cried out. "Damn you!"

Behind Nita about twenty feet was a fish rack that Nardo the Indian had used to dry fish he had caught. It consisted of two poles driven into the sand, and two horizontal boards nailed between them. The whole thing was only chest-high, and four feet wide. Pardal glanced at the rack, then grabbed at Nita again.

Nita pulled away from him, and fell to the ground. Pardal, grinning, fell to his knees beside her, and began unfastening the slacks at her waist. She fought him, but it did not help her much. The slacks came down, over her hips, then her thighs. Nita hit out at him fiercely, but he absorbed the blows without flinching.

In a moment, Nita was denuded of the slacks, and had only a wispy pair of panties on her hips.

"Well!" Pardal breathed.

He wanted to take her right there, in the hot sun. It was more than a man could stand, just looking at all those curves and the dark place between her thighs that showed beneath the sheer nylon cloth. But he had promised Cuesta. He had said he would wait for Torreon's return. Then, while Morales busied himself with the evening meal, and later prepared the yacht for leaving, Pardal, Torreon and Cuesta would take Nita to the men's hut and take turns with her.

Pardal dragged Nita to her feet. She was gasping raggedly, and had streaks of dirt on her body, and red marks from Pardal's rough hands. He pulled her to the fish rack, found a length of rope hanging there, and tied her hands to a cross-bar of the rack.

Nita slumped there numbly. Pardal grinned at her, taking a big hand and moving it harshly over her breasts, her hips. Irritated by the thin cloth, he ripped it off her in one quick movement. She jumped, weakly. "Oh, God."

Pardal shoved the hand between her legs, breathless himself, and fondled her there, looking directly into her face. She turned her head, avoiding his hungry stare.

"When Torreon returns from. . .hunting," Pardal breathed, "he will have a pleasant sight to greet him, heh?"

Nita moaned in her throat. Pardal looked past her, and saw Cuesta come and stand before the big hut, looking toward them.

"What are you doing with her?" Cuesta called out.

Pardal grinned. "Just getting her ready."

"Well, leave her for a moment. I want to show you these gems. I think they may be worth more than I thought."

Pardal nodded reluctantly. He took the hand away. "All right, I'll be right there."

Pardal looked into Nita's tear-streaked face. "Don't worry, we won't forget you, little pigeon. By nightfall you will be plucked clean." He laughed harshly, and she could smell liquor on his foul breath. He turned and headed for the big hut.

Nita slumped against the rack, naked in the sun. All she could do now was wait.

For all of it to be over.

A hundred yards away, in the cover of the jungle, Parrish and Tony crept up to the edge of the clearing. Birds had fled the trees before them, and even insect sounds had stopped. Parrish, recalling his violent days in the Asian jungles, knew that lack of sound could be a warning to an alert enemy. He hoped that Cuesta and Pardal were thinking of something else. Of that if they thought of the silence at all, they would attribute it to the approach of Torreon and Morales.

269

Just a short distance from the edge of the clearing, Parrish stopped and knelt on one knee, holding his hand up for Tony to stop. Tony came up and stood just behind him, holding the .45 pistol at ready. Parrish had rested the M-16 across the bent knee.

"I can see into the compound," Parrish whispered. "But there doesn't seem to be anybody moving around."

"We'd better get in there," Tony said nervously.

"Not too fast," Parrish said. "Too fast could be suicidal. And that wouldn't help anybody."

Kneeling there and scanning the clearing, Parrish could not see Nita who was hidden from view by a hut. He recalled a hot day very like this one, years before, when he and several other soldiers were creeping up on a Cong-infiltrated village. The Cong were believed to be expecting them, so it was a similar situation to this one. Except that Cuesta was expecting Torreon and Morales to appear from the trees.

He crouched there, watching and listening. He decided to circle around at the perimeter of the encampment, so that he and Tony would have a front view of that hut. He rose, and motioned Tony forward.

They moved off to the right, circling the clearing in the trees. Quietly. Slowly. They moved around in back of the hut they had shared with McGill, and beyond it, and then Parrish crept up to the very edge of the clearing.

When he got there, he stared hard toward the center of the compound. His eyes narrowed down, and a hard look came onto his handsome face. "Jesus!" he whispered.

Tony, beside him now, stared wide-eyed toward Nita, slumped against the fish rack. She was dirt-streaked and bruised-looking. Her hair was down and unruly, her nakedness burning under the sun.

"Nita!" Tony said hoarsely in his throat, and he

started forward.

But Parrish put a hand out and grabbed him. "No," he said quietly.

Tony looked at him wildly.

Parrish put a finger to his lips, and beckoned for Tony to follow him. Tony suppressed the emotions that were boiling through him like hot oil, and moved through the trees behind Parrish.

Parrish edged up to the tree line, kneeling beside a bushy shrub. Tony came up beside him, breathing shallowly now. They were nearer Nita, and had a frontal view of the big hut. As they watched, Pardal and Cuesta came out of the hut, and Pardal stared at Nita.

"Keep down!" Parrish whispered.

"That sonofabitch!" Tony whispered harshly. "What's he done to her?"

"Maybe nothing much, yet," Parrish replied.

Over at the hut, Cuesta looked toward the edge of trees, not far from Parrish and Tony. "I wonder what's keeping Torreon and Morales?" he said seriously. "They should have had time to fill that hole in by now."

"I think I'll go untie the girl and take her to the hut," Pardal said hungrily. "I've waited long enough for Torreon."

Cuesta turned to him. "All right, but help me move this table further into the shade first," he said. "I'm going to examine some of those documents out here, later."

The two went around to the side of the hut, and were momentarily out of sight. Suddenly, with a quickness that surprised Tony, Parrish moved out into the clearing. Tony hesitated only a half-second, then followed.

Nita, bruised and naked, sagged at the rack with her eyes shut against the sunlight. Then she opened her eyes, and saw Jake Parrish run up to her, Tony right behind him. Nita's eyes widened in disbelief as Parrish stopped before her. She started to speak, but Parrish put a hand gently over her mouth. "Where's Ana?" he whispered.

"Still in the small hut."

She glanced past Parrish to Tony with the pistol in his hand, and tears sprang into her eyes. Parrish was untying her hands, and in a moment she was free. Tony had gathered up her clothing, and they now hurried her to the women's hut. Parrish slid the bar from the door and swung it open slightly. Ana looked up at them blankly.

"Get in there and stay there until it's over," Parrish said quietly to Nita.

She looked down at the M-16 that hung at Parrish's side in his right hand. "All right, Jake." She looked over to Tony. "Please be careful!"

"I will, little sister," Tony said thickly, his eyes moist.

Parrish closed the door on her, and slid the bar back in place. When he turned back toward the big hut, Pardal had come around to the front again and was visible to them. He was talking to Cuesta. Parrish motioned to Tony, and they moved out of sight behind the women's hut.

Parrish led Tony around to the other side of the hut, and they watched Pardal.

"He's going to come down here," Tony said quietly.

Parrish nodded. "He hasn't noticed Nita's absence at the fish rack yet. But he will shortly. He'll come over here looking for her. He has only a pistol, so Cuesta must have the M-16 somewhere there. I'm going to have to leave you here to take Pardal."

Tony met his gaze with a scared one.

"Give me the pistol," Parrish told him.

Tony regarded him curiously, but gave the gun over. Parrish stuck it into his waistband, then held the M-16 up so Tony could see it. "You're going to have to use this after all. It's ready for firing, safety off, automatic fire. Fire only quick short bursts, or the gun will carry upward and off your target. Aim for center chest and. . ."

"Look," Tony said breathlessly. "Here he comes."

Parrish saw Pardal heading across the compound. He gave Tony the big gun. "Wait till he gets in close, and surprise him. Don't shoot toward the hut, Nita and Ana are in there."

Tony nodded, and then Parrish disappeared into the trees where he would find Cuesta.

Pardal, out in the middle of the compound, stopped short and stared in disbelief at the fish rack. "Hey!" he muttered. He just glared at it for a moment, then drew the .45 and began running toward it. When he got there, he examined the untied rope, and Tony saw a frown grow on his square face. Tony glanced toward the trees, hoping Parrish had reached the big hut.

"Sonofabitch!" Pardal said aloud. He looked at the sand under his feet for prints, but there were too many there for him to read what had happened. He came striding toward the women's hut, disappearing from Tony's view. Tony heard him pause, and he knew that Pardal was studying the bar across the door. Then Tony heard Pardal's gruff voice yelling to Cuesta.

"The girl is gone!"

Cuesta's voice came back from the far side of the big hut: "What?"

In the next moment, Pardal started around the hut, without waiting to reply to Cuesta. He came red-faced and sweating, the pistol out in front of him, watching the ground for prints. When he came into view of Tony, he looked very angry, and frustrated.

"Goddamn women!" Tony heard him grumble. He stared into the trees. "Are you out there, damn you? We'll come after you, if you are! You'd better come back now, while it will go easy with you!"

Then he turned and looked right at Tony.

Pardal was thirty feet away. Pardal had lowered the .45 to his side, and Tony had the drop on him. Pardal's eyes widened slightly, then narrowed down to hard slits.

"You!" he hissed out.

Tony held the automatic rifle trained on Pardal's chest, as Parrish had told him to do. But, with the gun hanging at Pardal's side, Tony could not pull the trigger. He froze. He had never killed a man before, not by himself.

Pardal saw the hesitation. "Are you alone?" His eyes darted from right to left, scanning the immediate area.

Tony knew he had to do it, before Pardal managed somehow to kill him.

"I'll bet you've never fired one of those things before," Pardal grinned. "They're very tricky. If you don't use them just so. . ."

As Pardal talked, he had raised the gun muzzle slightly. Now he jerked it up quickly, and fired a blast at Tony.

Tony had seen the movement and dropped into a crouch, the big slug from the .45 tugging at his sleeve but not hitting him. In the next split-instant, Tony was squeezing the trigger of the M-16. He rattled off a short blast and caught Pardal in the lower chest. The spray of hot lead exploded across Pardal, from lower left to high right, busting a floating rib, punching him under the heart, rupturing his aorta, breaking his collar bone. Pardal was flung into a tight pirouette, and then seemed to dive to the ground on his face. Tony, flushed in the cheeks now, came closer, his eyes glazed over slightly.

"You dirty bastard! You filthy coward!" He fired the gun again at Pardal's prone figure, raking lead across Pardal's back. The figure jumped and jerked under the impact. "You goddam murderer!" Another hail of hot lead clattered out of the gun, and new holes appeared in Pardal—in his thighs, buttocks, back, neck.

274

Finally Tony dropped the smoking gun to his side, and just stood over Pardal, breathing hard. An acrid odor hung thick and heavy in the air from the gunsmoke. Pardal's body was blood-splashed and mauled. A leg twitched as if pulled by a string.

From inside the women's hut, not far away, he heard Nita's voice. "Tony?"

"I'm all right, Nita!" he replied. Then he turned toward the big hut. It was surprisingly quiet.

Over behind the big hut, Parrish stood at the perimeter of the clearing. He had heard the rattling of the M-16, and hoped Tony had killed Pardal and was all right.

The compound was deadly quiet. In the jungle somewhere, a bird cried raucously. He looked toward the women's hut, but caught no sight of Tony. Moving to the hut's doorway, he suddenly lunged through it, the gun ready.

Cuesta was not there. Parrish frowned, looking around. There was a musty dead smell in there. The Fuentes trunk sat in the center of the room, its lid closed. But on a table at the rear sat a metal box from the trunk, and Parrish surmised it was a jewel box. He turned and stared out through the doorway.

Cuesta had reacted quickly to the shooting, and had taken evasive action.

Parrish moved back out through the doorway, and suddenly heard Cuesta's voice.

"Here I am, Parrish."

Parrish froze. Slowly turning his head, he saw Cuesta standing only fifteen feet away, pointing the other M-16 at his back. "Drop the gun. Without moving," Cuesta ordered him, in a quiet voice.

Parrish hesitated, sighed heavily, and let the .45 fall to the ground. He looked for Tony out of the corner of his eye, and still saw nothing.

"Now," Cuesta said. "Come over here, by the table. Slowly."

Parrish turned and faced Cuesta. Cuesta was shirtless, holding the M-16 carefully trained on Parrish. Parrish moved over to the table under the thatch canopy, not far from Cuesta.

"Very good," Cuesta said. "Frankly, I'm surprised at you, Parrish. I didn't think you had it in you. To take Torreon and Morales, that is. But now it's finished, isn't it?"

Parrish glared at him.

"Call out to the boy," Cuesta ordered him. "Tell him to come out in the open, unarmed. Tell him he has fifteen seconds. Then I will blow your head off your shoulders."

Parrish held Cuesta's gaze, hating him. He had hated few men in his life, but he hated Cuesta. Cuesta was not a revolutionary. He was a ruthless, cold-blooded adventurer who had gone through life killing and mauling and stealing. He was worse than Pardal or Torreon because he knew what he was.

"I can't do that," he told Cuesta evenly.

Cuesta scowled at him. "Do it! Now!" He moved the muzzle of the wicked-looking gun.

But Parrish knew that if he asked Tony to disarm himself, Tony would do it. Then it would be over for all of them. Cuesta would kill them without mercy, one by one.

Parrish eyed the table. It stood partially between him and Cuesta. He took a deep breath, trying to think of some way to give Tony time to get there to back him up. There seemed to be no way. Cuesta was impatient.

He met Cuesta's tough gaze. "Go to hell," he said clearly. Then he dived for the opposite side of the table.

In that same instant, Cuesta unleashed the M-16. It rattled loudly under the canopy, chipping wood off the table and punching hot lead into the ground beside

Parrish as he dived for cover. One slug grazed his side, another tugged at his shirt sleeve. He hit the ground hard and rolled quickly, infantry-like. Cuesta pulled off another short burst. More wood chipped up over Parrish's head as Cuesta moved to get a better angle on Parrish. Parrish rolled to the edge of the table, and saw the machete hanging there on a nail.

It was Nardo's. Morales had used it to chop up canned meat for tortillas. Parrish grabbed it and yanked it off the nail just as Cuesta came around the end of the table. Cuesta saw the big knife and laughed.

"You will go against me with that?" he said. "You're a fool, Parrish!"

But before he could shoot, Cuesta heard a sound behind him. It was Tony, coming up on the far side of the big hut. Cuesta had only seconds to make a decision.

The long glistening blade descended just as Cuesta turned. It hit him first across the face, splicing his nose away from his cheek and slicing through the bone of his jaw and chin. Then it cleaved him down along the torso, across the breastbone over the heart and down over the stomach and groin.

Cuesta's eyes widened in shock, and then he was stumbling backwards, falling. The M-16 banged off several wild shots as he fell, but none of them hit Parrish. Then Cuesta was on his back on the ground.

Tony came up just at that moment, the M-16 ready to fire. When he saw Cuesta lying there, he just stopped and stared. Cuesta was looking at Parrish, standing over him with the bloody blade, as if Parrish had performed some deadly feat of magic. Cuesta's insides were exposed. He had dropped the gun, and was grabbing at himself, his hands buried in a crimson mess.

"Why aren't you laughing now, you murdering sonofabitch?" Parrish growled out. He put a hand to the shallow wound at his side.

"Oh, Jesus!" Tony said, looking very pale. He

turned partially away.

Cuesta's jaw moved a couple of times, like a puppet's without its ventriloquist, and then his eyes glassed over.

Parrish dropped the machete. "Are you all right?" he asked Tony.

Tony turned to him and nodded. "I'm okay, Jake."

"Go release the women," Parrish said to him.

Tony set the gun on the table. "Yeah," he said.

It was only moments later that Tony brought Nita and Ana up to the big hut. Parrish had dragged Cuesta out of sight, and had washed off from a bucket of water.

Nita had donned her torn clothing and was presentable. She came with her arm around Ana, and Ana seemed to be more alert.

"But where's Luther?" she was saying, as the three of them came up.

"He's gone, Mother," Tony said quietly. "He's gone forever."

Ana stared hard at him.

Nita came over to Parrish, and he took her to him. Her eyes teared up as he embraced her. "Thanks," she said.

"Tony's the real hero," he said.

Tony was holding his mother close to him, "Like hell," he said.

"Your mother is going to be all right," Parrish told them. "I can feel it in my bones. She just needs time. . . and love."

"What do we do next?" Tony wondered.

Parrish turned to him, still holding onto Nita. "I figure we ought to avoid tangling with Mexican authorities if we can. There's gasoline stored in this hut, apparently brought by Nardo for the next leg of Cuesta's yacht trip. We can get back to Florida with it, at least to Key West. We'll tell them our story. The trunk, of course, belongs to the government of

278

Ecuador. We'll let the Mexican and Ecuadorian govern-
ments fight that one out."

Nita looked into Parrish's face. It was dirt-streaked
and sweaty, and it had fatigue written across its tanned
surface. But it looked very good to Nita.

"And after Key West?" she asked Parrish.

Parrish held her open gaze. "I'll be with you for just
as long as you'll have me, Nita," he said quietly. "I'll
be with all of you for as long as you want me."

"That ought to be a long, long time, Jake," Tony
told him.

Parrish looked from Tony back to Nita, and knew he
would never leave her.

"Tony," Parrish said, "let's you and I go try and
find a piece of canvas on the yacht. To wrap Luther in.
I'm taking him back with us for a proper burial."

Tony rose and nodded. He realized suddenly that he
loved Parrish like a brother. "Okay, Jake."

"Then we'll load that fuel aboard and get out of
here," Parrish added. "Before dark, if possible. This
isn't exactly my favorite place in the world, now."

Nita looked up at him. "I'll second that."

Parrish touched her lips gently with his, and then he
and Tony moved off together across the compound
toward the dinghy at the surf's edge. The sun was slant-
ing downward in the western sky, and the heat was
already less intense. There was a mild breeze off the
water, but the cobalt surface of the sea was hazy and
tranquil.

It would be a good night for crossing the Gulf.

Parrish welcomed what lay on the other side.

LOVE AND GLORY

They were brothers in the same squadron, fighting a private war all their own!

ROBERT LAWRENCE HECKER

LOVE AND GLORY
By Robert Lawrence Hecker

PRICE: $2.25   T51592
CATEGORY: Novel

Lt. Hal Bailey arrived in England to learn that he was assigned to an air squadron commanded by his arrogant brother, Major Luke Bailey. Luke had always considered his brother a coward, and his brother's actions could tarnish his excellent flying record. Luke was a ladies' man, and had once seduced the girl Hal was going to marry. This had changed Hal's life, and he still carried the hate. Soon, Luke began putting the pressure on Hal, and it became too much for both of them. Their rivalry burst into outright war and threatened the entire squadron when Hal, Luke's bombardier, refused the order to fight!

THE SEA RUNNERS
By Ralph Hayes

PRICE: $2.50   T51647   CATEGORY: Novel

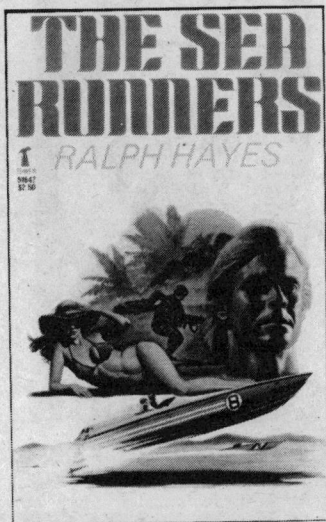

WILD RACES AND SWEET RISKS!
They were runners with a fast
crowd. But Steve Cahill out-dis-
tanced them all, running from his
past. He loved the wrong women,
befriended the wrong men, and
risked his life for a single prize. It
all happened on a lush island siz-
zling with life, and shadowed with
death!

Other Tower Books By Ralph Hayes:

51577 PROMISED LAND	—$2.25
51452 SHERYL	—$2.25
51442 EASTERN SHORE	—$2.25

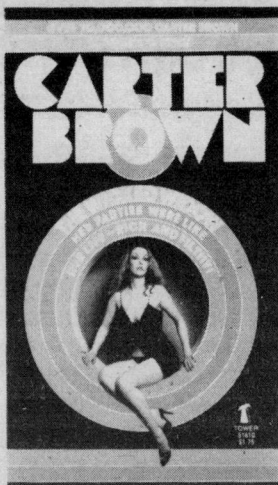

THE WICKED WIDOW
By Carter Brown

PRICE: $1.75   T51610   **CATEGORY:** Mystery

OVER 70,000,000 CARTER BROWN
<u>MYSTERIES IN PRINT!</u>

Wally Hamer was found murdered inside a Rolls, and Al Wheeler's investigation took him right to Minerva Trent, a gorgeous widow who rolled in cash and plenty of hay. He jumped into a sack full of kinky suspects, then something clicked—it was a gun at his head!

Other CARTER BROWN titles available:
SEE IT AGAIN, SAM $1.50   T51415
BUSTED WHEELER $1.50   T51414
THE STRAWBERRY BLONDE JUNGLE $1.50 T51405

THE GLORY TRAP
Dan Sherman & Robin Williamson

PRICE: $2.25   T51646
CATEGORY: Novel

"SOPHISTICATED AND DIVERTING!"
— *The New York Times*

He was a discredited and marked agent. She was a young British woman on the run. Together they fled into the vast European underground, living in shadows under the unrelenting threat of death! Explosive espionage suspense!

"ROUSINGLY GOOD ADVENTURE!"
— *King Features Syndicate*

"DAN SHERMAN IS A FIRST-RATE STORYTELLER!"
— *Morris West, author of* Proteus

IF NOT FOR LOVE

By Carol Franz

PRICE: $2.50
T51603

CATEGORY:
Historical Romance

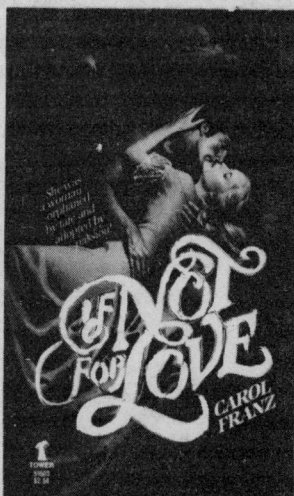

THEY RISKED A DANGEROUS LOVE!

IF — Katherine had not been orphaned, she would never have gone to work for the Cameron household, and would never have met the man whose love she yearned for.

NOT — until John Cameron was blinded by desire did he savagely seduce the woman who left him aware of the one thing he could never give her.

FOR — Katherine and John, the dream they pursued was shattered by a painful reality.

LOVE — trapped them, held them captive, and shackled them to a turbulent destiny!

1
TOWER
51611
$2.25

HIS TURF WAS HOLLYWOOD,
WHERE LOVE IS A PASTIME AND JEALOUSY
IS A WAY OF LIFE...

NEWSMAN

CHARLES PARKER

NEWSMAN
By Charles Parker

PRICE: $2.25   T51611
CATEGORY: Novel

A HOT NEW SLANT ON SIZZLING HOLLYWOOD!

JOCK FRASER   a handsome and pushy reporter,
who sticks his nose into the dirty doings of
Tinseltown's red-hot elite, and sniffs out a story that
would make a gossip columnist blush.

IVY CHRISTIAN   a knockout heiress who tries to
buy Jock's affection with a flashy Ferrari, a cool
million, and her warm self.

LEE-LEE   a six-foot-seven rock musician, who
gets high on some very special vibes.

PLUS   Sam the Illustrated Man, thieves,
PR men, producers—and, of course, a murderer!

THE GEHLEN PORTFOLIO
By Thomas Douglas

PRICE: $2.25   T51654
CATEGORY: Novel

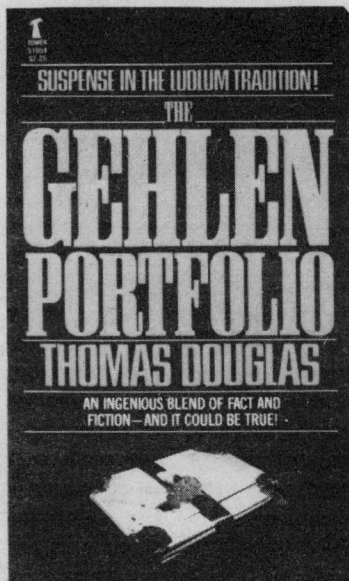

SUSPENSE IN THE LUDLUM TRADITION!

A shocking and tense novel of speculation, it combines fact and fiction to fill in the puzzling historical gaps in April, 1945. It begins with the death of a spy, and rockets to a mind-boggling international conspiracy!

BYE-BYE, LONESOME BLUES
By William Doxey

PRICE: $2.25   T51652
CATEGORY: Novel

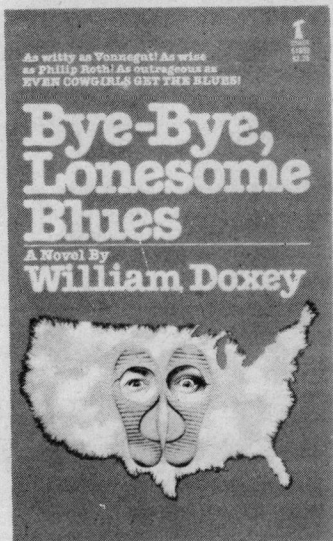

A JOGGER'S VIEW OF AMERICA AS SEEN THROUGH HIS FEET! Run with a special jogger as his sneakers bounce him across the nation, and soar as he takes you to uncharted highways of the imagination. An outrageous novel as witty as Vonnegut, and as crazy as *Even Cowgirls Get The Blues!*

SEND TO: **TOWER PUBLICATIONS**
P.O. BOX 270
NORWALK, CONN. 06852

PLEASE SEND ME THE FOLLOWING TITLES:

Quantity	Book Number	Price

IN THE EVENT THAT WE ARE OUT OF STOCK
ON ANY OF YOUR SELECTIONS, PLEASE LIST
ALTERNATE TITLES BELOW:

Postage/Handling	
I enclose...	

FOR U.S. ORDERS, add 50c for the first book and 10c for each additional book to cover cost of postage and handling. Buy five or more copies and we will pay for shipping. Sorry, no C.O.D.'s.

FOR ORDERS SENT OUTSIDE THE U.S.A., add $1.00 for the first book and 25c for each additional book. PAY BY foreign draft or money order drawn on a U.S. bank, payable in U.S. ($) dollars.

☐ **PLEASE SEND ME A FREE CATALOG.**

NAME_____
(Please print)

ADDRESS_____

CITY_____**STATE**_____**ZIP**_____
Allow Four Weeks for Delivery